Gone

LEONA DEAKIN

BLACK SWAN

TRANSWORLD PUBLISHERS
61–63 Uxbridge Road, London W5 5SA
www.penguin.co.uk

Transworld is part of the Penguin Random House group of companies
whose addresses can be found at global.penguinrandomhouse.com

Penguin
Random House
UK

First published in Great Britain in 2019 by Black Swan
an imprint of Transworld Publishers

A CIP catalogue record for this book is available from the British Library.

ISBN 9781784164089

Typeset in 12.5/14.75 pt Garamond MT Std by Jouve (UK), Milton Keynes
Printed and bound in Great Britain by Clays Ltd, Elcograf S.p.A.

Penguin Random House is committed to a sustainable
future for our business, our readers and our planet. This book
is made from Forest Stewardship Council® certified paper.

For my sisters, Elizabeth and Joanne.
Thank you for inspiring me to write.

We are all worms. But I do believe that
I am a glow-worm.

Winston Churchill

When evening closes Nature's eye
The glow-worm lights her little spark
To captivate her favourite fly
And tempt the rover through the dark.

James Montgomery

I

Fourteen-year-old Seraphine Walker's blonde hair fell in pretty ringlets. She wore a tight-fitting school jumper and a short skirt. There was something immediately enticing about her. But, like glow-worms shining hypnotic torches to draw in their prey, Seraphine Walker was not all that she seemed.

The school bell rang. Seraphine dropped her pencil. It hit the ground with a soft clack and tiny droplets of blood splattered from its point across the polished wooden floor. The caretaker lay beside the pencil, his hands to his neck and a crimson circle oozing from his crumpled body. He was almost certainly dying.

It looked beautiful. Was that disrespectful? Probably. But so was standing here watching every breath produce bubbles of blood that splashed across his chin.

Seraphine knew she should look away. But she couldn't. It was fascinating. She was struck by the urge to kneel down, to get closer, to see if the wound was neat where her pencil had met his skin, or loose and ragged. Logic told her it should be the former. She'd stabbed him quickly and decisively, so it should be a clean wound. She wanted to know for sure. Just a little bit closer.

'Seraphine? Seraphine?'

Mrs Brown was running across the sports hall. The Art teacher's huge bosom bobbed up, down, up, down, as her corduroy skirt whooshed against her boots. Her expression was one of panic and fear. Seraphine was surprised. She'd expected anger. Seraphine looked at Claudia, who sat sobbing, her arms wrapped around her legs and her head shaking against her knees. Mrs Brown sped past her without acknowledgement. Claudia raised her head and cried louder. Her eyes were red and her cheeks streaked with tears, but her expression was strange. No relief whatsoever.

Seraphine was good at reading people. Really good. But she couldn't always understand them. Why did they cry? Why did they scream? Why did they run?

And so she watched. She studied them. She mimicked. And fooled.

2

Coffee in hand and pyjamas still on, Lana sat at the small desk on the landing, ignoring the view of north London and staring instead at the laptop screen in front of her. She completed the day's trending Facebook quiz – *What kind of coffee are you?* – and then sat back, hugging her mug in both hands and waiting for the results to load. The screen was too bright and the curser pulsed to the beat of her aching temples. A more patient person would find the control settings and adjust the contrast, but Lana simply yanked out the power cord, sending the laptop into power-save mode and making the screen three shades darker.

The result was in: *You are a double espresso – too hot and strong for most to handle.* Lana liked the sound of that. Her daughter used phrases that were far less complimentary, with words like *irresponsible*, *crazy*, *a mess*. Jane would judge her for the wine bottle in the kitchen bin and the vodka at her bedside. At Jane's age Lana had been a promiscuous drug-user with at least three arrests for petty crime under her belt, so, compared with what Lana had put her own mother through, a judgemental, boring daughter was no big deal. A bit disappointing, but no big deal.

Lana shared the quiz result with her Facebook friends

and Twitter followers. Marj had posted a quote about good things happening to good people. Seventeen others had liked it. Lana typed a swift response – *Tell that to the 39 people killed in the Istanbul nightclub shooting* – and pressed Enter. People could be such dim, optimistic idiots.

There was a knock on the door. Lana padded downstairs with bare feet, wondering what type of person ignores a perfectly working doorbell to ram their meaty fist against a block of wood. *Instant coffee served with a truckload of milk and two sugars*, she concluded as she opened the door. There was nobody there. Lana checked for a delivery card or parcel left on the doorstep and found neither.

'Stupid kids,' she muttered under her breath as she went to boil the kettle again.

In the kitchen, she spooned ground coffee into the cafetière, filled it with water and then rinsed her mug in the sink. In the garden a large blackbird strained to pull its wriggling breakfast out of the ground. For a moment it looked as if the worm might have the upper hand, but then the bird replanted its feet a couple of times in a kind of avian death dance and, *ping*, out the worm sprang. Lana turned to fetch milk from the fridge – and there it was.

At the end of the hall by the front door a small white envelope lay on the carpet. It had been pushed against the wall when she'd answered the knock. Lana went to pick it up and turned it over. It shimmered as it moved. Her name was printed on the front, embossed in silver foil.

4

Her phone started to ring. She rooted for it in her pocket and checked the screen.

'Hi, babe,' she said, aware that her voice was hangover-husky.

'I wanted to wish you a Happy Birthday,' said Jane.

'Go on then,' said Lana.

There was a momentary pause. 'Happy Birthday, Mum. What have you got planned for today?' This was code for *Don't spend all day in the pub*.

Lana ignored her daughter's question. 'Is this card from you?'

Another pause.

'The card that's just arrived,' Lana continued. 'Is it from you?'

'What card?'

'Not to worry. Are you home normal time? Shall we go out for tea?'

Jane said something with her hand over the mouthpiece, then, 'Got to go, Mum. See you later. Have a nice day.'

A skinny single-shot latte – that would be Jane. Not too much caffeine, not too much fat; a sensible, boring coffee. Lana picked up the envelope. She lifted the flap and removed a white card. On the front it said *Happy 1st Birthday*.

Was it a joke? She didn't get it.

She opened it. Inside, it said:

YOUR GIFT IS THE GAME.
DARE TO PLAY?

Lana smiled. 'What sort of game are we talking about?' In the middle of the shiny white card a long strip of tissue paper contained a URL and an access code. Lana reached for her phone, opened the website and followed the instructions. A plain white webpage loaded and then in the same silver writing:

Hello, Lana,
I've been watching you.
You're special.
But you know that already, don't you?
The question is . . .

Lana scrolled down.

Are you prepared to prove it?

Underneath was a large red button stamped with the word PLAY. Then another phrase appeared. It scrolled across the screen, from right to left, again and again.

I dare you.

Like every player who had gone before and every player who would follow, Lana pressed the button. She felt no fear. She didn't stop to consider the consequences or to ponder the mysterious card. She simply wanted to know what came next.

3

Seraphine sat in the small, windowless room at the police station wondering if her answers sounded convincing, if they were normal. She had no idea how a normal person would talk about this sort of thing. She was relying on police dramas, books and her own imagination.

'So tell us again, Seraphine, how did you come to be in the sports hall this morning?' Police Constable Caroline Watkins had asked this question twice already. Her voice was high pitched and girly. She had her dark hair in a neat bun at the nape of her neck. Her make-up was thick but immaculate and each time she repeated a question her left eye twitched.

Seraphine shrugged. 'We were just bored,' she said for the third time.

'And you said the caretaker, Darren Shaw, followed you and Claudia Freeman?'

Seraphine nodded.

Watkins tilted her head towards the recording equipment.

'Yes,' said Seraphine.

'And the pencil?'

'It was in my pocket.'

Watkins looked straight at Seraphine. 'Oh yes,' she

said. 'From your Art class.' The smallest of smiles touched her lips.

'No,' said Seraphine. 'DT. Design Tech.'

'Of course. My mistake.' PC Watkins pretended to amend her notes. 'So, Mr Shaw approached Claudia in the sports hall. You said she was in trouble. What do you mean by that?' Watkins' eye twitched.

Seraphine repeated her response, exactly the same as before. 'He was holding her by the back of her neck and he had his hand down her top.'

'And you're sure this wasn't consensual?'

Seraphine paused for a moment to consider what that little bitch Claudia might have said. They were friendly, but Seraphine knew Claudia resented her popularity. How far would Claudia go to undermine her?

'Are you sure he was forcing Claudia against her will?' Watkins said.

'She's fifteen,' Seraphine replied, insulted at the implication that she didn't know the meaning of the word 'consensual'.

Watkins's cheeks flushed.

Seraphine's mother had been sitting in silence, as instructed – she was such an obedient sap – but now she spoke up. 'What are you implying?' she demanded, uncrossing her arms. 'We are a good family. My daughter would never hurt anyone. This man frightened her and she simply defended herself.'

'Is that right, Seraphine? Were you frightened?' asked Watkins.

'Yes.'

'He let go of Claudia and attacked you?'

'Yes.'

'And you lashed out with the pencil, in your own words, hoping to scratch him?'

'Yes.' Seraphine did not elaborate.

Watkins held Seraphine's eye.

She doesn't believe me, Seraphine thought. Dropping her gaze and hunching her shoulders, she sank down in her chair and picked at the skin around her fingernails. *I'm a fourteen-year-old girl and I'm scared. I didn't mean to hurt anyone. I was just trying to help my friend and now I'm being interrogated.*

For a moment she worried she'd failed to pull it off. Maybe her posture was wrong or her expression not quite right. Police officers were trained to spot a fraud.

But then Watkins folded up her paperwork. 'OK, that's enough for now. We'll take a break and PC Felix here will show you where the canteen is.' Watkins looked at Seraphine's mother. 'Something to eat will help with the shock.' Then she looked back at Seraphine, her smile warm. 'And then we'll speak again.'

Seraphine nodded. *I'm a vulnerable teenager in shock. I'm a vulnerable teenager in shock.* She found it helped to repeat the words in her head.

Watkins stood and turned away. Seraphine relaxed. This was going to be a breeze.

4

The second hand of the large consulting-room clock stuttered towards nine. Sitting upright in her chair, Dr Augusta Bloom watched it, feeling each tick bat away her anxieties, the things that might distract her from focusing on another person for a full hour. She knew this session would be challenging. She'd read the notes and knew what to expect. A traumatized victim called upon to defend actions that weren't intentional but primal.

Tick.

Tick.

Fourteen. You should have one foot still in childhood at fourteen. Innocence should drift away, little by little: Santa and the Tooth Fairy first; then the realization that your parents are flawed; then that people can be selfish; and finally that the world itself can be unfathomably cruel. Childhood needs to unravel slowly so that the mind can adjust. When it's ripped away in one brutal moment, it leaves behind the silhouettes of denial, anger and, ultimately, despair.

Bloom didn't have the power to turn back the clock and remove the trauma. But she could try to amplify the light inside a child's mind and turn down the volume of their distress.

*

Seraphine paused at the door to the small room and evaluated Dr Bloom. The woman sat in a high-backed chair with wooden arms. She had cropped hair the colour of oatmeal and wore black trousers and a green V-neck jumper that looked neat and smart. On her feet she wore flat black shoes; Seraphine's mother would describe them as sensible. The psychologist's feet only just touched the floor.

She's short, like me, thought Seraphine. *That could come in useful.*

'Hello, Seraphine,' said Dr Bloom. 'Come on in. Take a seat.' She kept her hands in her lap, clasped around a small black book. She waited for Seraphine to sit and then continued, 'How are you feeling today?'

Seraphine blinked a couple of times. 'OK,' she said. It was a safe answer.

'OK,' repeated Dr Bloom. 'Do you know why your mum has asked me to speak with you?'

'Because of the caretaker.'

Dr Bloom nodded. 'You know I'm a psychologist?' Bloom waited for Seraphine to acknowledge her question, then said, 'I work with young people who've been accused of committing a crime.'

'You work for the police then?'

'Sometimes. Although I mainly work with solicitors and their clients, or youth-offender teams, usually in preparation for a trial. But your mother has asked me to speak to you today because she's concerned about the effect of your recent experience. So I'm here to help you make sense of it. We'll take things at your pace. There's a glass of water and some tissues here, and if you wish to take a break at any point, just say and we will.'

Seraphine looked at the box of tissues. *I'm expected to need them*, she thought. 'What do I call you?'

'Dr Bloom will be fine. I understand you're quite a capable student and your teachers think you have a great deal of potential. Do you enjoy school?'

Seraphine shrugged.

'According to your mother, you're an accomplished athlete. She tells me you're in the netball team and have played badminton for the county. Is that correct?'

Seraphine shrugged again.

'And you took the lead in last year's school production, so quite the all-rounder.'

Seraphine shuffled in her chair. She needed to get a grip. She was acting like one of her stupid friends. She looked at Dr Bloom sitting straight-backed, her feet neatly side by side and her hands in her lap. Seraphine sat up. 'I'm good at Science and Maths.'

Dr Bloom nodded.

'And I enjoy sports.' She wiggled her right foot into place directly below her right knee.

'And you're an only child. Are you close to your parents?'

'Very.'

'That's good.' Dr Bloom smiled as though she was genuinely pleased by this response. 'Can you tell me what you mean by "very"?'

Seraphine moved her left foot into position beside her right. 'And I also enjoy Design Tech, because

Mr Richards is a good teacher.' *And he really, really sharpens his pencils.*

'I see.'

'Are you a medical doctor?' Seraphine asked, as she folded her hands over her thighs.

'No, but I have a PhD in Psychology. Do you know what that is?'

Seraphine nodded. 'Where did you study? I don't know whether to bother with university. It seems like a waste of time; I could just get on and earn some money. What do you think?'

'Would you say that you're closer to your mother or to your father?'

Neither, she thought. 'Both,' she replied. 'Equally.'

'And have they been supportive since the attack?'

Of each other. Like they were the bloody victims. Seraphine masked her irritation with a smile. 'They've been fabulous.'

'Fabulous?' Seraphine was very aware of Dr Bloom's brown eyes still fixed on her own. 'Well, you're very fortunate, Seraphine.'

Something about the way she said it made Seraphine think she meant the exact opposite.

'Can you tell me in your own words what happened in the sports hall?'

Seraphine took a deep breath. She had prepared for this. 'Claudia and I had gone inside and the caretaker followed us. It turns out he's been having it off with Claud for months. Not that she wanted to. He's been raping her. So he saw us go into the hall and decided he could have a go on both of us. Claudia tried to stop

13

him, but he came at me, trying to feel me up. He had me backed into a corner and I didn't know what to do. So . . .'

Seraphine paused: she needed to phrase it right.

'I had a pencil in my pocket and I hit him with it. I thought it might scratch him, hurt him, give us the chance to run. But it went straight in his neck, like *schloop*, and then there was a lot of blood. It was everywhere, and he was slipping and he fell and then he didn't stand up again. And that was that.'

Dr Bloom opened her notebook and wrote three or four words. 'Thank you. That's very helpful. And when the caretaker had you cornered' – she was still making notes – 'before you used the pencil. What were you thinking?'

'I didn't want that creep to rape me.'

Dr Bloom looked up. 'And how did you feel?'

'Absolutely terrified.'

Dr Bloom nodded. 'I'm sure you did. And in that moment, what did you see?'

'See?'

'Did you become alert to everything going on in the room or were you focused on one specific detail?'

Seraphine remembered staring at the beating pulse in Dreary Darren's neck. 'I don't think . . . I don't remember.'

'Did you shout or scream?'

'No.'

'Did Claudia?'

Seraphine shook her head.

'Why not?'

'He'd locked the doors. There was no point.'

'So you had no escape and no potential help coming?'

Seraphine nodded.

'He had you cornered and had made his intentions clear?'

'Yes.'

'And you felt absolutely terrified?'

'Yes.' Seraphine suppressed a smile. This was going well.

Dr Bloom paused and took a deep breath. 'What do you mean by terrified? Can you describe to me what that felt like?'

'Urm . . .'

Dr Bloom didn't fill the silence.

'How many sessions will we have?' asked Seraphine.

'As many as we need.'

'Typically?'

The doctor smiled. 'Do you consider this experience typical, Seraphine?'

Shit. I really need to watch what I say. 'Sorry. No. I just thought there'd be a number.'

'I'll know better when we've met a few times.' Dr Bloom closed her notebook. 'It might be useful for both of us if you kept a diary and wrote down your thoughts on this experience and our sessions. Just what you remember, any details that come back to you, and how you're feeling and adjusting.'

Dr Bloom lifted an identical notebook from the desk behind her and handed it to Seraphine. 'Maybe you could use this.'

Seraphine leaned forwards, took the book and placed it in her lap, folding her hands around it. She expected Dr Bloom to react to the very obvious act of mimicry. People often raised an eyebrow or flashed a micro-smile. But Bloom didn't respond at all. She quizzed Seraphine on her home and school life and Seraphine did her best to deflect and defer.

Seraphine left an hour later feeling rather smug about her ability to manipulate a psychologist. Until, halfway down the corridor, she remembered the tissues. *I was supposed to need the tissues.* She wouldn't make such a stupid mistake next time.

5

Bloom checked her coat pocket for her Oyster card as she approached Angel tube station. Then she caught sight of the commuters jostling towards the ticket gates and decided to walk the mile and a half back to Russell Square instead. Meeting a new client was always puzzling and the fresh air would help her to reflect on the session.

She took a right turn into Chadwell Street, planning to scoot around the edge of Myddelton Square and weave through the quiet back streets, and then her phone rang.

'G'day, Sheila.' Marcus Jameson had no Australian blood and yet, every day, his greeting was thus, complete with a suitably authentic accent.

'G'day, Bruce,' replied Bloom without even trying to conceal her distinctive Yorkshire lilt.

'What's occurring?' Jameson said, switching to Welsh.

Bloom wondered if a man with such a decorated history in the Secret Service should be more politically sensitive. But she expected his penchant for accents was like a pathologist's sharp humour, a coping mechanism to balance out the dark. Or perhaps she was over-interpreting. Perhaps he just liked accents.

'I'm on my way back now,' she replied. 'I should be with you in ten minutes or so.'

'How'd it go with the newbie?'

'I'm not sure.'

'Tricky case?'

'Tricky person, I think. But maybe that's unfair. Sorry. I shouldn't have said that.'

'It's OK to have a hunch, you know, Augusta. You can't live in an unbiased vacuum. Sometimes your gut simply knows.'

'Yes. Yes. That may be so, but the effort to be object-ive is never wasted. Now I need some time to think. I'll see you shortly.'

'Actually . . . I rang because I need a favour.'

Bloom pushed the phone firmly against her ear to drown out the traffic. This was new. In the five years they'd worked together at their little consultancy Jame-son had never once asked for a favour. He was one of those independent do-it-yourselfers. It was why she liked working with him. After counselling young offenders, she couldn't handle a needy business partner.

'I'm listening,' she replied.

'There's someone at the office I'd like you to meet. She needs our help. Her mother's missing and, well, it's a bit weird.'

'Will we be getting paid for our help?' Bloom turned into Margery Street.

'No. Not paid. That's why it's called a favour. Look, I'll explain when you get back. I just wanted to give you a heads-up, just so you don't feel ambushed.'

She knew Jameson was lying. He hadn't called to pre-vent her feeling ambushed. He'd called to plant a seed because he knew she couldn't resist a mystery. *Her mother's missing and, well, it's a bit weird.* There was always a mystery. Sometimes they were hired by families wanting to find out what had happened to their loved ones when the police hit a brick wall. Or by the Crown Prosecution Service; or a defence barrister, if the crime was of a particularly obscure nature.

They had met at a conference. Augusta had been speaking on the primary motives behind criminal exploits. Jameson had sought her out and joked that no one was better placed to investigate mysteries than an ex-spy and a criminal psychologist. And six months later they began doing just that.

They made a good team. They were different. Augusta figured Jameson had been *that boy* at school. She assumed he'd been popular, funny, head boy and captain of the rugby team. And, despite being the most disorganized person she'd ever met, he had the confidence to carry himself with a firm, quiet authority. She, on the other hand, was organized to a fault.

Their office was a rented basement in Russell Square beneath a glossy PR firm. It was small and dark and suitably discreet.

When Bloom arrived, she found Jameson at his desk. His dark hair was a little too long, his curls falling over his eyes. He was wearing jeans and a shirt, and, as always, no tie. A teenage girl sat next to him wearing faded skinny jeans with intentional rips. She had long brown hair tied in a low ponytail and wore a plain grey jumper.

'Jane,' said Jameson, 'this is Augusta.'

Bloom placed her bag on the floor and sat down behind her desk.

'Jane often stays with my sister Claire when her mother is deployed overseas,' said Jameson. 'Lana's in the Army. So we've known this one since she was a wee lassie. We've had many a fun BBQ and film night over the years, haven't we? She's my unofficial niece number three.' The girl smiled warmly at him. 'Can you tell Augusta what you told me, Jane?'

The girl's voice was strong despite her puffy red eyes. 'They said she left of her own accord and there's nothing they can do. Even though I told them it's all wrong.'

'The police,' clarified Jameson.

'This is your mum?' said Bloom.

Jane nodded. 'They said she'll come back when she's ready, but she's not well.' Jane looked at Jameson, then back to Bloom. 'She has PTSD. She served in Afghanistan and she's struggled since. She's gone missing overnight plenty of times, but she always comes home the next day.'

'How long has she been gone?' asked Jameson.

'How old are you?' asked Bloom at the same time.

'Sixteen,' Jane replied.

'And where's your father?' said Bloom.

'I don't have one.'

Bloom glanced towards Jameson.

'How long's she been gone?' he repeated.

'Over a week. She took all our money, left me nothing

for food or rent and no one's seen her. I've checked with everyone.'

'No calls? No emails? Nothing online?' asked Jameson.

Jane shook her head. 'No one will help me,' she said, her eyes still on Jameson. 'But Claire said you might.'

Bloom watched Jameson nod and felt uneasy. He'd never asked for a favour before, so she knew this was important, but investigating the lives of family and friends was fraught with danger, as she knew only too well.

'You said your mum was in the military?' Bloom said. Jane nodded.

'Then they will help you . . . eventually.' Bloom knew that particular machine wouldn't kick in until Lana was due back at work. 'But if your mum is in the habit of taking off unexpectedly then that's probably what's happened here.'

'But I haven't even told you the weird stuff yet.' Jane lifted her bag on to her lap and began to rummage through it.

Bloom looked at Jameson and raised an eyebrow.

Jane thrust a stack of papers at Bloom. 'There are more of them. I asked online if anyone else had gone missing like this and four people came back to me.'

Bloom kept her voice soft. 'Hundreds of people go missing every week.'

Jane waved the papers until Bloom reached out and took them. She spread the pages across her desk. Each contained a thread of email correspondence.

'There's a pregnant woman in Leeds whose fiancé had his car run off the road, then he just got out and walked away, and she hasn't seen or heard from him since. Another man in Bristol said his wife—'

'Where's the link?' Bloom said to Jameson.

Jane frowned.

'She means the thing that makes this more than random people going missing for random reasons,' said Jameson.

'They all went missing on their birthday,' Jane said, as though this explained everything.

'OK,' said Bloom, stretching out the word. She wanted to be kind.

'Show her the card,' said Jameson. He had a look in his eye, a quiet confidence. He thought this would be the clincher.

Jane handed over a white envelope. 'They all received one of these before they disappeared. Look . . .' She pointed as Bloom turned the envelope over and read the small silver writing. 'It says mum's name. Then all the cards have the same thing inside.'

'"Happy First Birthday."' Bloom opened the card. '"Your gift is the game. Dare to play?"' She turned it over, but there was nothing written on the back. 'Did anything else come with it?'

Jane shook her head.

'And they all received the same card?' Bloom flicked through the stack of emails again.

'The guy in Leeds left his in the car. His fiancé told me the police found it on the passenger seat.'

'Weird, isn't it?' Jameson said.

'And you showed this to the police?' said Bloom.

Jane nodded. 'They said it was evidence that these people chose to disappear and grown-ups were allowed to do that.'

'Maybe because it says "game" they dismissed it,' said Bloom.

'Have we seen anything like this before?' Jameson asked.

Bloom didn't need to respond to his question. He knew every detail of every case they'd ever worked on. Beneath that mop-haired head sat a hugely impressive brain. A brain that could see angles and manage complexity like none she had ever known. There was no one else she had even contemplated partnering with.

'And why happy *first* birthday?' Jameson said.

Bloom placed Lana's card back in its envelope. 'I expect if we knew the answer to that, we'd know what all of this was about.'

'So, what do you think?' Jameson said after he'd sent Jane to Costa for a latte. 'She was always a funny one, that Lana. A bit off, you know, never really around. Claire used to worry about Jane. The war really messed Lana up and that kid has paid the price. All the kids do.'

He wasn't subtle. She noticed the switch from talking about one sad little girl to the importance of standing up for troubled military kids in general, but she said nothing.

'I know what you're going to say. We're too busy. We can't afford to work for free. But this is a friend. You know why I wanted to do this work with you . . . to make amends, or do some good or . . . whatever. And if I can't do that for my friends and my family, what's the point?'

Bloom sighed. She wanted to think it through, consider all the angles, assess the risks. Their work often involved digging deeply into a person's private life, examining their hidden views, behaviour and motivation. How would that affect Jameson and Claire's relationship with this Lana?

'What would we do with our other work while we help your friend?' she said.

'We'd manage.'

'What would our clients say when we miss our deadlines?'

'We wouldn't. We'd make it work.'

'Do you really think snooping about in your friend's life is a good idea?'

'Lana's not *my* friend. And we'd be helping a vulnerable teenager find her mother.'

'An irresponsible mother who might well disappear on a whim again.'

Jameson rested his forearms on his lap and studied Bloom for a moment. 'You were intrigued, though, weren't you? I saw it on your face. Five people missing after receiving identical dares. It's not just one flaky mum going rogue. It's bigger than that.'

He wasn't going to take no for an answer. And he was right: she was intrigued.

'Speak to these other families,' she said. 'Make sure they're not just telling Jane what she wants to hear. I'll speak to Jane.'

'And you'll tell her we'll help?'

'No.'

'Augusta—'

'No, Marcus. Not yet. Not until we know if we can. We are not in the business of making false promises.'

6

Who the hell do they think they are? Pushing her around. Her!
They should watch themselves. Idiots. Stupid idiots.

, Seraphine paced the cold tiled floor of the police-
station toilet. Yes, she had stabbed him in the neck with
a pencil. Yes, she had pierced an artery. But the guy was
a creepy shit. He deserved it.

But now that bitch of a policewoman wanted to know
if Seraphine had *aimed* her weapon.

'Do you know where the carotid artery is located?'
Seraphine mimicked PC Watkins's high-pitched girly
squeak. 'Did you aim for the carotid artery? . . . Were
you trying to kill Mr Shaw?'

'Yes,' she rehearsed, her voice a slow sing-song. 'I
know where the carotid artery is. I learned it in Biology.'
They were trying to catch her out. Did they think she
was stupid? As if she would tell them the truth. Stupid,
stupid idiots.

Seraphine squeezed a few tears out of the corners
of her eyes. She stared at her reflection as she practised
the words. 'No, I didn't intend to kill him . . . No, of
course I didn't intend to kill him.' She remembered
the break in Claudia's voice when they had been confronted by Dreary Darren and tried adding it on the
word *kill*. 'No, I didn't intend to kill him.'

Nailed it, she thought, heading back to the interview
room before she forgot how to do it.

7

'Hello?' said Bloom, holding the phone to her cheek. She turned the kitchen radio down.

Jameson launched into the details without any traditional niceties.

'So three of the four other disappearances are legitimate. I spoke to family members and their local police stations. They all received the same dare-to-play card on their birthday, which was some time in the last three months. First was Faye Graham, a mother of two who turned forty-two on the fifth of January, then Grayson Taylor, a political science student who turned twenty on the tenth of February, then Stuart Rose-Butler, the father-to-be who deserted his car. He turned twenty-nine on the twenty-fourth of February.'

'And Lana's birthday was just over a week ago?'

'Yes. The ninth of March.'

'What's her surname?'

'Reid, spelled with an "e" and an "i".'

Bloom noted it down next to Lana's birth date. 'And the fifth person?'

'Seems to be a red herring. A girl called Sara James contacted Jane through Facebook and said her mother had gone missing too, but there were no details other than what Jane had already revealed.'

'Jane's message?'

'She asked if anyone knew of someone who'd received a white birthday card with a dare-to-play message and then gone missing.'

'Great,' said Bloom, pulling out a chair and sitting down.

'I know, but she's young and that's what they do these days, vent their every thought on social media. So I wondered if this Sara might be a fake, and sure enough the email came from an office building in Swindon. I checked and no one in the company knows of a Sara James.'

'Someone feeding off the drama? Or using it as an opportunity to groom?'

'Something like that. I'll keep looking, but for now we have four real disappearances. We may be too late for Faye and Grayson – they've been missing for a month or two – but Lana and Stuart have only been gone a few weeks.'

'That might still be too long. And the police officers you spoke to – were they doing anything?'

'Nope. Nada.'

'Any interest in a number of potential victims?'

'They said to keep them informed.'

'Of course they did.'

'Look, I know you're worried about our other work, but I've looked through the planner and we have no pressing deadlines in the coming week. The next court date is a fortnight away, and I've checked in with the solicitors and detectives on our cases and nothing's changed in terms of urgency.'

'I have my young-offender clients.'

'Tuesday mornings and Friday afternoons, right?'

Bloom murmured her confirmation. Counselling under-eighteens was important to her and Jameson knew that.

'We can work around that. One week. That's all I'm asking. Just to see if there's anything to it. I'll cover all the expenses.'

'There's no need to do that. We have enough in the account.'

'Is that a yes? Shall I arrange a meeting with Stuart's fiancée? She's the Finance Director at Leeds Bradford Airport, so back in your neck of the woods. She's also thirty-eight weeks pregnant.'

Bloom smiled. Jameson knew how to press her buttons. 'Fine. Yes. And let's meet with Jane again and conduct a full interview.'

'Consider it done,' Jameson said and then the line went dead.

Bloom turned Radio 4 back on. She wanted to catch Ian Rankin discussing the death of Inspector Morse creator Colin Dexter. She had loved watching *Morse* with her father when she was young. They'd competed to work out who'd done it, and then her father would turn lawyer and point out the flaws in the case. He was the reason for her fascination with the criminal mind.

She warmed the broccoli-and-Stilton soup she'd made on Sunday and sliced a loaf of farmhouse brown. Then she settled at the kitchen table just as Barrington

Pheloung's *Morse* theme began to play. The opening notes made her nostalgic; she wanted to be back on her father's sofa one last time. She wanted one more evening together.

8

Claire's conservatory was scattered with discarded soft toys and half-finished jigsaw puzzles. Bloom watched as the two girls ran around the kitchen island, squealing with delight. Claire kept telling them to keep it down. She had one of those fancy machines and was making coffee, frothing milk as she updated Jameson on her husband's new job. Bloom watched the interaction with fascination. As the only child of two intellectuals she hadn't grown up around banter or humour at all, so the trading of sarcastic asides and shared chuckles was as intriguing as it was alien.

'Sorry, Augusta. I'll take these noise-machines to the park so you can have some peace and quiet,' said Claire. 'Seriously, guys, shush a minute. You're giving me a headache.'

The girls fell silent but continued to run laps of the kitchen.

'Jane's not been so good the past day or so,' Claire said to her brother. As yet, Jane was nowhere to be seen. Claire had shouted up the stairs when Bloom and Jameson had arrived, but that was over fifteen minutes ago.

Jameson carried his cappuccino to the seat opposite Bloom, then placed a mug of tea in front of her. 'How d'ya mean?'

Claire glanced at the stairs and lowered her voice. 'Staying up late, lying in late, not eating.'

'Sounds like you as a teenager.' Jameson took a sip of coffee. It left a white moustache of milk that he licked away.

'Yeah, because you were the dream child,' Claire said to her brother before smiling at Bloom. 'What d'ya reckon's going on? Is Lana in trouble or has she just lost her way?' Claire turned around. 'Girls!'

'Sorry, Mummy,' her daughters sang together.

'It's a weird one, sis.' Jameson was halfway through his coffee already. The man inhaled the stuff. 'The other people who've received these cards have been missing for a good few weeks now and the first one for two months.'

'What do you think?' Bloom asked. 'Is this game something Lana might play on a whim?'

Claire spoke quietly. 'Lana's had a rough time recently. Since Afghanistan she's been struggling. She's been on a few more tours – driving, this time – but it's not easy. I don't know what happened out there, but she's having a hard time coping.'

'You think she might want to escape?' asked Bloom.

'She wouldn't leave Jane. She's a good mum.'

Jameson tutted. 'What're you talking about, Claire? You're always moaning that she's a terrible mother.'

Claire tilted her head, raised her eyebrows towards the hallway and spoke through clenched teeth. 'Not when I can be overhead I'm not.'

Jameson dropped the volume of his voice. 'OK, but it

won't help us if you hold back. We need to know what's really going on with Lana.'

'Fine.' Claire kept her voice low as she spoke to Bloom. 'Lana's incredibly good fun but utterly flaky. She can't be trusted to pay her bills or do her shopping and that's not down to the PTSD. She's been like that as long as I've known her.'

'How long's that?' said Bloom.

'About ten years. She and Jane moved here not long after Dan and me. They live at number seventeen. It's split into flats.' Claire glanced towards the hallway. 'She puts a hell of a lot on that young girl. What with the drinking and the constant absences, it's a wonder Jane hasn't gone off the rails herself.'

'She's been lucky to have you and Sue,' said Jameson.

Claire gave her brother a smile. 'Sue lives across the road,' she explained to Bloom. 'She and I have taken turns to have Jane over the years, but it's fallen on me and Dan a bit more lately. Sue and Mark are going through a divorce.'

'Has anything happened recently to make you think Lana is struggling any more than usual?'

Claire frowned and shook her head. 'If I'm honest, I actually thought she was getting better.'

Bloom knew that people with depression often seemed to be doing better in the weeks and days before they took their own lives.

'Tell Augusta about the men,' said Jameson to his sister.

Jane appeared in the doorway.

33

'Hi sleepyhead,' said Claire. 'Want a cuppa?'

Jane nodded. She had made a small effort – she was dressed – but not much. Her hair hung limply around her face and her leggings and long-sleeved T-shirt were only one step away from pyjamas.

'How ya doin', sport?' Jameson said to Jane. She responded with a weak smile.

'Marcus can fill you in on the rest,' said Claire, herding her children into the hallway. They put on coats and shoes and then left for the park.

Jameson turned to Jane. 'We need you to tell us as much as you can about your mum. You need to be totally honest. We need to hear everything. OK?' Jameson's voice was gentler than normal. It was obvious that he cared a great deal about this young girl.

Jane curled her feet under her legs and nodded. 'Where do you want me to start?' Her voice was still croaky with sleep.

'Just tell us what your mum's like,' pressed Jameson.

Jane looked out into the garden. 'Mum's a bit crazy, completely nuts sometimes, but . . .'

Jameson waited.

She looked at them both. 'She tries her best. Dad left her with nothing. She was on her own at twenty-one, a single mum with a two-year-old and no job.'

Most sixteen-year-olds thought twenty-one-year-olds were ancient. Bloom guessed these might be Lana's words, rather than Jane's own.

Jane continued, 'She applied for an office job at the Army base but she did so well on her tests and they liked

34

her so much that she joined up.' She shrugged. 'So she's been away a lot and I stayed with Claire and Sue. I'd be excited to see her when she got back, but she was always distracted. She just wanted to sleep. Or go out and party.'

'Sounds tough,' said Jameson.

Jane stared into her tea. 'I try to take care of her and look after the house.'

'Course you do.' Jameson smiled at Jane. 'Has your dad ever made any contact with you or your mum?' This would be a key line of inquiry if the police looked into Lana's disappearance.

Jane shook her head. 'Mum made sure he couldn't find us. He was a druggie. He stole money from her. Once, when I was a baby, she left me with him and when she came back I had a bruise on my face. And she promised she'd never let him hurt me again.'

'So did he leave? Or did she throw him out?' Bloom asked.

Jane frowned, then nodded. Bloom picked up her pen and scribbled in her notebook, *Dad left or kicked out?*

'And how was your mum before she went missing? She was on extended leave?' Jameson said.

'Yes, because the PTSD was getting worse.'

'Did she receive any treatment?' said Bloom.

Jane shook her head. 'I don't think so.'

'But they put her on extended leave?' said Jameson.

Bloom wrote down, *Leave without treatment?*

'And how was she doing?' Jameson asked again.

'She was OK. Always drinking too much and spending all day on the computer, but her mood was good. She

35

wanted to go out for tea on her birthday. It would have been nice, but then . . .'

Jane sounded like the parent. Bloom wondered how long it would be before the girl disappeared. Children responsible for alcoholic or drug-dependent parents often fled as soon as they could and never looked back.

'Do you know if she'd upset anybody?' she asked.

'No more than usual. You know Mum,' Jane said to Jameson. His raised eyebrows and smirk suggested he'd seen this aspect of Lana first-hand. Jane mirrored his smirk. It was a shared joke. She turned to Bloom. 'She never backs away from a fight.'

'Never,' said Jameson, and Bloom wondered how many arguments there'd been between Claire – and by extension Jameson – and Lana over the years.

Bloom continued, 'Did your mum seem particularly worried about any of the fall-outs? Scared, even?'

Jane shook her head. 'I don't think Mum's ever been scared of anything. If I was worrying about something, she'd just tell me to stop being stupid. "What's there to be scared of?" she'd say.'

Plenty, thought Bloom. Sometimes those who felt no fear were the most frightening of all.

9

Dear Dr Bloom,

This morning PC Watkins came over to tell us that Darren Shaw isn't dead. He's in a serious but stable condition. She said this will help my case immensely. But then the school phoned to say I was excluded and couldn't attend any of the upcoming trips. I told Mum how important my classes are and how much I love Art. She's ringing the headmaster now to convince him to let me go. Claudia's going, so I don't see why I shouldn't. It's not as if I can't catch up with the work. I could probably get away with missing the whole term and still pass my exams.

    I'm not sure the police and school really understand the meaning of justice. I mean, the whole thing was the caretaker's fault. I didn't ask him to follow us into the hall and get all pervy. So why punish me and my poor parents who've done absolutely nothing wrong?

    I might do some research into miscarriages of justice. I'll let you know what I find out as it might be helpful for your job.

Seraphine

Jameson placed two cups of tea on the table in front of Bloom. They were passing Peterborough and would arrive in Leeds to meet with Libby Goodman, Stuart Rose-Butler's fiancée, in an hour or so.

Bloom lifted the lid from one of the insulated red cups.

'Ah,' Jameson said, twisting her cup around. 'I think you've got mine.' Bloom looked down. On the side of the cup it said: *What can I say? I'm hot.*

Bloom twisted the second cup. 'They both say that.'

Jameson frowned. 'Disappointing.'

Bloom shook her head disparagingly. She took a small sip and looked out of the window at the Cambridgeshire countryside. 'So what else is there to know about Lana?' she asked.

Jameson poured three little milk pots into his tea. 'Like I said, I hardly know the woman. I've spent plenty of time with Jane – Sunday lunches and whatnot, because she's always at Claire's – but I've only met Lana a few times. But from what Claire says . . .' He shook his head. 'From what I can tell, she's trouble. Claire watched Lana seduce Sue's husband. It's the equivalent of Lana going after Dan. I mean, she probably wouldn't, because Claire can be bloody scary, but Sue is this sweet, gentle woman.'

'And that's why Sue and her husband are divorcing?'

'Absolutely. And Mark wasn't Lana's first married man. Claire thinks Lana enjoys the thrill of proving she can have any man she wants. She never sticks with them. She pursued Mark for months, slept with him and then that was that.'

'She's never made a play for you?'

'Why would she? I'm not married. Nothing to prove.'

Bloom mulled it over. Lana was competitive – that was clear – otherwise there'd be no thrill in seducing another woman's husband. But plenty of people liked the chase. And very few would drop everything to play a bizarre game. 'What's Lana's motivation? Why would she play this game? If that's the reason our people have disappeared, we need to understand why.'

'Maybe she didn't have a choice.' Jameson opened his packet of biscuits and offered one to Bloom.

She shook her head. 'Right. Did they choose to do it – it had some personal appeal – or . . .'

'Were they forced to do it? Blackmailed.'

'Or were they abducted? The birthday message could be nothing more than a calling card. There may be no game at all.'

'Just some sicko showing off?'

Bloom made a few notes in her book. 'If they did voluntarily accept the dare and play a game, then what are we dealing with? All of the participants would be highly competitive, very impulsive. Jane said her mother didn't play computer games, but she could be wrong. This might be something targeted at enthusiasts.'

'You mean they may have asked for access to the game?'

'Or visited a specific website. Have you heard of this Blue Whale game? The one in Russia?'

Jameson's expression darkened. 'You don't think it's similar, do you? Targeting unhappy kids and coercing them into committing suicide?'

'I hope not. But Lana's PTSD could make her a candidate for something like that. Let's try and find out if Stuart was similarly vulnerable, if he was depressed. And if he's in the habit of going missing, or losing touch. If he's impulsive or impressionable. And if there's anything going on that would make him susceptible to coercion.'

'Could these people have crossed the wrong person?'

'We need to find the link.'

Bloom's phone buzzed on the table and she headed out of the carriage to answer it.

Five minutes later, she returned to her seat. 'That was the PC who attended Stuart Rose-Butler's road-traffic accident.'

'How'd you find him?'

'Contacts.' Bloom smiled. 'He said they treated it as abandonment initially. But after a couple of days they spoke to his partner, Libby, and his employer, the ASDA in Pudsey – he's a shelf-stacker – and a few friends. It seems Stuart was prone to flitting between jobs. His parents passed away when he was young and Libby and his friends have only known him a few years. The officer said they passed it on to CID as a missing-persons case

40

but were pretty sure he'd done a runner due to impending fatherhood.'

'Sounds like a stand-up guy. What about the game?'

'Well, this is interesting. One of the witnesses said they saw the driver of the other vehicle involved in the collision hand a card to Stuart.'

'Really? Someone may have seen who's doing this?'

'Possibly, but the other two witnesses had no recollection of such a handover taking place. The other car was gone by the time the police arrived and they didn't follow it up.'

'Good police work.' Jameson drained the dregs of his tea.

Libby Goodman lived in a neat little house in Horsforth, on the outskirts of Leeds. It had a small, pretty front garden filled with daffodils. Bloom knocked on the wooden door and a heavily pregnant woman with tight dark curls opened it.

'Libby Goodman? I'm Dr Bloom. We spoke. And this is Marcus Jameson.'

'Yes. Hello. Come on in.' Libby walked through to the lounge with one hand tucked beneath her belly. Bloom and Jameson took the two single chairs, leaving the sofa for Libby. It was useful to have her swivelling between them, facing only one of them at a time, so that the other could observe her reactions.

'Thank you for seeing us, Libby,' Jameson said, his charm turned up to ten. He explained about Jane and Lana, how he knew them and why he and Bloom were looking into Stuart's disappearance. Then he asked Libby to tell them about the day Stuart went missing.

They had shared breakfast, she'd given him a birthday gift and then she'd waved him off before tidying up and getting ready for work. She'd been irritated because Stuart had forgotten to wish her luck with a big presentation she had that day. The police arrived just after she'd showered, so half an hour or so later. When she'd seen them step out of the car and put their hats on, she'd known it was bad news. She'd been convinced Stuart was dead, so their revelation had been quite a relief.

'But you haven't heard anything from him since?' said Jameson.

Libby glanced at Bloom, then shook her head. 'I left messages, loads of them, but he's just disappeared. No one's heard a thing.'

'And is that unusual?' Jameson asked.

'Very.'

Bloom cleared her throat. 'I hope you don't mind my asking, Libby, but was everything OK between the two of you?'

'Fine.'

'And was Stuart OK? Had you noticed anything different or unusual about his behaviour?'

'He wouldn't leave me, if that's what you're asking. I told the police and I can tell you too. He was fine.'

'But was there anything unusual about his behaviour in the last few weeks?' Jameson repeated.

Libby sighed and shook her head. 'No. Nothing unusual. Nothing at all.'

Jameson nodded and then continued, 'Had he been worried about anything in particular or fallen out with anyone?'

'No.'

'Has he ever gone off without telling you before?'

Libby shook her head.

'And how long have you been together?'

'Nearly two years. It was just after I started as Finance Director at the airport. It was a pretty lonely time, if I'm honest. People didn't like the fact I'd been promoted so young. Stuart worked in the cafe and he was the only person who'd look me in the eye and smile. He was charming. Then he was asked to leave and I was devastated.' Libby glanced at Bloom. 'But three days later I came out of work and found him waiting by my car with flowers. We've been together ever since.'

'I like his style,' said Jameson with a kind smile. 'How would you describe Stuart, Libby? What sort of person is he?'

'He's . . . perfect. I mean, for me. I don't mean he's, like, the perfect man. Certainly not.' She smiled. It was the first heartfelt smile they'd seen and it turned her from bland to really rather pretty. 'I'm a bit obsessive and he's the total opposite. Which works. He makes me laugh. He shows me I'm taking life too seriously. He does these menial jobs because he hasn't worked out what he wants to do yet, but he could be anything. He's bright and super-confident.'

'You said Stuart was asked to leave the cafe at the airport?' said Bloom.

43

Libby looked away. 'That was all a misunderstanding.'

'Oh?'

'They thought he'd done something he hadn't. I got it all cleared up, but he wouldn't go back after how they'd treated him and I can't say I blame him.'

'What sort of misunderstanding?'

'I really don't want to talk about it. It's not relevant.'

Bloom and Jameson exchanged a glance, a look that said *later*.

'So Stuart is a bit of an extrovert,' said Jameson. 'Pretty laid-back, charming, confident and bright?'

'It sounds like I'm bigging him up, doesn't it? I suppose I am.' Libby stroked her hand around and around her bump. 'But I hope this little one turns out like Daddy rather than neurotic Mummy.'

'Was Stuart excited about becoming a father?' Jameson continued.

Libby rested both hands on her bump. 'Yeah.' She swallowed. 'It's different for guys, I think. It doesn't become real to them until the baby's here, does it? But he was excited.'

'Are there any old friends he might be staying with?' said Jameson.

'He's not great at keeping in touch with people. Not like me. I've known my two best friends since nursery school. Another way we're opposites, I guess. But I checked everyone I could think of. Like I say, I'm obsessive.'

'Nothing wrong with that, is there, Dr Bloom?' Jameson didn't look across to see his colleague's reaction, deliberately focusing on his notebook instead.

'You said Stuart *was* excited about becoming a father,' said Bloom. 'Rather than *is* excited.'

Libby raised her chin to the ceiling for a few seconds. When she looked back at Bloom there were tears in the corners of her eyes. 'I'm not stupid, Dr Bloom. He's been missing for nearly a month. How long do the police allow before they suspect foul play? Three days?'

Jameson cut in. 'That tends to be in cases of abduction, or specifically for vulnerable people and children.'

'He took no money. No clothes. No passport or driving licence. They're all still here. He hasn't used his phone, been on social media, written anyone a bloody postcard. He's dead. You know it and I know it too. I'm a single mother. I don't even know why we're talking, to be honest. This is all too late. Where were you three weeks ago?' Libby stood and Bloom thought she was about to ask them to leave, but she didn't. She just walked over to the window and stared out of it.

'You don't set any store by this game, then?' asked Jameson.

Libby looked back at him.

'You told Jane Reid that Stuart had received a card like Jane's mum Lana. A birthday card, daring him to play a game.'

'I never saw it. The police told me about it. I expect it's just marketing for a stupid computer game. Stuart certainly loved those.'

'Stuart was into gaming?'

'The bigger the guns, the better. Maybe it's best he's not around to influence this little one, after all.'

45

'Just one final question, Libby, and then we'll leave you in peace,' said Bloom. 'As far as you know, has Stuart ever suffered from depression?'

Libby frowned. 'No. Why would you ask that? Why does everyone assume he's taken off because he was unhappy? He wasn't unhappy. We were great.'

'Did you believe her?' Jameson asked as he and Bloom climbed into the back of a taxi. 'When she said they were happy?'

'Didn't you?'

Jameson ran a hand through his hair. 'I don't know. I want to. She seems like a lovely lady. It would be nice if they were happy, but . . .'

'You think she might have her rose-tints on?'

'I know you hate my gut feelings, Augusta, but something was off.'

Bloom told the driver to head to Leeds station. 'I only object to gut feelings that aren't fully explained or explored, Marcus. If you have a hunch it's probably for good reason. Let's dig deeper.'

Across the Pennines, Stuart Rose-Butler walked into The Principal Hotel, Manchester's recently refurbished five-star option for businessmen and wealthy visitors. He stopped beside the full-size statue of a horse in the centre of the lobby with his hands in the pockets of his suit trousers. His newly acquired tattoo was covered by the sleeve of his Ted Baker shirt, the Breitling watch Libby had given him for his birthday just visible below the cuff. The tattoo was a half sleeve, a large melting clock face that had won him the previous round and boosted him to level two. He was on a roll.

He watched the stairs and waited. He wasn't a patient man, but he knew a bad choice would destroy his winning streak.

A dark-haired woman in a suit descended into the lobby twenty minutes later. She was thin, scrawny rather than athletic, stressed rather than fit. Her make-up was heavy but neat and her tailored black suit looked expensive. There were no rings on her fingers. Stuart reckoned this wealthy forty-something hadn't seen any action in the bedroom for a long, long time.

As she walked towards the reception desk, her right shoe lost traction on the polished floor and she lurched sideways before quickly righting herself. She glanced around – had anyone spotted her ungraceful movement? – and her gaze halted at the man with his hands in his pockets standing perfectly still.

Stuart smiled. He could stop a woman in her tracks when he smiled right. And everything banked on him doing it right.

11

'Hello, Seraphine. How are you?'

Dr Bloom was sitting as before: hands clasped in her lap, back straight and feet and knees squeezed together.

Seraphine took her seat opposite and mimicked that posture: back straight, legs together, diary held in her lap. The sparse little room contained only their two chairs, a small table in between them with a water jug, two glasses and a box of tissues, and a low cabinet with two deep drawers.

'I started the diary for you,' Seraphine said, holding out the book.

Bloom shook her head. 'I don't want to see it, Seraphine. You can talk to me about what you write, but the diary is for your own private reflections. No one should read it but you.'

'Why?'

'So you can be totally honest with yourself. If we know another person is going to read what we write we tend to moderate the content. For a diary like this to be of use you need to write the truth.'

Seraphine placed the diary back in her lap. This changed things. She had been planning to use the diary to show Dr Bloom just how normal she was. But if the woman was never going to read it . . . Seraphine couldn't see the point of it.

'Have you been thinking any more about your experience with Darren Shaw? Or your discussions with the police?'

Seraphine shrugged. She was confident that the police were convinced that she'd acted in self-defence. There would be no benefit in repeating her story here.

'You heard that Mr Shaw is recovering well, I take it? How do you feel about that?'

'Relieved, obviously.' Seraphine knew she was supposed to feel relieved. 'I didn't mean to hurt him,' she added.

Dr Bloom was silent. She stared at Seraphine with a sort of blank expression. Seraphine couldn't work it out at all.

'It will help my case too, the police said.'

'Of course. Without a death, murder becomes attempted murder, manslaughter becomes grievous bodily harm.'

'But I was only defending myself. He's a pervert. He attacked us.'

'And that's exactly what that is: your defence.'

'You don't believe me?'

'I believe you acted calmly in a very stressful situation. I also noted that you described the incident in a matter-of-fact way; there was no drama or emotion. But I can also see that you really don't like it when anyone suggests that Mr Shaw is the victim.'

'Because *I* was the victim. Me.' Seraphine shuffled in her chair and looked out of the small window. 'He was lucky I didn't really hurt him.'

'That's an interesting thing to say.'

Sometimes this happened. People pulled her up on specific words or sentences. She didn't understand why.

'I heard that when your teacher came to your aid in the sports hall she described you as surprisingly calm,' Dr Bloom said. 'The police suspect this was due to shock.'

Seraphine remained silent because there was no question to answer.

'But what I'm most interested in is Claudia's account of events. Have you been told what your friend said?'

'How do you know all this? You said you didn't work for the police.'

'I don't, Seraphine. I work for you and your family. Your mother told me.'

Of course her stupid mother would fuss about everything in front of the psychologist; anything to get some attention. Seraphine took a deep breath to suppress her rage. This was not the place for it.

'Do you know that Claudia disputes your statement?' asked Dr Bloom. 'She says that you attacked Mr Shaw before he had showed any interest in you.'

Seraphine smiled. She had been through all of this with PC Watkins. 'I think Claudia suffers from that thing people get for their abusers. She doesn't like the idea that he wanted me too.'

'Stockholm syndrome?'

'Is that what kidnap victims get?'

Dr Bloom nodded. 'They form an attachment to their aggressor. So are you saying Claudia's account is wrong?'

'Yes.'

'She also recalls you saying, "Why don't you pick on someone your own size?" to Mr Shaw. Is that incorrect too?'

'No,' replied Seraphine. 'I said that.'

'Why?'

Seraphine shrugged. 'It's what people say. It's a saying.'

'Were you suggesting that you are his size?'

Seraphine smiled her sweetest smile. She had practised it in front of the mirror. 'Obviously not. I'm a girl.'

'I didn't think you meant it physically.' Bloom poured water from the jug into the two glasses. 'Do you think about the incident much?' she asked.

'Sometimes.'

'In what way?'

Seraphine didn't understand. She shook her head.

'Tell me what you think about when you remember it. It's not a trick question, Seraphine. I'm just trying to understand what stood out to you about the experience.'

The blood. The thick, red, glistening blood. There was so much blood . . . 'I think of him on the floor.'

'After you stabbed him?'

Seraphine nodded. 'He was wriggling around on the shiny wooden floor. His hand was gripping his neck. I think he was trying to stop the bleeding.'

'Anything else?'

'Then his hand flopped on to the floor and he went still. I could see where the blood was coming from – it was spilling from the side of his neck – but I couldn't see the actual hole.'

'Did you want to see the hole?'

Why wouldn't I want to see the hole? 'I wanted to know if it was smooth or ragged.'

'Why did you want to know that?'

Seraphine frowned. She had hoped Bloom would understand, that she was more intelligent than your average normal. But maybe not. 'Because it's interesting.'

Dr Bloom nodded. She got it now. 'And how often do you think about the incident?'

All the time. It's the most fascinating thing that's ever happened to me. 'A bit.'

'Did you think about helping him at the time?'

'He didn't deserve any help.'

'Why not?'

'Because he's a pervert. A rapist.' Seraphine couldn't be sure, but she thought she detected the briefest of smiles on Dr Bloom's lips.

12

Harry Graham's Opticians was a stylish double-fronted shop in the Clifton area of Bristol. It looked more like a photographer's studio – with its dove-grey window frames and thin white lettering – than a clinic.

Bloom and Jameson arrived just after five in the afternoon, as the dark-haired receptionist in red FCUK glasses was clearing up her desk. The inside was as stylish and minimalist as the exterior. Glasses were displayed like jewellery in cases that hung on the walls and fronted the receptionist's counter. She called for her boss, who emerged from an office at the back of the store.

Harry Graham was a tall, slender man with fair hair and a soft West Country accent. 'Come through,' he said, checking his watch. 'This won't take long, will it? I have to pick up the children.' As he led Bloom and Jameson into the spacious office at the back of the building, the phone on the desk rang. He held up his index finger apologetically and answered it. He had a brief, terse conversation about contact lens deliveries and then hung up abruptly. 'Sorry about that,' he said. 'We appear to be having some supplier issues this week. That's the third cock-up in as many days. I don't know how these people run a business.' He shook his head and let out a sigh. 'Ever had one of those weeks?'

'Frequently,' said Bloom with a smile. 'We'll try not to take up too much of your time. We were hoping you could supply some more information about your wife, Faye. We've discovered a few other individuals who've gone missing under similar circumstances and we're speaking to the families to see if there's a link that might help us find out what's happened to them.'

'You said you were private investigators?'

Jameson answered, 'Of a sort. We're helping out because I know one of the families involved.'

'What do you think's happened to them?' asked Harry.

'Truthfully?' said Bloom. 'We don't know. We don't think this game that was mentioned in the birthday card is a marketing ploy; there are no gaming or tech companies taking responsibility. So we're trying to find a link between the missing people. We're hoping this will shed some light.'

Harry nodded. 'Look. This is going to sound awful, but I'm going to be totally honest with you. I was relieved when Faye disappeared. We aren't happy together. We haven't been for years. We should have called it a day a long time ago, but the children are still so young, so you don't, do you?'

'Do you think Faye chose to disappear?' Jameson asked.

'I did, yes. That's why I didn't push it with the police. I reported her missing after the first week, but I expected she'd turn up when she was ready.' Harry rubbed his right eye. 'She's not been happy for a long time. I tried to help her with the children and talk to her about things, but . . .' He stopped, dropped his hand to his side and looked at them both. 'I don't think she liked being a mother. She loved the kids, don't get me wrong, but that day-in, day-out routine and the responsibility, it made her . . . oh, I don't know.'

'Frustrated?' said Jameson.

'More than that. It made her . . .' He looked up at the ceiling. 'I'm just going to say it. It made her vile. Not a nice person to be around. She was always angry and short-tempered, everyone and everything annoyed her – particularly me, it seemed. She was always saying that her life would be so much better without me in it and . . . well . . . I must sound like the worst husband. I know my children are missing their mum, but I think this space is good for all of us.'

'So, having children changed Faye?' asked Bloom.

Harry nodded. 'Before Fred, Faye loved travelling and trying new things, not what you'd expect from an accountant. She was incredibly good fun, everyone always wanted her at a party.' He smiled, trying to make light of his low self-esteem. 'She was totally different before. And the awful thing is I'm not even sure she wanted a family. I know I did, but I can't remember now if she wanted that too . . .'

'You think she had children to make you happy?' asked Jameson. Bloom was always impressed that he could ask such direct and personal questions without sounding rude or intrusive. It was something about his tone.

Harry paused. 'I really hope not. I hope that's not on me.' A deep frown creased his forehead.

'You still think she disappeared of her own accord?' asked Bloom.

'It's getting on for three months now. That's a long time, isn't it? To not see your children or check how they are?'

Faye Graham's fury burned in her veins. This new player – some jackass called SRB – had only entered The Game three weeks ago but he was already at level two. It had taken Faye nearly two months to reach the second level, and from the stats that were posted each week, she knew that she'd been the fastest riser until this shitty little upstart had come along to steal her crown.

She had taken her eye off the ball. In January, she'd been focused and obsessive. She had checked the website constantly, analysing the stats and the posts from other players, detailing their various achievements.

For every new challenge, the game matched you with an opponent. If you won, you moved up to compete against a higher-level player. The loser moved down a level and was paired with a lesser competitor. It was survival of the fittest. And it was constant. As soon as you completed one challenge, there was another waiting, and the threat of a competitor who could achieve the goal better or quicker. There was no time for anything else. It was exciting and addictive. Faye hadn't felt this alive in years.

Her mistake had been choosing her stupid-ass husband as a target for the latest challenge.

She'd enjoyed cancelling his suppliers, calling up his clients to say he was under investigation for misconduct, spreading rumours about him on professional forums. She wished she'd done it years ago. All those days bored at home with the kids. She could have been having fun.

But she had enjoyed it too much. She hated him too much. And she'd lost sight of the game.

Now she was falling behind. It was all Harry's fault. He had ruined her long before she had ruined him. He had ruined her body, convincing her to have children, and then ruined her career by encouraging her to look after the kids. She'd thought he would be successful and rich, but he had been boring and unambitious and, to top it all, an irritating arse.

She had to make sure Harry could never ruin her again.

13

Back in the office, Bloom and Jameson were waiting to hear from Geoff Taylor about the disappearance of his son Grayson.

As they waited for his call, Bloom pulled together a summary of the case on her iPad. She was creating an electronic incident wall, with everything they'd learned so far. They had a virtual wall for every case and they added fresh information and new hypotheses as the investigation progressed. It was an invaluable tool for collating their findings and sharing critical information.

'There are literally no commonalities,' said Jameson, peering over Bloom's shoulder. 'Our victims are different ages, different genders, and work in different professions. We have a thirty-five-year-old soldier signed off with PTSD, a forty-two-year-old self-employed accountant and mother of two, a twenty-nine-year-old shelf-stacker and a twenty-year-old politics student who all disappeared from different places across the country. The two women are parents, the two men aren't – but Stuart is about to be a father and we don't know for sure that Grayson hasn't fathered a child. But still, that feels a bit tenuous. The women are professionals and the men aren't.'

'It's a heterogeneous group. But with no diversity of ethnic background and all from England,' said Bloom.

'So why these four people?'

'And why on their birthdays? That's the biggest link so far.'

Jameson pursed his lips. 'I've checked their birth-places, but they're spread across the UK. I'll check their social media footprint again. Look for hobbies. I've started tracing previous jobs and am waiting for a call from an old mate.'

Bloom knew that when Jameson said 'old mate', he meant a contact with the highest level of security clearance. A person who could access most of the details of most of our lives, should they so wish.

The office phone began to ring.

'That'll be Geoff Taylor,' said Bloom.

Jameson answered, pressed the speaker button and introduced himself. He was beginning to explain the background to the case when his mobile flashed on the table. Bloom saw that the incoming number was blocked and nodded for him to take it. It was probably his 'old mate'. Jameson headed into the hallway and Bloom took over the phone conversation.

'Can you tell us about Grayson's disappearance, please?' she asked.

Mr Taylor explained that his son had gone missing after meeting a girl on a night out. He'd hoped he was simply losing time in her student bedroom. But some of Grayson's friends had tracked down the girl and she said she'd last seen him outside a club at the end of the night.

'Have the police checked the CCTV?' Bloom found it easier to gauge a person's response over the phone. The lack of visual stimuli made it easier to detect a lie: the deceit was evident in what a person said – the hesitations, the lack of details, the inconsistencies – rather than in the tapping of a foot or a shifty look to the left.

'Yes, but only on that street. They said that anything more would be a strain on resources. They saw Grayson walk away from the club, but not which way he went at the end of the road. They haven't let me look at the footage. They told me, and I'm quoting here, "There's literally nothing of interest to see."'

Bloom exhaled . . . *Nothing of interest to see.* The insensitivity of some officers infuriated her. She understood that they became desensitized, but this footage could be the last sighting of Grayson. And, if the worst had happened, it might be Geoff's final chance to see his son.

'So you're confident he walked away alone?'

'That's what they're saying,' said Geoff.

'Tell me about Grayson, Geoff. There are four people who have gone missing and we're trying to find out if they have anything in common.'

'What do you want to know?'

'What sort of person is he?'

'He's a very intelligent boy. He takes life seriously. I had a few problems with him when he was younger, right after he lost his mum, but we came through it and he's grown into a fine young man.'

'What kind of problems?'

'The usual. Just what you'd expect from a teenage boy

burying his grief. He'd get angry, smash things up – but who wouldn't in those circumstances?'

'Of course,' said Bloom. 'He's studying political science, is that right?'

'That's right. He's in his second year – he's doing very well. He's very passionate about how the world is run. I suppose he's like me in that sense. He takes an interest, you know? But he sees angles I don't. He thinks critically about things and sees the darker side of people's motivations.'

Bloom could see Jameson pacing back and forth in the hallway outside their office. He was thrusting his right hand up and down and she knew he was getting annoyed.

'Was Grayson enjoying university?' she asked.

'Oh, yes. Definitely. He's very popular. They're a great group of lads. They've been fantastic helping me find this girl. He had no reason to go off, no reason at all. It has to be this bloody dare.'

Jameson came back into the room. His face was flushed and he gestured at Bloom to wrap up the call.

'This has been very helpful, Geoff. I'm sure we'll need to speak to you again, but this should be enough for now.' She noted down a few final details, then said goodbye and hung up.

'Go on,' she said to Jameson. 'What's happened?'

'So it turns out Lana Reid is not a serving soldier. Not in the Army or any other military service. In fact, she has never been a serving soldier. She's never even applied for a civilian job. I mean . . . what the hell? My sister's known the woman for nearly ten years. Claire looks after her kid while Lana's posted overseas.' Jameson continued to pace. 'And before you ask, no, she is not part of some Secret Service operation. I checked.'

'I see,' said Bloom.

'It makes no sense. I've seen her in uniform. The day she left for her last tour. I was at Claire's when she dropped off Jane. She had all the gear and an Army-issue bag in her car. I saw it.'

'And the bag was on show in the car rather than in the boot?' asked Bloom. Had Lana staged it? But if Lana wasn't in the forces, where was she going? What was she doing? 'This changes everything. Lana is a serial missing person. And she's also keeping a big secret. There's potential for blackmail.'

Bloom picked up her phone, googled Sheffield University, scrolled down the Contact page and dialled the number for Grayson's department.

'Politics department, Margaret speaking,' said a woman with a soft voice.

'Good afternoon. My name is Dr Augusta Bloom. I'm part of the team investigating the disappearance of one of your students, Grayson Taylor. He's a second-year political science student. Can I please have the contact details for his personal tutor?'

'I'm not sure I—'

Bloom interrupted, choosing her words carefully. 'My team provide specialist support to police forces across the UK, including the South Yorkshire Force.' She wasn't lying. She waited for a moment.

'OK,' said the woman. 'Let me just . . .'

Bloom wrote down the name and number. 'Thank you for your efficiency, Margaret. Much appreciated.' She hung up and dialled the number she'd been given, turning the loudspeaker on.

'Hello?' said a male voice.

'I'm looking for Grayson Taylor's personal tutor,' said Bloom. 'Have I come through to the right person?'

'You have,' he replied. 'How can I help?'

Bloom introduced herself and explained the situation. Grayson's tutor ummed and aahed politely.

'You see,' he said eventually, 'I'm not sure he was having a *fantastic* time. He failed his first year after missing three exams and was in the process of retaking them when he went missing. But he hadn't attended any lectures or tutorials since October. I challenged him about that just before Christmas, and, well . . .'

'Go on,' said Bloom. 'This is all very helpful.'

'He said that if I pushed him to attend he would make an official complaint to the Vice-Chancellor.'

'About what?' asked Bloom.

The tutor took a moment to respond. 'My competence. Grayson said I was incompetent.'

Jameson shook his head. 'Charming,' he muttered.

Bloom thanked the tutor for his time and hung up.

'Just as I thought,' said Bloom. 'So what does this tell us? Two of them are lying. Lana about where she's been going and what she's been doing all these years, and Grayson about how well he's doing on his course. Faye Graham's husband said she'd been unhappy, so maybe we do have a group of people who all want to run away.'

'Libby may be lying about Stuart being happy.'

'Possibly. But I don't think Geoff was lying to me. He believes his son is doing great, because that's what Grayson is telling him. You don't think Jane is lying, do you? She can't know that her mother has been faking this Army job.'

'God, no,' said Jameson.

'And I didn't get the impression that Faye Graham had told her husband she hated being a mum. It was his best guess based on her behaviour.'

'So the families are in the dark?' Jameson said.

Bloom smiled at her colleague until he nodded and said, 'The families are always in the dark. Do you know who I'd like to hear from?' she added. 'The person who sacked Stuart Rose-Butler from Leeds Bradford Airport two years ago.'

Jameson nodded. 'Yeah, Libby was cagey about that. I'll get on to it.'

'See if we can speak to them tomorrow morning. I've got to get to my session in Islington now.' Bloom checked her watch and began to gather her things. 'Make it a video conference if you can. I'd like to see their expression when we ask about Stuart's dismissal. I expect it will show us what they think of him.'

'You've got a theory building, haven't you?' said Jameson. 'I can see it.'

14

Seraphine sat in the consulting room and listened to Dr Bloom and her mother talking on the other side of the door. Mum was doing her usual performance: 'This is all about me, me, me.' Seraphine heard her say, 'What's wrong with her? Why is she not responding to this? Is she repressing something? I don't want her growing up with issues.'

Seraphine smiled. *Issues.*

'Penny, please be reassured that I'm doing all that I can to help Seraphine.' Dr Bloom sounded authoritative. Seraphine made a mental note to practise that same tone of voice.

'But what's she saying? What's she thinking? I can't get a word out of her,' said her mother.

'I'm afraid I can't reveal what's being said in the sessions. Seraphine needs to know that she can trust me.'

'But I'm her mother – you have to tell me.' She sounded emotional. Seraphine knew tears were imminent.

'If I'm to really help your daughter, as you'd clearly like me to, I need her to know that she can tell me anything and that I won't tell a soul.'

Seraphine suspected that Dr Bloom knew she was listening and that this conversation was really for her benefit.

Bloom continued, 'Does Seraphine usually talk to you?'

No answer.

'So her reticence is normal? Try to take some comfort from that. I would be far more concerned if your daughter were acting out of character.'

A few moments later, Dr Bloom opened the door and entered the consulting room. She sat back in her seat with her legs crossed and her notebook open on her lap.

Seraphine sat as she had on previous occasions with her back straight, her feet and knees together and her hands in her lap. She didn't know what the doctor's new posture meant so she wasn't yet sure whether to mirror it.

'Good morning, Dr Bloom.' Seraphine smiled sweetly. 'How are you?'

'I'm well, thank you. And you?'

'I got the results of my mock GCSE Maths paper back today. I got an A star.'

'Congratulations. You must feel pleased.'

Seraphine did feel pleased; elated, in fact.

'What's happening with the investigation?' asked Dr Bloom.

'Nothing. They're still waiting for Dreary to wake up and tell them his version of events.' Seraphine clocked the question in Dr Bloom's raised eyebrows. 'We call the caretaker Dreary Darren . . . because he is.'

'Dreary Darren. Who came up with that?'

'We did.'

'You and your friends?'

Seraphine nodded.

'Tell me about them.'

'They're . . . normal.'

'Good normal or bad normal?'

Is there any such thing as good normal? 'Just normal.'

'Nice?'

'Yeah.' *Why not?*

'Is Claudia part of the group?'

Bitch face. 'Yes.'

'And are you close to Claudia?'

'We hang out in school.'

'And out of school?'

'A bit, but I like to do my own thing. Claudia and Ruby always want to do pyjama parties and each other's make-up. It's boring.'

'So what do you like to do?'

'Have fun.'

'How?'

Seraphine shrugged. 'Do stuff. Try stuff. Learn stuff.'

'How do you compare to your friends? Let's say on a scale of one to ten, with ten being high, how would you rate yourself?'

Ten. 'Probably seven or eight.'

'And your friends?'

'Three.' *Apart from bitch face, who'd be minus three.*

'What makes you an eight?'

'Well, I'm definitely smarter . . . I get much higher grades . . . and I think I'm prettier. I don't need make-up, for instance. Plus they moan and cry and giggle over stupid stuff. Most of the time they talk nonsense.'

'But you don't?'

Seraphine shook her head. 'I don't see the point.'

'Do you feel different, Seraphine?'

'Different?'

'To your friends and your family. Do you ever feel you have a better grasp of the world and how it works than those around you?'

Seraphine felt uncomfortable for the first time since she'd walked in. Had she made a mistake? Did other people not think themselves superior to their friends? Maybe she should have given them a seven or eight too. She said nothing.

'My PhD focused on young people, teenagers much like yourself, who are in many respects outstanding. And I mean outstanding in both senses of the word: they have some superior abilities and attributes, but also they stand apart, like an evolutionary branch that has veered off in its own direction.'

Seraphine had suspected she was superior to her friends for quite a while. For example, she knew it was easy to get someone to do what you wanted if you went about it the right way. But her schoolmates didn't seem to see that. But maybe, as the doctor said, that was because they weren't as bright as her.

Dr Bloom's light-brown eyes stared, as if peering directly at the thoughts in Seraphine's head. 'Do you often find you remain unemotional about things, Seraphine?'

Seraphine couldn't work out if this was a trick question, so she stayed quiet.

Bloom clasped her hands together as though praying.

'It's a very strong characteristic, in my experience. The type of quality people look for when employing air-traffic controllers, for instance, people who need to remain calm in a crisis. Would you say you're like that?'

Seraphine liked the idea of being calm in a crisis. 'I suppose.'

'Other than your recent experience with Mr Shaw, when was the last time something really upset you?'

She couldn't think of an example. 'I don't know. I don't really cry. They tried to stop me going on the Art trip at school, which made me angry, but Mum spoke to them and sorted it all out.'

'So you're going now?'

'No. They wouldn't let me while I'm not in school. But it's been cancelled now.'

Dr Bloom's eyebrows rose ever so slightly and then reset themselves. 'And now no one is going?'

Seraphine nodded. 'Mum spoke to them, and now it's not happening.' If she couldn't go, why should the rest of her class? She was the best artist by far.

'You said you don't really cry. What did you mean?'

'Well, Mum cried for a week when the dog died. She's a bit of a drama queen.'

'Were you upset about the dog dying?'

Seraphine thought about it. 'He'd had a good life.'

'You didn't miss him?'

'I didn't miss taking him for walks in the rain or having to feed him every night. Although I suppose my pocket money went down as a result of losing those jobs, so that was annoying.'

69

Bloom nodded and smiled for the first time. 'Seraphine, I think you may possess some of the qualities of these outstanding teens. And, if it's OK with you, I'd like to spend our next few sessions exploring whether that's the case. Will you have a think about that for me before we meet again?'

Seraphine left the room feeling a little taller. *I knew I was special,* she thought as she walked out of the building and into the sunshine, *I knew it.* She was starting to like this psychologist. Dr Augusta Bloom might be the first person she had met who deserved her respect.

15

The train home was quiet. Bloom placed her handbag on the seat beside her and circled her shoulders. Jameson had been right to insist they look into Lana's disappearance. There was definitely something odd going on.

But the extra workload was exhausting. Bloom could happily sit in a room of people and say not a single word, but the thoughts in her head were rarely quiet. It was the curse of the introvert to think, rethink and ponder every aspect of every experience. An additional case simply added to the noise.

Bloom took out her iPad, opened a new section of the storyboard and started with Lana. She typed Lana's key characteristics into the left-hand column.

Emotionally unstable with (possible) PTSD/depression. Impulsive. Goes out, stays out, drinks too much. Extroverted. Likes social media, partying, and being in the pub.

Bloom supposed the latter two could also be symptomatic of alcoholism. In the right-hand column she listed the things she knew about Lana's circumstances.

Rents a small house in Wembley so must have, or have had, some income. Goes away for long periods of time, up to six months, but not with the military. Has one dependent child, 16-year-old Jane, and has been a single mother since Jane's father left or perhaps was kicked out.

Bloom stopped and looked at that last sentence again. Something didn't quite add up. Jane had talked about Lana being abandoned and forced to cope alone, and then, only a moment or two later, had described her mother as a heroine booting out an abusive father. In both narratives, Lana came out looking good. Which wasn't necessarily unusual – we all tend to cast ourselves as the leading actor in our own stories. But Lana was known to be erratic and impulsive. Would she have had the wherewithal to successfully rebuild their lives, or, alternatively, to escape from an abusive ex?

Bloom didn't have the answer, but she knew not to ignore the question. She often spotted important gaps and links long before she could explain why they were significant. The trick was to note these gut feelings (as Jameson would call them) and to examine them ruthlessly.

As the train pulled into her station, Bloom made one last note.

Find Jane's father.

16

Rural towns and villages had parks filled with mummies and their buggies and walkers with their dogs. But Russell Square moved at a pace. Even the woman doing yoga on the grass was moving as quickly as possible from one position to the next. Outside the green oasis of the square, the hum of traffic coming and going, starting and stopping, provided a percussion accompaniment that never stopped. Inside the square, the constant flow of people entering and exiting at all four corners, dodging other walkers while flicking through their messages or talking incessantly into their phones, throbbed to the beat of the traffic. This was a place where things happened. Perhaps not literally, but in the minds and digital realities of the square's brief visitors.

She looked around. There were only two types of people who inhabited the square for any length of time: the workers employed to keep everything clean and serve drinks in the cafe at the northeast corner, and the watchers. The watchers sat at the few tables outside the cafe, sipping flat whites or loose-leaf tea as they took time to think or simply to watch the world pass by in a flurry of feet.

She was one such watcher. She sat in the chair farthest from the cafe door, next to the fence. This was her favourite chair, partly because the scent of the six-foot-high privet reminded her of summer, but mainly because this position offered the best view of the square and everyone in it. Watching the normal people was one of her favourite pastimes. Wasn't it strange that people with the gift of empathy rarely looked at one another? She looked at them all the time. Watching them was how you learned to fit in.

But today she wasn't simply watching; she was searching. She perched on the edge of her seat, her hands locked above her knees. Black coats, blue coats, red, purple and yellow coats passed by, a rainbow of normal people doing normal things. She craned her neck from side to side, worried she might miss her target. But then she found what she was looking for. A vision in bland, from her mousy hair to her sensible shoes. It was the woman who had taught her to hide.

17

Bloom crossed Russell Square with her head down and her pace steady. At the gate she slowed to check for traffic and then, halfway across the road, she caught sight of a young woman standing outside her office in a fitted blue-leather jacket, skinny jeans and Converse trainers.

'Dr Bloom,' shouted the woman. 'Do you have a comment to make about the Jamie Bolton case?' The young woman held out her iPhone, the Record function clearly activated.

'No.' Bloom tried to pass but the journalist blocked her. The verdict on the Bolton case had been announced that morning. The defence barrister had rung Bloom personally to thank her for her input as an expert witness.

'The family say you're to blame for letting a child abuser walk free. What do you have to say about that?'

'Jamie Bolton was found not guilty,' Bloom said.

The journalist straightened, and continued with renewed purpose. 'Because of your testimony.'

Bloom sighed inside. 'I have no comment.' She side-stepped the woman to get to her office door.

'Is that what you'll say when the next child is attacked?'

Bloom turned to face the woman, looking her square in the eyes. She was no older than twenty-five. 'Did you attend court?' asked Bloom. The woman's blank expression revealed that she had not. 'Did you bother to do your research and read the judge's summary before coming here to hassle me? Is the truth at all important or are you simply chasing cheap scandal?'

'Why did you defend a child abuser, Dr Bloom?'

'You need to ask yourself what type of journalist you want to be. It might be easier to find work down in the gutter press, but don't you want more from your life? If you are any good at writing and investigating, put it to good use, for pity's sake. Don't just do what's easy, do what matters.'

'Why did you defend a child abuser, Dr Bloom?'

Bloom shook her head at the woman before turning and entering the building. Jameson was talking to the Terminal Manager at Leeds Bradford Airport via video link. She quickly removed her jacket and sat down beside him.

'Jerry, this is Dr Bloom,' said Jameson. 'Jerry Moore is in charge of all the cafes and concessionary stands landside at LBA.'

The man on the screen was in his mid-thirties. He had a thin face and a rather unflattering beard. The hair on his head was dark and smooth but his facial hair was coarse and frizzy.

'G'morning,' he said, his voice slightly higher than she'd expected.

'Jerry was telling me that he remembers Stuart Rose-Butler well. That they were all pretty shocked to discover he and Libby were a couple,' said Jameson.

'Yeah, a right shock that was at the Christmas do. She's such a lovely lady.'

'How would you describe Stuart?' said Bloom.

Jerry leaned back in his seat. 'It's safe to say I didn't like the guy. I wasn't the TM when Stuart started work here. I was his colleague, so I saw both sides. He'd properly suck up to anyone in management, but to the rest of us he was a bully.'

Bloom thought of the picture she'd seen of Stuart on Libby's mantelpiece. He was well-built and good-looking. Guys like that could often be dismissive of the Jerry Moores of the world. 'A bully in what sense?'

'Nothing in-your-face. But he was always putting people down, taking the credit, showing off – you know the type. I expect he was angry about being a nobody. He hated it when I was promoted. Whoo,' said Jerry with wide eyes and a shake of the head, 'that made him furious.'

'And how did he lose his job?' asked Jameson.

'It was only a matter of time. He rarely did any actual work. He'd ponce around making the rest of the team do it and, you see, I knew that, so I paid attention. But then he shot himself in the foot, didn't he? He stole the money from one of the charity boxes we have by the tills. Said he only borrowed it to buy lunch, but in the cafe they got a free lunch so we knew that was a load of bull.'

'So you fired him?'

'Yep. Stealing is gross misconduct, so he was a goner.'

*

After the conversation with Jerry Moore, they called Faye Graham's boss at Fisher & Wright Tax Accountants in Bristol. It was equally enlightening.

'Faye was a phenomenal accountant,' said John Fisher, the firm's managing partner. He wore a crisp white shirt, a thickly knotted grey tie and a suit jacket. 'We thought we'd struck gold with her but, to be brutally honest, she turned out to be a bit of a nightmare.' Fisher described how both colleagues and clients had complained about Faye's unreasonable demands and dismissive treatment over the years. One client refused to work with her after it transpired she'd been over-claiming on the expenses attached to their account. She hadn't been stealing as such, but she'd opted for expensive lunches, and taxis over trains. 'I never saw it myself, but my secretary, Lisa, said Faye could be very intimidating. People in the office were scared of her. It was a relief when she left to start a family. I think that suited her better. She always talked about how happy she was at home.'

Bloom noted Jameson's raised eyebrows and tried to keep her expression neutral.

'There's definitely something off about these people,' she said afterwards. 'Lana's been an absent and somewhat irresponsible mother. Harry described his wife as vile and her boss thought she was trouble. Grayson's tutor said he'd threatened to report him for incompetence. And Stuart's boss described him as a manipulative bully.'

Jameson shuddered theatrically. 'Yeah, but that's what happens when you look at people under a microscope.'

'Well, yes, I expect if I took a look at you . . .' Bloom said with a smile.

'Explains why you're such a closed book. No one gets to analyse you, do they?'

'I have no idea what you mean.'

'Course you don't, Mrs I've-got-my-private-life-locked-up-tight.'

Bloom glared at him and he chuckled and held up his hands. 'I had to have a little dig about before we started working together. I had to check you weren't dodgy, didn't I? Don't look at me like that. You did the same, no doubt.'

'I certainly did not.'

Jameson returned to his desk and opened up one of the tabloid websites.

'So you and Jamie Bolton have gone viral, I see.' He waited for Bloom to look across at his screen before pressing Play. 'The girl's father did an interview outside the court.'

A red-faced man in an ill-fitting suit spoke into the camera. 'The psychologist told them that a twenty-five-year-old man grooming my ten-year-old daughter was normal, and they bought it. Bloody disgusting. What's the world coming to when they take the word of cranks like that over the facts?'

Bloom sighed. 'That explains the journalist outside.'

'What? Here?'

She nodded. 'It's like none of these people sat in court and heard a word that was said. Not only does Jamie Bolton have the mental age of a ten-year-old, his brain damage means he has little-to-no sex drive – *facts* which came from the neurologist.' Bloom pointed at Jameson's screen. 'And it was that man's precious little girl who suggested they play strip poker because she had seen her mum and dad playing it "all the time".' Bloom used finger quotes for the last phrase; it was a direct quote from the alleged victim.

'Hey, you don't have to justify your testimony to me,' said Jameson. 'I'm on your side.'

His phone rang and he rushed to answer it.

'Alright, sis?' he said. He listened for a moment. 'Shit.' With the phone still in his hand he opened the BBC News website. On the screen was a picture of Harry Graham and the headline read:

BRISTOL OPTICIAN STABBED
TO DEATH IN HIS HOME

18

Chief Superintendent Steve Barker took Bloom's hand in both of his: a solid, firm handshake designed to instil trust and simultaneously remind you of his rank.

'Now then, Dr Bloom, how the devil are you? I always hoped we'd get you out to our neck of the woods someday.' Barker had been a delegate on one of Bloom's College of Policing courses two years previously. She ran a module on The Psychology of Crime for up-and-coming leaders.

'I'm very well, Steve, and I hear congratulations are in order.' He'd just been promoted to the rank of Assistant Chief Constable for Avon & Somerset Police.

Barker leaned closer and lowered his voice. 'Thank you. No one was more surprised than me.' His attempt to play it down was undermined by the excitement in his eyes. 'I won't start for another few months. ACC Wilks doesn't retire until the end of May.'

Barker led Bloom behind the police station's reception desk, swiped open the door and gestured for Bloom to follow.

Bloom lowered her voice to match his. 'I'm not surprised at all, Steve. You were always going places, from what I could see.'

'You're too kind. Now let's get you set up with Carly. Awful business, this. Just awful.'

Detective Inspector Carly Mathers from the Child Protection Team sat on a large cushioned chair looking down at her phone. Bloom could see through an internal window behind her that a standard square office next door had been furnished with comfy chairs and decorated in soft yellows and greens. An Ikea shelving unit along the side wall was filled with books and toys and the window was framed with bright-green curtains. On the floor a large round mat in the same bright green covered half of the carpet. An un-uniformed woman sat in one of the chairs and on the mat sat a boy of around eight or nine, and a younger girl. They were building towers of Lego.

'Carly, can I introduce Dr Bloom?'

The DI sprang from her seat and deposited her phone in her jacket pocket in one smooth movement. 'Good morning, Sir,' she said to her boss. She turned to face Bloom. 'Dr Bloom, DI Mathers.' She held out her hand. Mathers was tall, with her hair cut in a no-nonsense chin-length bob. She wore a smart shirt and trouser suit, tailored but not overly so. It was a look Bloom recognized. She had taken the same approach herself years ago when working to gain the respect of her mainly male police colleagues.

Bloom shook her hand. 'Thank you for letting me sit in.'

'The Chief Super said we'd be foolish not to.'

Bloom saw the quickly masked look of irritation on

the DI's face. She couldn't blame the woman. DI Mathers was highly trained and no doubt very competent, and there was nothing more irritating than a boss telling you how to do your job or, God forbid, suggesting that you might need help. 'I'll endeavour not to interfere with your investigation, Detective Inspector. I'm here because Harry Graham's wife, Faye, is someone we've been trying to trace.'

'Yes, I heard Mrs Graham had been reported missing. Do you think this is related?'

'I've no idea at the moment.'

DI Mathers nodded slowly. 'I heard about a game. What is it? A Blue-Whale-type thing?'

'Blue Whale? What's that?' asked Chief Superintendent Barker.

'It's an online Russian suicide game that's resulted in over a hundred deaths,' replied Mathers. Bloom wasn't surprised that the Child Protection Team had been briefed on Blue Whale.

'Goodness,' said Chief Superintendent Barker.

'There are some sick bastards out there.' DI Mathers rolled her shoulders. 'They get these kids to do tasks that keep them up and make them sleep-deprived, then when they've got them hooked, they tell them to top themselves.'

Bloom spoke up. 'It's awful and we're hoping what we're looking at is nothing like that, but this thing with Harry Graham—'

'That's not what we have here. A suicide,' said Chief Superintendent Barker.

'No, Sir,' said DI Mathers. 'Harry Graham had multiple stab wounds, too many to have been self-inflicted. And we found the knife upstairs in the boy's bedroom. Mr Graham was downstairs.' DI Mathers followed her boss's eyes into the room behind her, towards the two children building Lego towers. 'So we're pretty sure there's a third party involved.'

'This monster went upstairs to find the children?' asked Chief Superintendent Barker.

DI Mathers shrugged. 'That's what we need to find out.'

Steve unbuttoned his jacket and placed his hands in his pockets. 'So what are we dealing with here, Bloom? Is this some nutter killing the families of players who fail a game?'

Bloom shook her head. She didn't know the answer to that. 'Have the children said anything?'

DI Mathers glanced through the window and shook her head. 'The Chief Super wanted me to wait for you.'

'Let's go then.' Bloom shook hands with Barker again and followed Mathers into the next-door room.

'Wow, Fred,' said DI Mathers. 'That's a great tower.' She sat on the edge of the seat previously occupied by her colleague, who had now left, and turned on the video-recording equipment with a remote control. 'Are we OK to have a little chat while you two are building?' Bloom could tell immediately from the warmth of her tone and her friendly expression that Mathers knew what she was doing. 'This is Dr Bloom.'

'Hi, Fred. Hi, Julia. I'm Augusta.' Bloom sat down.

The boy had dark hair and a more olive complexion than his fair-haired younger sister. He wore jeans with a red T-shirt that had an aeroplane on the front. Julia wore pink leggings with a purple dress covered in unicorns.

'Your name is August,' said Julia with a giggle of delight.

'That's right. And yours is like July,' said Bloom.

The little girl frowned.

'Augusta is like August. Julia is like July.'

Julia beamed at her. 'Yes, like July!'

'Her birthday is in July.' Fred was looking at Augusta with wide eyes.

'Maybe that's why your mummy and daddy picked the name.'

Fred looked at his sister, then back at Bloom. 'When's your birthday?'

Bloom smiled. 'Can you guess?'

'August,' both children said together.

DI Mathers winked at Bloom, then began gently probing the children for details. She started with what they'd had for breakfast yesterday morning and who had been there.

'Weetabix and just Daddy,' said Fred.

Then she coaxed them towards lunchtime, when their father had been attacked while making cheese sandwiches with slices of apple on the side. Bloom sat listening, watching and hoping they didn't hit a brick wall of silence anytime soon.

'Fred, where were you and Julia when your daddy was making lunch?' asked Mathers.

The young boy paused, holding a yellow rectangular block above his tower. 'We were helping.' He put the yellow block in place and pushed it firmly down.

'You and Julia were in the kitchen?'

The boy nodded. Julia continued to build her own construction in silence.

'Can you tell me what happened next?' Mathers leaned forward in her chair, her forehead almost touching the top of Fred's head.

The boy continued building. 'Mummy and Daddy had a fight.'

Mathers exchanged a look with Bloom, and then said, 'Mummy was there?'

Fred nodded.

Bloom sat further forward in her chair. So Faye was alive yesterday, three months after she'd disappeared. That was good news, if not a little unexpected.

'Was there anyone else there with Mummy and Daddy?'

Fred shook his head and stood up to place two more bricks on his tower. 'Just me and Julia.'

Bloom's heart rate quickened. Perhaps it wasn't good news, after all. She had a bad feeling about this.

Mathers' voice softened. 'How do you know they were fighting, Fred?'

The boy crouched beside the toy box, and discarded several bricks before selecting two more to use. Bloom noted that each of the selected bricks was red. Julia continued to build a random structure entirely from orange blocks.

'Fred. How do you know they were fighting?' The boy

stood looking at his tower. 'It's OK, Fred. I know this is hard to talk about. You're being very brave.'

Fred shook his head quickly.

'Take your time, sweetheart.'

Fred gave another shake of his head.

Mathers looked at Bloom and her expression said, *Take a break?*

Bloom was about to nod her agreement when Fred began talking, his words running into and over each other, his babbling hard to follow.

'I'm not brave. Daddy shouted run. I took Julia. I didn't know where to go. I ran. I had Julia's arm. She fell and I dragged her upstairs. I got behind the bed. Put Julia behind me. Then Mummy came.' He looked at Mathers for the first time. 'Then Mummy came.'

'It's OK, Fred. You're safe here with us. It's OK,' said Mathers.

Fred looked back at his tower.

'Then Mummy came . . . ?' repeated Mathers softly.

Fred said nothing for a minute or so, an achingly long silence. 'I was scared,' he whispered eventually.

'Of what, Fred?'

Fred's eyes filled with tears. 'Mummy hurt Daddy.'

Oh no. Could murder be the final dare in some sick game? Who would design such a thing? Who would agree to play it? She and Jameson were out of their depth, if so. They investigated crime after it happened. They didn't stop it in its tracks.

Mathers swallowed and placed a hand on the little boy's arm. 'Did you see Mummy hurt your daddy?'

87

The little boy nodded. 'I was scared.'

Mathers looked at Bloom but kept her hand on the boy, stroking his arm with her thumb.

'I cried,' said Fred.

'That's OK. Lots of people cry when they're scared, honey. You're being very brave.'

Fred looked at his sister. Julia was still playing with her bricks, seemingly entirely oblivious to the conversation taking place less than a metre away. 'I'm not brave,' he said again.

'You're very brave for telling me, Fred. Very brave.'

Fred began to cry, choking on his sobs, his eyes fixed on his sister.

'Can I ask?' said Bloom to Mathers, before looking at Fred. 'Fred, why do you think you weren't brave?'

The boy looked her way.

'You took your sister and hid her behind you. Is that not brave?'

Fred shook his head.

'Why not?'

'Because . . .' He looked back at his sister. 'Because I cried.' His voice shook and his breath caught in his throat.

'That's enough for now,' said Mathers, her tone clearly intended for Bloom.

Bloom ignored her and watched the boy as he in turn watched his sister. 'What did Julia do?'

The boy looked at Bloom with wide eyes. 'She waved Tigger at Mummy,' he said.

'Tigger?'

Fred nodded.

Bloom reached for a small soft toy, a tiger with a dress on. 'Can you show me what Julia did?'

The boy took the tiger and held it out in front of him, facing Bloom. 'Grrrrrr,' he said, as he shook the toy from side to side.

'And you thought this was brave of Julia?'

'Yes,' said Fred, looking at his feet. 'Because . . . Mummy stopped.'

Bloom felt a tightening in her chest. 'Mummy stopped doing what, Fred?'

The boy looked up. 'Chasing us.'

'You think your mummy was chasing you?' asked Mathers.

Bloom continued with her line of questioning. 'And when Julia waved Tigger at your mummy, she stopped chasing you?'

'Yes.'

Bloom looked at Julia building her orange Lego tower on the edge of the green mat. She was small for six, with an angelic face and honey-coloured pigtails. Bloom couldn't help but think of elfin Seraphine Walker fighting back against her would-be rapist. She looked at Fred again. 'What did your mummy do then?'

Fred looked at Julia. 'She said, "Good luck to ya."'

DI Mathers frowned at Bloom. But Bloom had a horrible feeling she knew what Faye had meant. She just needed to check one final thing.

'Fred?' She waited for the little boy to look her in the eye. 'When your mummy said that . . . was she talking to both of you, or just to Julia?'

'Just to Julia,' he said without hesitation.

'What do you think?' asked DI Mathers as they stood in the small kitchenette waiting for the kettle to boil. 'It's unlikely a child would make up a story that dark, isn't it? It looks like Faye Graham stabbed her husband in front of her children.'

Bloom filled her cup with hot water.

'She has to be some kind of crazy. That can't be a game,' Mathers continued.

Or she simply didn't care, thought Bloom, but decided to keep that hypothesis to herself. She wanted to be sure before she said anything. She needed to sound out Jameson first and look at this from all angles, because if she was right, this game was much worse than anything they'd anticipated.

'The game started with a dare,' she said. She needed to give Mathers something. 'The card said *Dare to Play*, so it may be a sequence of dares, culminating in murder. If the dares increase in severity each time, it's possible the player could become desensitized to the reality of what they're doing.'

'You can't incite people to murder just by giving them a set of dares. People have more sense than that, surely?'

'Depends on the person.'

'So if the likes of Blue Whale attract kids who are already

suicidal, this game could attract people who want to kill someone?' The DI stood straighter as her theory picked up pace. 'Maybe you don't have the know-how or the guts to bump off your husband, so you sign up for this game.'

'There were problems in the Graham marriage, as I'm sure you'll uncover in your investigation,' said Bloom.

'But would you do it in front of your kids?' Mathers leaned back against the work surface. 'That's the bit I don't get.'

'If you needed the game to give you the motivation to kill, that would imply you had some reservations, which doesn't fit with then doing it so brazenly in front of your children.'

'Exactly. So she must have been crazy or off her face, as I said.'

Bloom took a sip of her hot water. 'Or she intended to kill the children too.' She knew this must have occurred to Mathers as well. She was an experienced detective and interviewer and there had been no mistaking Fred's fear. 'You're probably aware of this, but there are five key motives for any crime. Necessity: she had to do it to survive. Need: spoils like money or drugs, perhaps. Habit. Emotion – but I don't think this was a crime of passion. And personality, which can be anything from insanity to getting a kick out of it.'

'Is she a crazy nutter?' finished Mathers. 'What about drugs, though? What if someone gave her something that caused her to hallucinate?'

'I'd still expect a trigger motive. Let's say she did take

something. Why go home? She'd been missing for nearly three months.'

DI Mathers nodded.

'Look. These are all hypotheses. I'd keep looking at it from all angles. All I'm saying is that human beings are motivated animals. We tend to have a reason for our actions, and if you can establish the most likely motivation for Faye Graham there might be a chance we can stop this game in its tracks.'

'If it is to do with the game.'

'Indeed,' said Bloom, while thinking, *Oh, this is definitely to do with the game.*

19

'So what's the deal?' Jameson was halfway through a ham and cheese baguette and there was a pint of squash on his desk.

'Any luck with Jane's father?' Bloom asked. She'd been poking holes in her theory all the way back to London, but without any luck. Even if she hadn't voiced it aloud yet, she knew it was true.

'No. Jane's not even sure of his surname. It's a needle-in-haystack thing.' He didn't elaborate any further.

Bloom sighed, took off her coat and sat down. Jameson said nothing. He knew how to make her talk.

She took a deep breath. 'Faye Graham went home to kill her husband and children. I don't have evidence that she was there for the children too, but I'm confident that was her intention. She stabbed their father, then chased them upstairs with a knife. She only stopped when her daughter waved a tiger at her and growled.'

'Sure, that sounds likely to stop a psychopath,' said Jameson.

Bloom said nothing.

Jameson looked at her and his eyes widened. 'You're joking. You think Faye is a psychopath?'

'Four people go missing. They've nothing in common, but they seem to be playing the same game. But why? Who would do that? Certainly not a doting fiancé and prospect-ive dad, or the loving mother of two small children. A student might be daft enough, but the others? It would take a special set of circumstances. Or a certain kind of person.'

'No. Surely not. You're not suggesting they're all . . .'

'Stuart was the perfect partner. Grayson the success-ful son. Lana the flawed but courageous single mother. And Faye the talented accountant. But dig a bit deeper and they're all facades. Stuart was a bully, Grayson a dropout, Lana a liar, and Faye was vile.'

'And how is that different to the rest of us? You're a successful psychologist but a social disaster. I'm charm-ing company but a career dropout. People are good *and* bad. That's what you're always saying to me. Faye might well have been out to kill her whole family, and that might mean she's psychopathic, but that doesn't mean the rest of them are.'

'You mean Lana?'

'Yes. I mean Lana.'

Bloom rested her hands on the desk in front of her, and then spoke softly. 'From what you know of Lana, would you say she showed a degree of irresponsibility?'

'You know I would, but—'

'How about a willingness to live off others? Rely on her daughter to keep house, for example, or on friends to raise her child?'

'Well OK—'

'Would you describe her as impulsive or easily bored?'

Jameson frowned. 'Sometimes. Claire would probably say so.'

'How about failing to take responsibility for her actions, or lying repeatedly?'

Jameson said nothing.

'And have you or Claire seen any remorse or guilt from Lana for the way she's treated Jane?'

'This is crazy, Augusta. Come on. You're exaggerating. Surely.'

'Has Lana Reid ever struck you as having superficial charm, or a higher than average sense of self-worth, or shallow emotions, or—'

'I know, I know. A lack of empathy. I get it. She hits a lot of the indicators.'

Bloom waited, allowing the idea to ferment in her partner's mind. Then she said, 'Happy First Birthday.'

Jameson sat back in his chair.

'It's obvious, really,' she said.

Jameson started to shake his head, then faltered, frowned and met her gaze.

'There are two phrases commonly found on cards for one-year-olds. Happy First Birthday, and—'

'You Are One,' said Jameson.

'You are one,' repeated Bloom. 'You are one what? One of us? One of them? I'm thinking these people have been profiled and selected for something. And with an estimated one per cent of the population possessing psychopathic tendencies, if I'm right, there'll be more of them playing.'

Jameson walked straight past Russell Square tube station and into the Marquis Cornwallis pub. He needed a drink.

Bloom's hypothesis was unnerving. She wasn't one for outlandish theories, and she rarely committed herself to an idea unless she'd thought it through. But this felt oddly knee-jerk. Like something he would throw out as a joke. Like something she'd scoff at. A whole bunch of psychopaths playing a game? Together? And for what purpose? To what end? Jameson thought of the terror plots he'd worked on in MI6 and shuddered. Those had been normal people radicalized to do crazy things. What might someone without a conscience be willing to do?

The Cornwallis was light and airy despite its dark wooden floors, Victorian fireplaces and chunky wooden tables. The window seats were inhabited by large groups of smartly dressed drinkers. Jameson saw Steph at the bar. He raised a hand and waved. Steph worked in the British Medical Association offices around the corner and could often be found here on a week night. She was petite and perky with curly red hair and a dirty laugh. They'd had a few flings – nothing serious, just fun, which had suited him fine. After spending his twenties and early thirties hiding his profession from every woman he dated, he'd become a fan of informal, no-strings relationships. He hoped Steph might take the edge off his day.

'What's occurring?' said Steph in a terrible Welsh accent.

Jameson smiled. He liked that she tried. 'Fancy a drink?' he said. 'I've had a shitty day.'

'Sounds like a blast. Count me in.' Steph held up two fingers to the barman. 'Peroni, please.' She turned to Jameson. 'Wanna talk about it?'

'Nope.'

'Good.' The beers arrived and they clinked their bottles together. Jameson lifted the bottle to his lips and then paused. A woman was approaching, sidling up behind Steph and placing a hand on her shoulder.

'I'm heading off now, Steph,' she said. 'Thanks for inviting me.'

Jameson wanted to look at the woman, but he didn't want to be seen to be looking.

Steph swivelled on her bar stool. 'Are you sure? We're only just getting started. We were going to grab some food later.' Steph looked over at Jameson. 'You up for that, Marcus?'

Before Jameson could respond the woman said, 'That's very kind. Maybe next time though.' He couldn't stop staring at her blue eyes. The smallest of smiles touched her lips. 'Nice to meet you,' she said. Four words clearly meant for him.

Jameson watched the blonde woman walk away as Steph began talking about some actor she'd seen on the train.

'Who was that?' he said, interrupting Steph's story.

'One of the doctors seconded to the BMA. Sarah something. I can't remember now. She's nice. A bit boring, but pleasant enough.'

Jameson continued to drink his beer and catch up with Steph, but he no longer hoped for an invite. That sexy smile and the 'Nice to meet you' had distracted him. And he thought it might be nice to run into Dr Sarah Something again. Very nice indeed.

20

Chief Superintendent Steve Barker called at 7.30am, just as Bloom was finishing her morning run. She'd emailed him the night before – a summary of what they'd learned so far – so she'd been expecting to hear from him.

'I'm setting up a task force following the death of Harry Graham,' he said. 'I've taken a look at what you sent me on this game and I can provide some additional resource to help track down the other players. I don't want any more deaths on our hands.'

Bloom stood at her sink, filled a glass with water and took a large sip. 'Thank you, Steve,' she said. 'Will that be based out of your HQ?'

'To begin with. I've spoken to my counterpart in the Met and if we can show this is of national interest they may be willing to gold-command it, but for now you're stuck with me.'

'No problem at all. Marcus and I can head over later today if you like. For a briefing. Then take it from there.'

'You said in your email you had a working hypothesis?' Bloom had mentioned a theory, but hadn't explicitly mentioned psychopaths.

'We do, but I'd rather go through it face-to-face. It's somewhat sensitive and more than a little controversial.'

'Right. I shall expect nothing less then, Dr Bloom. Shall I organize a briefing for this morning?'

Bloom and Jameson arrived at Avon and Somerset Police Headquarters in Portishead three hours later. Bloom had collected Jameson from his home in Wembley en route. He had offered to drive, but she didn't want him coming to her home to collect her. In the five years they'd been working together, he hadn't visited once. She knew it bugged him.

They were met in reception by DI Carly Mathers. Bloom introduced Jameson, and then they headed to the designated incident room. Chief Superintendent Barker was sitting with half a dozen plain-clothed officers. On the far wall pictures of Faye and Harry Graham, Lana Reid, Grayson Taylor and Stuart Rose-Butler had been stuck to a whiteboard. Under a smiling photograph of Faye and Harry were two gruesome images of Harry's bloodied body. Below that, Fred and Julia grinned out from their school photograph, their innocent faces unaware of the horrors to come.

'How are Fred and Julia?' Bloom asked Mathers.

'Social Services have placed them in a foster home. Faye's mother died years ago and her father's in a home. Harry's parents live in Spain. They're flying over this afternoon, so perhaps they'll take them in.'

'Good morning,' said Barker in a manner that demanded attention. 'Welcome, Dr Bloom – and this must be Mr Jameson.' Barker shook Jameson's hand. 'I'm delighted you're working with us on this.'

Of course, the case now belonged to the police. Senior officers always took ownership when things became interesting.

Barker continued, 'Let me introduce the team. You know Detective Inspector Mathers. We also have DS Phil Green.' Barker gestured to a tall, skinny man in a grey suit that matched the colour of his short hair. DS Green nodded a hello. 'DC Craig Logan, who is our technical wizard. Anything to do with cybercrime, he's your man. He's just finished a secondment with the National Crime Agency in their National Cyber Crime Unit.'

'Good morning,' said DC Logan, the youngest person in the room by some margin. He wasn't much more than twenty-five and his pockmarked skin suggested he had suffered severe acne as a teen.

Barker gestured to another two officers, one male, one female, sitting at the desks behind him. 'And finally we have DC Raj Akhtar and DC Kaye Willis, two of our most experienced CID officers.' The two older DCs smiled at Jameson and Bloom. 'So as I was saying, Dr Bloom leads one of our most popular courses at the National Training Centre on the Psychology of Motivated Crime. I attended three years ago and it was a fascinating and thought-provoking experience. She is also an expert witness for the CPS and along with Mr Jameson here provides specialist investigation support. Is that about right?' He looked at Bloom.

'Spot on. Thank you, Steve.' Bloom deliberately referred to senior officers by their first name when working alongside the police. Civilians weren't required to address officers by their rank and it reminded the team that Bloom and Jameson weren't part of the normal hierarchy.

'I couldn't find much background on you, Mr Jameson,' said Barker.

Jameson smiled. 'Ex-MI6,' he said.

Bloom felt the usual ripple of nervous energy spread across the room. The police, in particular, were often suspicious of Jameson's Secret Service past.

After teas, coffees and packets of biscuits had been delivered by Steve's PA, Bloom took centre stage.

'We know that Faye Graham was the first person to receive one of these birthday cards. That was on January the fifth. You've probably seen the photograph I sent over last night but, for confirmation, it reads "Happy First Birthday" on the front, and then "Your gift is the game. Dare to Play?" on the inside. There's no other information, but there is a small tacky patch at the bottom of the card. The other three cards have the same patch so we're assuming something was stuck here originally.'

'Why "Happy First Birthday"?' said Barker, who was perched on the corner of one of the desks, his highly polished shoe resting on a chair.

'Oh, she'll come to that,' said Jameson.

Bloom knew that Jameson had reservations about her hypothesis, so she was interested to see how the team reacted. 'Faye Graham went missing that very day and hadn't been in touch until she returned to the family home earlier this week. We understand from her son – Fred – that she then stabbed Harry Graham to death.'

This was clearly not news to the team.

'Was there any phone activity for Faye Graham while she was missing?' asked DC Kaye Willis.

'She didn't contact her family or her employer. We would need a warrant to access her phone records,' said Bloom.

'I'll get on to that,' said Willis.

'And let's check call histories for the others too,' said Jameson. 'I've looked at the social media accounts of all four and there's been no activity since they went missing, but we need a more sophisticated examination of their activity over the last year or so. I want to know if they were accessing any particular groups or sites of interest.'

'On it,' said DC Craig Logan, making a note in his book.

'Thank you,' said Bloom. 'Grayson Taylor, a twenty-year-old politics student at Sheffield University, received the same card and went missing after a night out to celebrate his birthday on February the tenth. Stuart Rose-Butler, a twenty-nine-year-old shelf-stacker from Leeds, then disappeared from the scene of a road-traffic accident on the morning of his birthday on February the twenty-fourth.'

'We've an eye witness who claims they saw the driver of the other car pass a white card to Stuart before driving away,' said Jameson.

Bloom continued, 'We've made a request to West

Yorkshire Police to send us the contact details of all three eye witnesses at the incident, but if you could speed things up that'd be helpful.'

'I'll speak to them,' said DC Raj Akhtar.

Bloom nodded. 'Then finally we have the disappearance of Lana Reid on March the ninth, again her birthday, and this is where we came in. Lana's daughter Jane approached us for help.'

'I've known Jane since she was a child,' said Jameson. 'My sister often took care of her when Lana Reid was deployed overseas in the Army. Except we've recently discovered that Lana doesn't and never has worked for the military in any capacity.'

'So what was she doing?' asked Barker.

'We've no idea.' Jameson picked up a pen from the desk beside him and turned it over in his right hand. 'It's a mystery.'

'So what are our working theories?'

Jameson looked at Bloom. He clearly wasn't planning to participate in this part of the briefing.

'As far as we can tell,' began Bloom, 'there's nothing circumstantial linking the four missing people. They are different ages, different genders and have different professions. Some have children, some don't. They were born and live in different locations and, according to their families, they don't know each other. There is some suggestion that they were all unhappy, but we have no evidence of significant problems such as debt, depression or mental health issues. What we do know is that they were all living a lie. As Marcus said, Lana was not really in the military, Grayson was failing his degree, Stuart has no known history beyond the two years he has been with his fiancée, and Faye told her employers she was happy at home but her husband said she was vile.'

'Standard,' said DS Green.

Jameson smiled.

Bloom continued, 'What I've been asking myself is why they would take up a dare just because a random birthday card challenges them to. Why leave their lives to play this game? And I think there are three options. The first is blackmail. Someone has discovered their secrets and is threatening to expose them. Faye Graham might have decided to call the blackmailer's bluff by killing her husband.'

'Harsh, but I've seen crazier things,' said DI Mathers. 'We should dig deeper into their pasts, see what dirt we can find.'

Bloom nodded. 'The second theory is that these people play the game because it promises them something. If we lay this theory on Faye, it could be that she wanted to kill her husband, and this game prepared her mentally and physically for that challenge.'

'In which case, we might have other innocent victims coming our way. And the third theory?' said Chief Superintendent Barker.

'This is where things get a little more concerning,' said Bloom.

'This is your controversial theory.' Chief Superintendent Barker glanced around, checking that everyone was listening.

'I've noticed that our game players display certain traits; traits that concern me.' Bloom stood, picked up a pen from the tray below the whiteboard and wrote a list of keywords as she spoke. 'Stuart, Faye and Grayson have all been described to us as sociable and charming. We also know that all four players were competent liars. Stuart was described as manipulative and a bully by his ex-employer, and we know that Lana deceived her own daughter and the likes of Jameson's sister over a considerable time period. When we spoke to Harry Graham, he said his wife was often angry and aggressive. And we have a report from Grayson's tutor that he threatened to make his life difficult if he was forced to attend lectures. Then we have parasitic lifestyles and a failure to take responsibility. Lana relied on others to raise her daughter, and Stuart happily lived a very comfortable life with his wealthy fiancée while struggling to hold down a menial job himself. Then, of course, we have the level of irresponsibility and impulsiveness needed to walk away from your home, your family, your job and your life to take up some dare . . . So we have a list of traits which sound worryingly familiar.' She read the list on the whiteboard aloud. '*Charming, liar, manipulative, bullying, parasitic, irresponsible, impulsive.* We could easily add *prone to boredom* and *lack of realistic goals* to the list, as we have seen hints of this in all four missing persons.'

'Looks like a description of your average criminal scumbag,' said DS Green.

Bloom nodded. 'That may be.' She took another pen from the tray, this time a red one, and proceeded to write a second column of words: *inflated ego, emotionally shallow, lack of guilt, lack of empathy*. She looked at the faces around the room. Carly Mathers was frowning, DS Green scowling.

'Have you heard of Antisocial Personality Disorder?' Bloom asked. She pointed at the second list. 'Because if we add in these last four traits, that is exactly what this board describes.'

'Isn't that . . . ?' started DI Mathers.

'Yep,' interrupted Jameson, with a deadpan tone and a neutral expression. 'Psychopaths.'

'It's estimated that one in every hundred people possesses antisocial personality traits. These people live among us in astounding commonality,' said Bloom.

'One in every hundred?' said DS Green. He was clearly the sceptic of the group; it was always healthy to have at least one.

'It's a spectrum. We probably all have some of these characteristics, and some of us will be more extreme on, let's say, impulsiveness than others. But some people possess all these qualities at a more extreme level. It's like any human difference. It doesn't mean they're all serial killers and most won't ever commit a crime.'

'So . . . what? They just do nothing?' said DS Green cynically.

'Much like the rest of us, yes.' Bloom replaced the red pen in its tray. 'They live their lives the best they can. Some know they are different and hide it, some simply believe they're normal and assume other people think and feel the way they do.'

'I'd say those last characteristics, the ones in red, are the real traits of a psychopath. And you haven't seen any evidence of any of those in our four players,' said DI Carly Mathers.

Chief Superintendent Barker answered for Bloom. 'Because those are much harder to observe. They're about how that person feels: a lack of guilt, a lack of empathy, a big ego.'

'Exactly,' said Bloom. 'We can't judge those things without speaking to the individuals themselves.'

DS Green was nodding but the scowl remained. 'So let's say all four are psychos. Why the hell would they play a stupid game?'

'People who possess these antisocial traits experience emotions less keenly than the rest of us. They rarely feel scared, coerced, or motivated to fit in, and so their decisions are calculated on the basis of *What do I gain?* Life is a game to them. They're often highly competitive, feel superior to their fellow human beings, and make decisions from a totally selfish position.'

'So a game would appeal to them more than it would to a normal person?' said DC Kaye Willis.

Bloom chose not to challenge the concept that there is any such thing as a normal person. 'More than that. If I'm right, this game has been designed specifically *for* them. I think someone has selected people with these traits and invited them to play.'

'Selected how?' Barker asked.

'I don't know. That's where I need your help.' Bloom looked at DC Logan. 'Could it be something online?

Somehow tracking their decisions and behaviours? Or even getting them to complete a questionnaire?'

'How the hell do you do that without people getting suspicious?' DS Green said.

'People are completing questionnaires all the time,' replied DC Logan. 'For marketing purposes. All those pop quizzes. "What type of animal are you?" Things that trend on social media. They're all designed to collect our personal data.'

'So someone could place their own questionnaire into the mix to identify psychopaths?' Jameson seemed to be coming around to the theory.

'It's possible. I can look at the online activity of these four people and see if they completed any quizzes or questionnaires,' said Logan.

'Perfect,' said Bloom.

'And how sure are you of this theory?' said Chief Superintendent Barker. 'How much effort should we be putting into this theory compared to the other two?'

'I think it would be sensible to pursue all three for the sake of open-mindedness. But there's one more element that I think adds weight to the third option.' Bloom reached into her handbag and pulled out a card she'd bought at the petrol station. It had a picture on the front of a bunny driving a red train and at the top it said, YOU ARE ONE. 'I think "Happy First Birthday" is a play on words, or perhaps even a joke. I think it sends a message; it says, "I've been watching you and have identified that *you are one*." Being chosen would make the dare even more intoxicating to a self-centred, highly competitive risk-taker.'

DC Kaye Willis leaned forward in her seat. 'You're saying we have four psychopaths out there playing some sick game and no idea why?'

Jameson smiled at Willis and then looked at Bloom. 'Oh no. What Dr Bloom is saying is that someone is selecting psychopaths to play a game, and that an estimated one per cent of the population are psychopaths. So we have way in excess of four players. If she's right, of course.'

There was total silence.

21

With the girls at school, Claire's kitchen looked much less cluttered: no toys on the floor or crayons covering the table. 'So where's Jane gone?' Jameson asked.

'Shopping in town with her friends. Not that she has any money, poor thing. I've given her twenty quid but that won't get much more than some lunch, will it? Tell me, what's with all the secrecy? Why *I need to speak to you in private?*' Claire asked, deepening her voice in a pretty convincing impression of her brother.

Jameson suppressed his rising panic. He didn't like the idea of Jane being out unsupervised. Faye had murdered her husband. Could Lana hurt her own daughter?

'It's our latest theory. There's a chance Lana might have been selected to play this game because of her personality type.'

'What d'you mean?'

'You know the stuff you've been complaining about? That she's an irresponsible mother, that she drinks too much and has crazy one-night stands. There may be more to it.'

'Go on.' Claire slurped her tea noisily, just like their mother.

'You're not going to like this, sis, but Lana's been lying for years. She's never been deployed oversees by the Army because she's never been in the Army, or the Navy, or the RAF, or any military organization for that matter.'

Claire held the mug below her mouth. 'What?'

'She's not and never has been employed by the military or the government, neither overtly nor covertly. An old colleague I worked with at River House checked every database. He ran her information through all their systems using personal details, photo recognition, biometrics such as fingerprints and DNA – and nothing.'

'But she sent me photographs from Afghanistan.' Claire got up and grabbed her iPad from the kitchen worktop. 'She's been on five tours. I looked after Jane for three of them.' Claire passed the iPad to her brother. The picture on the screen was of Lana squatting in camouflage trousers and a sand-coloured T-shirt beside two male colleagues, all holding cigarettes and smiling into the camera.

'Can you send me this?'

Claire took the iPad back and tapped the screen a few times. 'Done.'

'This is going to sound weird – and I don't want you to panic – but would you say there's anything sinister about Lana?'

'Sinister?'

'You know. Dark and twisty. Fucked up. That type of thing.'

'She's certainly dark and twisty. She's a bit fucked up – lots of drink and drugs – but I've always thought she was suffering from PTSD. She said she had PTSD. That she'd seen some terrible shit and that it changes a person.'

'But she hadn't seen anything. Did she ever show guilt?'

Claire shrugged. 'I'm sure she did feel guilty.'

'But did she show it?'

'What are you getting at, Marcus? Stop being cryptic and spit it out.'

Jameson shook his head. 'I can't, sis. Not until we know more. It wouldn't be fair on Lana or Jane. Last question though: what do you know about Lana's past? Where did she live before she moved here? I've been trying to track down Jane's father but I don't even know his name.'

'I've got his name somewhere. Lana gave me Jane's birth certificate years ago. I needed to get her a passport.'

Jameson raised his eyebrows quizzically.

'She was staying with us one summer and we were planning a holiday. Give me a minute. I've still got it upstairs, I think.' Claire got up and left the room.

Jameson waited, hoping he hadn't given too much away. There was still a chance that Bloom was wrong about this. They might not have to tell Jane that her mother was a psychopath.

Claire came back into the room with a long slip of pink paper. 'Here you go. I knew I had it.'

Jameson took the birth certificate, wishing he was as organized as his sister. Their mother was the same. He skimmed the page and there, beside the word 'Father', it said 'Thomas Lake'.

As Jameson opened his car door, he saw a familiar figure sitting on the wall in front of Claire's neighbour's house.

'Claire said you'd gone into town with your friends.'

Jane looked at him with swollen red eyes.

He sat down on the wall beside her and put an arm around her shoulder. 'What's happened?'

'I heard Claire on the phone to you earlier. You wanted to speak to her without me there. Mum's dead, isn't she?'

'Oh, Jane.' He hugged her a little tighter. 'There's no news on your mum, good or bad, I'm afraid.'

'So why did you need to speak to Claire alone?'

'Look, sweetheart, you know Claire and Dan think of you as part of the family, as do I, so whatever happens you have a home.'

'Answer my question. I want to know what's happening. She's my mum.'

Jameson took a deep breath. Jane had a right to know what they'd learned, but he would stick to the facts. 'We found out that your mum isn't employed by the Army and never has been.' He paused to let that sink in.

After a few moments, Jane said, 'So where's our money been coming from?'

Jane was a practical girl. He had expected a torrent of denial. 'We don't know,' he said.

Jane frowned. 'Why would she lie?'

The million-dollar question. 'We don't know.'

'What *do* you know?'

'We know . . .' Jameson hesitated. He chose his words carefully. 'We know that Faye Graham is alive three months after her disappearance. So there's a good chance your mum and the others are too.'

'Someone killed her husband, though. I saw it on the news. How do you know he didn't kill Faye too?'

'We're pretty sure Faye is still alive.'

'How can you be? Is she home?'

'I'm sorry, Jane. We're working really hard and have a team of police officers helping us now. We're going to do everything we can to find your mum, and in the meantime I'm trying to locate your father.'

Jane jumped down from the wall. 'No!' she said. 'I don't want you to! I don't want him anywhere near me. And you said I'd always have a home here. I don't want him in my life. I want my mum.'

'OK, OK.' Jameson held up his hands. 'Don't worry. I need to try and find him; I need to ask some questions about your mum's past.'

Jane placed her hands over her mouth and her eyes widened. 'You think it's him, don't you? You think he's got her!'

'No, Jane. We don't. We don't think that at all.'

Jane looked at him. 'I don't believe you. You're lying.'

Jameson was hiding more than he was saying. He pushed himself off the wall and placed his hands on Jane's shoulders. 'You asked for our help, Jane, and we're doing everything we can, but you're going to have to trust me. Can you do that?'

22

Dear Diary,

That bitch Claudia is going to regret messing with me. She won't know what I've done — I'm too smart for that. But she'll wish she'd stayed in her place.

She thought she could twist this to her advantage. She thought she could take the group. She told them I was a weirdo, a monster or something, even though it was me who saved her from being raped again. Not the sort of thank-you I'd hoped for.

But here's the thing. She needs to learn to be careful. Dreary Darren Shaw knows it — the pencil in his neck caused a stroke so he's pretty much a vegetable — and now Claudia will know it too.

It didn't take much. Just a few calls to the other girls. I told them how hurt I was that Claudia was lying. I told each of them that I'd only phoned them, that they were my bestie, and they bought it because they all love me. Then I told them a few of the things I'd heard Claudia saying to Dreary Darren. Like how much she loved him and how much she wanted him. All lies, of course, but a little doubt was enough . . . and poor little Claudia became a freak.

And believe me, there's more to come for that little traitor.

Seraphine sat back and re-read her diary entry. Dr Bloom was right. It was liberating to write simply for yourself. She could stack up all her victories in one little book, then re-live them and enjoy them whenever she fancied.

Bloom was sitting with her feet curled beneath her on the large chair in the corner of her bedroom reading *Go Set a Watchman* when her phone rang. She didn't mind being interrupted. She wasn't even sure she liked the book. It was no *Mockingbird*.

'Bloom,' she said, by way of hello.

'Augusta. This is Steve Barker. I'm sorry to ring so late, but I've had a call from our Chief Constable asking why we're looking into these birthday-card disappearances.'

'How did they know about it?'

'When DC Logan started trawling the internet for related clues, a red flag went up.'

'So they were aware of the case already?'

'Yes and no. It turns out one of our own is missing too: a DCI from the Merseyside force. He didn't turn up to work three shifts in a row so his boss sent a couple of PCs to check his home. They found one of these cards.'

'When?'

'Last week. Wednesday. The DCI has something of a chequered record. He's been investigated three times. As a young PC he was implicated in the Hillsborough cover-up. Then there was an allegation of attempted rape ten years ago. It was from a witness on one of his cases; she dropped the charges. And he was recently investigated again. There were rumours he was taking back-handers from a local crime family to look the other way.'

'I see.' Bloom opened her tablet. 'Can you give me his name?'

'Detective Chief Inspector Warren Beardsley.'

'Anything else from your Chief Constable?'

'That we need to be careful what we say. And to who. His priority is public relations.'

The line went quiet for a moment and then Barker said, 'I've got a horrible feeling you might be right about this, Augusta.'

While Bloom was speaking to Chief Superintendent Barker, Lana Reid was struggling to get comfortable in a shop doorway beneath a stolen blanket that smelled of stale beer and urine. She'd picked bad marks; that was the problem. A banker and a barrister. It was too ambitious. They weren't keen on her drinking – bedtimes were early; work in the morning – and they were ruthless too. The barrister had kicked her out two hours ago and refused to give her the things she'd accumulated over the past two weeks. He'd said it was collateral for the shit he'd put up with. She was supposed to be fleecing him, stealing his money, manipulating him.

It was the drink. She needed to stop. She was better than this. She should be flying through this game.

Sometimes she couldn't cope with the boredom of suburban life as a single mum. So she took off – just for a few months – and created a separate life. She found a bloke, strung him along, manipulated him, lived off him, call it what you will. She was good at finding affluent, needy men who would fall for her particular brand of sexy, the vulnerable heroine. She enjoyed the role. But she could never desert Jane completely. Jane was her child, her responsibility, and so, eventually, she always returned home.

24

Jameson considered taking the main road to work, past the British Medical Association building, but instead followed Bloom's normal route, left off Euston Road and through the quieter back streets. It was a fortuitous choice. A few minutes from the office, he came across a small independent cafe called Fork. Nestled in between tiled partition walls, its pale wooden panelling and large arched windows reminded him of the cafes of continental Europe. There, in the queue at the counter, stood Dr Sarah Something. She was wearing a simple black dress and black heels that showed off her toned calves. Her blonde hair was in a neat bun.

'Hello again,' Jameson said, joining the queue.

She turned. 'Oh,' she said, bemused. 'Hello.'

'Marcus Jameson. We met the other night at the Marquis. You were there with Steph Chambers.' He was only slightly disappointed that she hadn't remembered him.

'Sorry,' she said, smiling. 'I've met so many new people recently. They've all merged into one!' She turned back to the counter to order a flat white.

Ouch, thought Jameson.

'Yes?' said the girl behind the counter.

'Large latte to go, please,' he replied.

'Just one size.' The girl had a strong Eastern European accent. She waved her hand at the blackboard behind her.

Sarah collected her coffee. She'd be leaving any minute. He handed over a fiver, then called to Sarah, 'Is the coffee good?'

She looked back at him. 'Excuse me?'

'Is it good? The coffee? I've never been here before.'

'Yes.' She pulled the door open.

'Maybe I'll see you here again, then,' he said.

With just a small nod of her head, she was gone.

Jameson took a sip of his coffee. She was right. It tasted pretty good. A second reason to make this his regular coffee shop.

'G'day, Sheila,' Jameson said as he walked into their small office.

'G'day, Bruce,' replied Bloom. 'Sit down. You'll want to hear this.' Jameson perched on the edge of his desk. 'We have another player. A DCI from Merseyside. He went missing last week and colleagues found the card in his flat.'

'A copper?'

'And a dodgy one at that. He's been investigated for everything from corruption to attempted rape.'

Jameson whistled.

'There are more psychopathic traits higher up the corporate tree. So I expect this won't be our last player in a position of power.'

'I reckon I've worked for a few in my time.' Jameson

switched on his laptop. 'I have a name for Jane's father. Thomas Lake. Claire knew it all along.'

'How did she take the news?'

'About Lana? She couldn't believe it. She showed me a photograph Lana had sent from Afghanistan. I should have an email from . . . Yep. Photoshopped, according to my man. He found the original.' Jameson leaned in closer to his screen. 'She swapped in her own head. Did a pretty good job, too.'

'She's resourceful. I can't argue with that.'

'So where the hell has she been going all these years?'

'It's not unusual for psychopathic personalities to live double lives – triple lives even. She could have another family running in parallel. Some male psychopaths have dozens of children via multiple marriages, sometimes all over the world. They're an impressive bunch; they cover their tracks.'

'You really love psychopaths, don't you?'

Bloom tutted. 'I have a healthy interest. And it's my job. And,' she continued, 'it makes sense to understand those who might struggle to understand and think like us.'

Jameson turned back to his laptop. 'Like I said, you love them. Whereas I'm freaking out that the conscienceless are out there murdering their loved ones.'

'We don't know that. I find it hard to believe that Faye was the first to start playing and the first to finish. There must be others.'

'Maybe. But murders happen all the time. The police

might have missed the link. We should get protection for Jane and the other families. If we can't convince the police to foot the bill, I've got a few old mates who work privately now.'

'I think you do our crime-fighters a disservice. If there'd been other linked deaths, I'm sure we'd know.'

'Can we take that chance? We should assume that the other players will do a Faye.'

'OK. Talk to the police, then.'

'And what made you suspect Faye was a psychopath? It wasn't the kid waving the tiger?'

'It was, actually. I'd noted some common traits from our interviews, but nothing too alarming. But when Fred described Julia's lack of fear, things clicked. I asked myself why Julia's fearlessness stopped Faye. Faye would have seen that Freddie was afraid. She might have recognized such fear, but I don't think she'd be able to relate to it. But when Julia strode forward and growled – *that* she could relate to.'

'She saw herself in Julia?'

'I think most six-year-olds would instinctively know that something was wrong. Julia might not have witnessed her father's murder, but her mother would have been covered in blood and carrying a knife.'

'But she wasn't scared.'

'Exactly.'

Jameson looked horrified. 'Can a child even be a psychopath?'

Bloom exhaled slowly. 'Some would say so. Personally, I think we're born with certain tendencies that are either exaggerated or negated by our experiences. But there may be a few characteristics that are fixed from birth.' She thought about Seraphine. The girl had described her parents on numerous occasions as fabulous, but the description always felt too overstated to ring true, and she could never back it up with any examples of how they were fabulous. The true nature of Seraphine's home life remained a mystery.

'So potentially psychopathic traits can be inhibited in the right circumstances?'

'I didn't say that. There's evidence that the brain of an adult psychopath functions very differently to that of other adults, but it's impossible to say whether those differences are innate. Some share your fear – they argue that psychopaths are the natural predators of our species – but they're also our wildest adventurers, our risk-takers, those willing to sail across an ocean with no knowledge of what's on the other side.'

'So you're saying they contribute? That they're essential?'

'They work as surgeons, soldiers, firefighters, entrepreneurs. Many contribute positively to society. Sure, some steal, some murder, but most don't. I think the problem here is that the game seems to be encouraging antisocial choices.'

'We need to stop thinking about the game.'

'Pardon?'

'You said that "the game" encourages antisocial choices. But it's not "the game", is it? It's the person behind the game.'

'Right.'

'Because they're a psychopath, too. That's what you're thinking, isn't it?'

Bloom looked at Jameson. She liked that he was quick; it was one of his most attractive qualities. 'I expect so. To recruit latent psychopaths—'

'And corrupt them?'

Bloom nodded. 'You'd need a solid understanding of what motivates them.'

'So what's the motive? You think they're being primed for something?'

'That's my fear.'

'Christ, Bloom.'

'And sending them all off home to kill their husbands or wives is too ... pedestrian. What's in it for the puppeteer?'

'Power?'

'Perhaps,' said Bloom. 'But I think it's more than that. This game is ambitious; it's outlandish. There's more than power at play.'

25

'Dr Bloom is right,' said DC Craig Logan.

Jameson rolled his eyes. Bloom shrugged. She couldn't help it.

They were on a conference call with Chief Superintendent Barker, DC Logan, DI Carly Mathers and DC Kaye Willis. DC Logan had trawled the internet for questionnaires that might profile psychopaths and had found a few that might fit. There was one on Psych Central – 'The Psychopath Test' – and a few floating around on various social media platforms: 'What 80s Film Would You Be?' and 'Are You a Genius?'

'And I'm afraid I've uncovered another forty people who disappeared after receiving one of the cards,' DC Logan continued. 'And the number is rising.'

'*Forty?*' said Barker, his voice tinny. 'As in four zero?'

'Yes, Sir. Four zero. I repeated Jane Reid's online approach, asking if anyone's loved ones had gone missing after receiving a strange birthday card. I posted the enquiry via multiple accounts across multiple platforms. And I've confirmed at least forty further disappearances.'

'Not as a police officer, I hope?' Barker asked.

'No. With a dummy persona. A young man looking for his sister. I didn't include any specific details – the look of the card, the exact wording or the existence of a sticky patch – so I've been able to filter out the frauds.'

'When did the first person receive a card?' asked Jameson.

'That's the weird thing. The first was over a year ago.'

'So what's the next step?' asked Barker.

'Craig and I will continue to monitor the responses,' said DI Mathers. 'And if Dr Bloom and Mr Jameson could take a look at the questionnaires?'

'We'll do that straight away,' said Bloom. 'Were any of them completed by our original four players?'

'Yes,' replied DC Logan. 'I'll send over a list of who did what, but in short, all four completed at least one of these quizzes.'

'Are you on the dark web, Craig?' asked Jameson.

'Yes,' said DC Logan. 'No references to the Birthday Card Game there, as far as I can tell. And if there was a website or forum, I'd have found something by now.'

'On that note,' said DC Kaye Willis, 'I have an update on Faye Graham's phone usage. Not much to find there either. Just after she went missing, she accessed 315 megabytes of data, but there's been no activity since then.'

'They probably dump their own phone and get an unregistered one,' said DC Logan. 'They could use it to access whatever they need to play.'

'Can we find out what the 315 megabytes were used for?' asked Jameson.

'I've requested details from the phone company. We should have that today or tomorrow,' said Willis.

'Good work,' said Barker. 'Let's speak again tomorrow.'

'So they've given it a name,' said Jameson, after hanging up. 'The Birthday Card Game. Catchy.'

'Or not.'

'Forty players.'

'And rising,' said Bloom.

They spent the next few hours analysing the questionnaires from DC Logan. Those identifying as psychopath tests were too obvious and therefore too easy for respondents to manipulate. The profiler would need potential players to answer questions honestly, so they couldn't know the motive behind the questions. The social media quizzes were more promising. They included 'How Persuasive Are You?', 'The Five-Minute Personality Test', and Bloom's personal favourite, 'Which Greek God Would You Be?' The latter included clever questions to determine vengefulness and ruthlessness. The four players Bloom and Jameson had been investigating had each completed several similar quizzes and posted their results online. Bloom flagged the quizzes and sent them back to DC Logan with a note to find more like these. An accurate profile would require numerous questionnaires.

26

Jameson had struck up a rapport with Alina the Latvian barista over the last few days, but there'd been no sign of Dr Sarah Something. He was sitting flicking through the *Metro*, hoping she might appear, but he needed to get to the office to carry out telephone interviews with the witnesses to Stuart's car accident along with DC Akhtar. With luck, they might have a description of their games master by the end of the day.

'Thanks, Alina,' he called as he headed outside.

At the end of the block, walking towards him, was Dr Sarah Something.

'Hello,' she said. Her tone sounded polite but her eyes screamed *stalker*.

'You were right about the coffee,' said Jameson. 'Shame about the name.' He smiled up at the cafe's sign.

Sarah looked at it and frowned.

'The owners aren't English,' he said. 'They don't realize how easily Fork can sound like – well, you know.'

'I see,' said Sarah, looking up at the sign again.

'Anyway,' he said, 'have a nice day.' He turned and walked away as quickly as he could.

The telephone interviews were wholly unsatisfactory. The first interviewee was convinced that a tall, slim, olive-skinned man in an expensive suit had exited the other car and handed a white envelope to Stuart while he sat in his damaged vehicle. She said that no words were exchanged and the tall man then returned to his white Land Rover Discovery and drove away. She suspected it was to do with drugs. The second witness contradicted much of what the first had said. He had been in his work van and had slammed on his brakes to avoid hitting Stuart's car when it was shunted into his path. He remembered a fair-skinned man of average height exiting a white Land Rover Discovery and exchanging details with Stuart. He remembered a small piece of paper being handed over. He'd assumed it was a business card. The third witness saw the collision and then pulled up to call emergency services. By the time he got out of his car, the white Land Rover was gone. He approached Stuart to tell him the police were on their way. He didn't see Stuart leave.

'People never see the same thing,' said DC Akhtar. 'Best-case scenario is they don't directly contradict each other.'

'But they did,' said Jameson, feeling frustrated. The only consensus was that a white Land Rover had hit Stuart's car and that both drivers had left the scene before the police arrived. 'How do we trace this guy?'

'No one took down the Land Rover's registration. The West Yorkshire force are checking CCTV but I wouldn't hold my breath.'

'Before you go,' said Jameson, 'can I ask you to check your database for someone? His name's Thomas Lake.

Probably aged between thirty-five and forty-five. He may have been arrested for drink or drug offences fifteen or so years ago in the Greater London area.'

'Thomas Lake. Got it.'

'You'd better look at domestic abuse or any violent crimes too. He had a temper, by all accounts.'

'Who is he? Another player?'

'I hope not. He's Jane Reid's father. I've checked the electoral register for Greater London and he's no longer on it, so he must have moved.'

'I'll see what I can do.'

While Jameson and DC Akhtar were interviewing the witnesses to his accident, Stuart Rose-Butler sat in a rented BMW in a car park near the maternity ward at Airedale Hospital in Yorkshire. He had been keeping tabs on Libby through Facebook and had seen the messages of congratulation appear yesterday afternoon. Apparently he had a son.

He'd planned to go in, but had changed his mind on the drive. He'd progressed up the league table at a pace and life was sweet. He was living in the swanky apartment of Harriet Goodway, the woman he'd selected in the lobby of The Principal Hotel, and was gradually siphoning money from her savings account. He'd infiltrated her small group of friends and was creating as much conflict and chaos as possible. He was pretty confident he could get Harriet's closest friend into bed.

It was liberating to be living life on his own terms and finally using his talents. It would be foolish to walk back into his old life with Libby. He would have to give up this freedom, sacrifice the thrills. And in the eyes of his competitors, he would be a dropout. And he never wanted to be a dropout again.

So he sat in the car park with a hat pulled low over his forehead and waited. He just needed one look at his son and then he would leave.

27

Like butter wouldn't melt. Her granny used to say it all the time, but Seraphine hadn't understood before.

'I know what you mean by "outstanding",' Seraphine said. 'I found your PhD thesis.'

She'd expected an apology. That was what usually happened when she caught someone out. But Bloom simply sat and smiled, *like butter wouldn't melt.*

'I said I know what you mean. I know what you've been doing.'

'And what is that, Seraphine?' said Dr Bloom, her smile fixed in place.

'Trying to catch me out. You've been trying to trick me.'

Dr Bloom tilted her head a little to the left. 'And why would I do that?'

She was so calm. Why was she so calm? Seraphine felt herself growing angrier and angrier. 'So you can tell my parents and my teachers and the police probably.'

'I see,' replied Dr Bloom. 'Let me reassure you that I won't be doing any of those things.'

Seraphine stared, but Dr Bloom didn't react. Again, this was unusual. People almost always looked away from Seraphine's stare.

Dr Bloom leaned forward in her chair. 'What do you think I mean by "outstanding"?'

'That I'm some kind of monster.'

'And why would you think that?'

'Because that's who you studied ... serial-killer psychos.'

Bloom sat back and finally frowned. 'No, I didn't. I studied teenagers and young adults with specific traits. They were not serial killers; none of them had ever committed a murder.'

'Why?'

'I'm interested in what it takes to be human. And I wanted to study one extreme aspect of mankind, one that I think is very revealing.'

'No. Not that. I mean why didn't they murder anyone?'

'Because they chose not to.'

'Or maybe no one pissed them off enough.'

Bloom's lips curled just a little. 'Or that – yes.'

'And you think I'm one of these psychos, just because I defended myself?'

'It's totally irrelevant what I think. What matters is what *you* think, or what you know about who you are and how you differ from other people. You said I'd tricked you, but I've not revealed anything new to you. You already knew that you were different. You work hard to cover it up, and may I say, you do so with an impressive level of self-control for someone so young.'

'So why am I here if you're only telling me what I already know?' Was she giving too much away? 'If that's what's happening.'

'So that you have one person who's on your side and willing to help you.'

'Help me what?'

Bloom looked at her and said, 'Help you to choose, Seraphine.'

28

Chief Superintendent Steve Barker had scheduled daily conference calls. Bloom dialled in and listened to the music on the other end of the line. She had planned to rush back from her one-to-one to dial in alongside Jameson, but things had taken longer than expected.

She put in her earphones and scanned through her emails as she waited, opening one from the Crown Prosecution Service solicitor. They were charging her client with inflicting grievous bodily harm. There was no evidence to suggest wounding with intent.

Barker introduced himself and Bloom closed down the email.

In a sobering update, DC Logan revealed that the Birthday Card Game had at least 109 players. He had finally tracked down the game's website deep in the dark web and, so far, it was totally inaccessible. DC Kaye Willis was yet to hear from the various phone companies regarding the data usage, but she had confirmed that Stuart, Grayson and Lana had all downloaded something similar in the first few hours after disappearing. As Barker set out the priorities for the next few days, Bloom received three missed calls from the same London number. Someone was keen to speak to her. She listened to the voicemail message. A Dr Claude Fallon from the Health and Care Professions Council asked her to return his call as a matter of urgency.

The governing body for professional psychologists was a passive regulator. Bloom had never received a call from them before, not since they'd taken over from the British Psychological Society. But she did as requested and returned the call.

'Dr Claude Fallon.' The man had a deep voice and an assertive tone. Bloom guessed he was in his fifties, perhaps older.

'This is Dr Bloom returning your calls.'

'Ah yes, Dr Bloom, I'm afraid we have something of a problem. We've received a rather serious complaint regarding your suitability to practise.'

'Excuse me?'

'Yes. We've forwarded it on to our Health and Care Professions Tribunal Service. The HCPTS.'

'Without speaking to me first? What's it about?'

'It's a rather delicate matter, so we felt it should be handled by the professionals at this stage. I would advise you to secure some professional advice for yourself . . . legally, I mean.'

Bloom's shock gave way to anger. 'Who made this complaint? What exactly is it about?'

'I'm afraid I can't say any more over the telephone.'

'You can summon me to a tribunal but you can't tell me why? That's ridiculous. I demand to know.'

'The HCPTS will be in touch to talk you through the process and provide the necessary details. This is simply a courtesy call.'

'A courtesy call?'

'Like I say, the HCPTS will be in touch,' said Dr Claude Fallon and then he was gone.

This made no sense. Who had she worked with recently? Who might have an issue with her advice? Who would hold such a grudge?

Each question led to one answer: Dave Jones, the man who had accused asexual Jamie Bolton of grooming his twelve-year-old daughter, Amy. This was all she needed.

29

Lana hated to admit it, but her latest opponent was out of her league. PV had already posted evidence of his latest triumph, pictures of an old lady he'd defrauded asleep with a large purple bruise across her eye. He'd also attached evidence of the cash she'd handed over for whatever fake job he'd promised to do, and a bank statement showing a transfer of £42,300 from her legitimate account to his ghost account. Lana hadn't even identified a target. She was going to drop down the league table – again – and have a lower-level opponent assigned, someone who, like PV, would walk all over her. Why couldn't she stop drinking? She had lost thirteen of the last twenty-four hours to the bottle.

The answer came to her with total clarity.

She couldn't do it alone. She couldn't stay sober alone. She needed help.

Jameson was standing outside Fork trying to access the game. *One hundred and nine confirmed players,* he thought as he followed the link and instructions sent over by DC Logan. He downloaded the Tor browser bundle needed to access encrypted websites via his phone. The site opened with a bright white screen and three boxes requesting your full name, date of birth and unique user reference. The only other content was three lines of silver writing at the bottom of the page that read:

HAPPY 1ST BIRTHDAY.
YOUR GIFT IS THE GAME.
DARE TO PLAY?
YOU HAVE ONE CHANCE AND
ONE CHANCE ONLY.
THE GAME MUST START TODAY.

'Good morning.'

Jameson looked up to see Dr Sarah Something standing in front of him.

'Dr Sarah Something.'

Her laugh was low and husky. Jameson liked it. A lot.

He shrugged. 'That's how Steph introduced you.'

'I see.'

'It makes you sound like a comic-strip sidekick.' Why was he saying these ridiculous things?

'You looked engrossed,' she said, nodding to his phone.

'Yeah. Work. It's a little crazy at the moment.' Understatement of the century.

'What do you do?'

Their first proper conversation and here, just a few moments into it, was his first lie. 'I'm a researcher,' he replied.

'University?'

'Freelance.'

She looked at him. Her light blue eyes were captivating. 'Can I get you a coffee?' she asked.

'No, thanks,' Jameson replied. 'I've got to . . .' He held the phone up; he needed to finish this.

'It's no problem. I'll get you a take-out. What do you have?'

'Just a latte.'

'Just a latte it is then, James.'

'Jameson. Marcus Jameson.'

She held out her hand. 'Something. Sarah Something.'

Jameson laughed and shook her hand, this first physical contact pinching in the pit of his stomach. He wondered if she'd felt it too.

She opened the door to the cafe and he called out, 'In case you were worried, I'm not stalking you. I just like the coffee.'

Just before the door closed behind her, he heard her say, 'Disappointing.'

'Why are you smiling?' Bloom asked as Jameson walked into their office with a takeout cup and a small paper bag.

'Because it's a good day, Sheila,' he said. 'I bought croissants.'

'Have you seen Logan's email?'

'Yup.' Jameson sat down and passed a pain au chocolat across the table.

'We can't get any further without an access code. It's locked up tight.'

'I don't like the name,' said Jameson through a mouthful of croissant. 'The Birthday Card Game sounds like it's for toddlers. I vote for a rebrand. The Psychopath Collector? Maybe it'll get more attention.'

'Why would we want attention?'

'Not from the public. From the police.' Jameson wiped his mouth with a paper napkin. 'DC Akhtar couldn't get any CCTV from Stuart's accident from the West Yorkshire force. Not a priority, apparently. Well, maybe they'd pay more attention if they knew we were looking for hundreds of psychopaths.'

Bloom nodded and took a bite of the croissant. 'Thanks for this.'

Jameson winked at her.

'What's with you today?' she asked. 'You're all . . . odd.'

'I've got a date.'

'Oh, I see. Well, so long as your social life is tickety-boo . . .' She felt unreasonably irritated. He was allowed to go on dates, after all. But in light of what they were dealing with, romance seemed pretty unimportant right now.

'Hey! Don't get grumpy with me because you're lonely and single. Be pleased that I can find good stuff to balance out the shit.'

'I am not lonely and single.'

'You are single though.'

'Yes, and happy that way, thank you very much.'

'Do you even know that for sure?' Jameson finished his croissant and brushed the flakes into his waste-paper bin. 'When was your last relationship?'

Bloom turned back to her work. She was not having this conversation. 'There's something I need to tell you,' she said. 'I had a call from the Health and Care Professions Council yesterday. They've received a complaint about my competence to practise and have put me under investigation. I had the formal letter this morning.'

'Blimey,' said Jameson. 'I thought you were about to tell me you were a lesbian.'

Bloom looked at him. She was definitely irritated now. 'And would that be such a problem?'

Jameson held his hands up and flashed her his don't-take-offence smile. 'Not at all. Some of my favourite women are lesbians.'

'You're better than that, Marcus.'

'Sorry, Mum.' He smirked and took a sip of his coffee. 'Are you worried? Is there anything to this complaint?'

Bloom passed him the letter. 'Dave Jones thinks I had an inappropriate relationship with his daughter. He's claiming that I met her informally outside the consultation rooms and even at my home.'

'Wow.'

'I didn't.'

'Well, no. Of course you didn't. You're . . . Bloom.'

'No need to be glib.'

'I'm not! I'm just saying you're the most straight-laced, moral person I know. Even our local vicar has more questionable ethics than you.'

Bloom raised her eyebrows.

'I was a choirboy. Didn't know that, did you? Dad was really into the Big Man.'

Bloom couldn't help but smile. He was the best cure for a terrible day. 'They won't find any evidence because there isn't any, but it's going to tie me up in an investigation.'

He handed the letter back. 'We'll sort it. And here's a question that's been bugging me. This website is a fortress, right? And our psychopath players all disappear eventually. So why bother with these cards? Why not email people? Or text them? Or even better, WhatsApp? That bloody thing has end-to-end encryption so we'll never find out what was going on.'

'I've wondered that myself. They must want us to know what they're doing. Without the cards we wouldn't know that the disappearances were linked or how many players there were. The recipients are told to remove something from inside – whatever the sticky patch holds in place, I'd guess directions to the website and their unique user reference – so why not tell them to destroy the card too? At the last count we have one hundred and nine people who simply left it behind to be found.'

'So it's a calling card, after all.'

'It's a *Look at me, aren't I clever?* card. That's what it is.'

'They're showing off. They might mess up at some point.'

'We're dealing with a very high-functioning psychopath here, so probably not. Most people make mistakes when they become emotional and forget to follow their own rules—'

'But psychopaths don't get emotional.'

'Not as often, no. The one angle we have is ego. They might get carried away with their own brilliance and become complacent. The question is, how do we make them do that?'

Jameson thought for a moment. 'We make them think they're winning. They need to believe that we have nothing and know nothing because they're simply too clever. It's a Romanova play.'

'Romanova?'

'It's what we called an operation in MI6 that required psychological manipulation. It's from the Black Widow. The Marvel comics? Natasha Romanova? Have you seen that scene in *The Avengers* where she's tied to a chair being interrogated, but in fact she's interrogating them? I can see from the look on your face that you haven't, but you get the gist.'

Bloom did get the gist, but until they knew who was masterminding the game, tactics were worthless.

30

In Yorkshire, Stuart Rose-Butler – or Stuart Lord as he now preferred to be known – walked out of Leeds train station and towards Park Square in the city's financial district.

The streets surrounding the park were silent apart from the occasional passing car and, when he reached it, the park was empty. There were Georgian buildings on either side, all with large windows and grand doorways. Most were occupied by firms of solicitors or barristers' chambers. Stuart checked the message again.

We are very impressed.
Meet me in Park Square, Leeds, tomorrow at 1.30pm.

And that was it. No name. No description. Stuart looked at his watch: 1.28pm. He took a seat on a bench and waited.

Exactly two minutes later, a tall man, thin and olive-skinned, strolled into the park. Stuart recognized him immediately. He stood as the man approached him.

'Good afternoon, Sir.' The man held his hand out and his shake was so firm as to be painful. 'Sebastian Forbes.'

Sebastian wore a tweed jacket and a navy tie with what looked to be a diamond-encrusted tie pin. Stuart was glad he was wearing his new Armani suit. 'Good after-noon,' said Stuart, making his accent as refined as possible. Sebastian no doubt knew his history, but things had moved on and he wanted them to see it.

'And by what name shall I address you?'

Stuart had been instructed to change his identity sev-eral challenges back. He had thought long and hard about his new name. 'Stuart Lord.'

'From a Butler to a Lord. Very good. Please, come with me, Mr Lord. There are some people keen to meet you.'

Sebastian Forbes led Stuart to a building a few roads away. There were no signs outside and no doorbell, just a shiny black door. Forbes knocked firmly, just once, and waited. A second or two later the door opened on an automatic hinge. The two men entered an elaborate hall-way. The tiled floor led to a wide staircase and, as the door closed behind them, Stuart could hear voices com-ing from upstairs.

'What is this place?' Stuart said as they walked up the stairs.

'This is a place that doesn't exist. It's a place you've never been to, where you will meet people you have never met.' Sebastian Forbes stopped at the top of the stairs and looked back at Stuart, two steps behind. 'Do you understand what I'm saying?'

'Sure. I never came here.' Stuart had experience with the criminal underworld; he'd forgotten plenty of places before this one.

The large sunny room at the front of the building

screamed money despite the subtle décor. Leather chairs in groups of two or three were set around wooden tables and, at the far end of the room, a black glass bar ran the length of the wall. A man in a red bow tie and white shirt stood behind it, mixing a drink in a cut-glass tumbler. In front of the bar, three men and two women stopped talking and looked Stuart's way.

'May I introduce Mr Stuart Lord,' said Sebastian Forbes, taking the drink from the barman.

Stuart shook their hands. Each said, 'Welcome, welcome,' but they didn't give their names.

The younger woman handed Stuart a cold glass of lager. 'Your tipple of choice, I believe?' He took the glass, and she said, 'You are not yet one of us, Mr Lord, but you have shown great potential, a certain degree of class in your manner of operation.'

For a brief moment, Stuart felt stupid. He had been so engrossed in his new life and the pure, unadulterated pleasure he'd been taking from each and every challenge that he hadn't thought to consider *why* he'd been invited to play the game. He raised himself to his full six foot two and squared his shoulders. It was a recruitment drive. Of course it was. And this was the final interview.

31

It was nearly midnight. Bloom knocked at the door.

'Jane's missing,' said Jameson, pulling it open.

'I know,' said Bloom, stepping into Claire's hallway. 'Since when?'

'She left school at lunchtime to go to the sandwich shop, but never came back. They thought she'd gone home and the stupid teachers didn't check because they knew she was having a tough time.'

'She left school alone?'

'Apparently. Dan and I are about to head out, search the streets. Claire's called all her friends, but we'll knock on some doors anyway. We've tried the hospitals.'

'You've told the police?'

'Claire rang them, but they're saying it's only been a few hours and most teenagers come back.'

'Did Claire tell them about Lana?'

'Yeah, but Claire doesn't know everything, does she?'

'OK. You go. I'll call Barker and then stay with Claire.'

'Thank you.'

Bloom pulled out her phone and called Steve Barker. She'd be waking him up, but this was urgent.

'Hello?' he said groggily.

'Steve,' she said, 'it's Augusta. Lana Reid's daughter has been missing for the last twelve hours or so.'

'What?'

'Jane Reid is missing.'

There was a brief pause, then Barker said, 'What do you need?'

'We need the local police to take it seriously. We need them to know who Lana is and what she might be capable of. My next call is to Superintendent Briggs at the Met, but I'll need to tell her everything.' Briggs was another of Bloom's course delegates and one of the most impressive police officers she'd ever met.

'I know Briggs. She's a sensible copper. Tell her what you need to and I'll speak to her tomorrow to keep this tight.'

Bloom thanked him and then called Grace Briggs, who, as luck would have it, was wide awake and dealing with a major firearms incident. Bloom filled her in as quickly as possible – the psychopath collector, the Graham family, the disappearance of Jane Reid – and Briggs promised a high-priority call-out to all officers.

Bloom headed towards the kitchen. Claire was pacing round and round the kitchen island.

'Claire?' said Bloom quietly, not wanting to scare her.

'Augusta. Thank you for coming.'

'Of course. What can I do? Have you eaten anything?' Bloom asked, switching on the kettle.

Claire shook her head.

'Can I ask you some questions?'

'Please. Anything at all.'

'When was the last time you spoke to Jane?'

'This morning at breakfast. She always helps me with the girls.'

'And how did she seem?' Bloom put teabags in two mugs.

'Normal – just normal. I've been wracking my brain for something I missed, but there was nothing. I know she's been subdued this last week, but she's a tough little cookie.'

'Would she go anywhere without telling you?'

'Jane's the most mature young girl I've ever met. She always tells me where she's going and who with. She's never out later than eight thirty, and, most importantly, she talks to me. She told me she was upset that you and Marcus were looking for her dad. She tells me everything.'

'Did she say why that upset her?' asked Bloom.

'He's a loser, isn't he? She doesn't want anything to do with him, and I suppose she's scared that if her mum doesn't come back, he might have some claim to her.'

'Might that make her run away?'

Claire sighed. 'We talked it through and she seemed fine. I said no one would force her to see him and that Dan and I would make sure she got to choose if the worst came to the worst. I thought she was OK with that.' Claire started pacing again. 'I've no idea what I'm doing, you know. How am I supposed to help her? What if I've said the wrong thing?'

'We'll find her,' Bloom said. 'Have you considered where Lana might have taken Jane, if that's what's happened?'

Claire stopped in her tracks. 'Is that what you think's happened? Marcus was asking me all these weird questions about Lana the other day, whether I thought she could be sinister, but he wouldn't tell me why.'

'I see,' said Bloom.

'I think I should know the whole story, don't you?'

'Let's sit down,' said Bloom, handing Claire a mug of tea. 'I promise I'll tell you everything. But let's wait for Marcus to get back.'

They sat in silence, cradling their steaming mugs and both stealing quick glances at the clock. An hour later, the front door opened and Jameson and Dan walked in.

Claire jumped up. 'Have you found her?'

Dan shook his head, his curly blond hair falling over his eyes. 'Sorry, love. We came back to see if there's any more news.'

Claire sat back down. 'No. But Augusta promised you'd tell me what's really going on.'

Jameson gave a small nod. They both knew that it was pointless to hide the truth now.

'Claire,' said Bloom, 'we think the people selected to play this game may have psychopathic personality traits.'

Dan sat on the arm of his wife's chair. Neither spoke, and so Bloom continued. 'There are many people who possess these traits and most of them function very normally. They may sometimes surprise us with their actions or their views, but lots of non-psychopathic people do that too. The main thing that differentiates psychopaths from others is that they lack a conscience or any real empathy. They experience emotions more dimly than the rest of us. This makes them more rational on the one hand, but also unconcerned about the impact they have on others.'

'Why is someone selecting them? Who would hunt psychopaths?' asked Claire.

'We can't be sure. We don't yet know the content of this game. But my guess is these people are being groomed for something specific, something related to their unique talents.'

'We know of one player who's emerged from this game—' said Jameson.

'Are you sure you need to cover this?' interrupted Bloom. Jameson glared at her. 'Sorry, carry on,' she said.

'Faye Graham who disappeared in January turned up at her family home last week.'

'Well, that's great news, isn't it?' said Claire.

'I recognize that name,' said Dan at the same time.

'She stabbed her husband to death,' said Jameson.

'Jesus, Marcus.' Claire stood. For a moment Bloom thought Claire might throw her tea at her brother. 'Shit,' she said in a faraway voice as she sat down again.

Dan took his wife's hand. 'What are the police doing about this?'

'They're helping, but it's not easy. At the end of the day, these people have disappeared of their own accord and, other than Faye, we have no evidence of any wrongdoing.'

'A woman killed her husband!' Dan looked furious.

Bloom sat forward in her chair. 'Yes, and the police are trying to find her.'

'Is that what Lana's going to do to Jane?' said Claire.

'Not if I have anything to do with it,' replied Jameson.

'Faye Graham has two children who remain alive and well despite being home at the time of the attack,' said Bloom. She felt Jameson turn towards her. He knew her theory about why those children were spared and that she was avoiding that detail deliberately.

'So what's the plan?' asked Dan.

'I need to join this game.' Jameson turned to Bloom. 'I need you to get me in. I need to become one of them, get selected, and see what the hell is going on.'

'How am I supposed to do that?' Bloom asked. As if she had the power to manipulate a game embedded deep within the dark web.

'We have all the questionnaires and quizzes. I'll complete as many as I can as though I'm a psychopath. You can tell me what to say.'

Bloom shook her head. 'They won't just be using the quizzes. They'll be looking at your whole online history, the choices you've made, the views you've expressed. That's what I'd be doing.'

'You see! You know what they'd do, so you can get me in.'

'We'd have to fake a whole persona, a whole background, not to mention a birthday that's coming up soon.'

'We'll get DC Logan to help.'

'It's too risky. We've no idea what you'd be asked to do.'

Claire spoke up. 'Marcus can do this. He's done it before. He has medals for it.'

'What?' said Jameson, startled.

'You told Dad.'

'On his deathbed,' Jameson said through gritted teeth.

'Well, he had a little time to show off about your medals before he popped off. He was proud. So am I, for that matter.'

'It's called the Secret Service for a reason, Claire.'

'Then you should have kept your big mouth shut.'

'He was dying.'

'And you still had to show off.'

'I wasn't showing off. I was explaining why I hadn't been around and why I'd been so distant. I thought he deserved to know.'

Claire ignored her brother's indignation and looked at Bloom. 'He can do this. You have to let him do this.'

Bloom looked at Jameson. It was a foolish idea. An absolute long shot, at best. But maybe, just maybe, it would work.

32

The day of Jameson's accident started so well.

The police called Claire because a girl matching Jane's description had been seen at King's Cross station. They couldn't tell if she was alone – she was surrounded by commuters – but they were confident that she had walked through the station concourse. They were checking CCTV to confirm that she hadn't boarded a train.

Jameson knew there was nothing he could do but wait and so he set off on a bike ride. The cortisol was making him jumpy and irritable. If he wanted to pass himself off as an authentic psychopath, he needed to know how they operated, what they thought and what they felt. Bloom had recommended Robert Hare's *Without Conscience*, a study of psychopaths from the man who invented a way to identify them, *Confessions of a Sociopath* by M. E. Thomas, an autobiographical insight into life as a sociopath by an American lawyer, and *The Wisdom of Psychopaths* by Oxford University's Professor of Psychology, Kevin Dutton. Jameson parked his bike and downloaded *Confessions of a Sociopath* to his phone.

Two hours and fifty pages later, he arrived home. There was no more news about Jane. What the hell had she been doing at King's Cross? The police had tried to trace her phone, but it was switched off. He had a bad feeling. Jane wasn't the type to play truant. She was responsible. Running away simply didn't make sense.

After taking a shower, Jameson headed into town to meet Sarah. He'd been tempted to call it off – he wasn't sure he'd be good company – but in the end he'd decided to go. It had been a long time since he'd wanted to see a woman as much as he wanted to see Sarah, and he'd just be sitting at home waiting for news, so why not sit with her? It might take his mind off things.

On the tube, he reflected on the first few chapters of *Confessions of a Sociopath*. He wasn't entirely sure how he felt about it. The author, a self-confessed sociopath, was articulate, intelligent and, on occasion, witty. But there was an underlying tone of frickin' scariness. There was something so removed about how she viewed the world and other people, as though they were pawns in an elaborate game of chess.

Jameson stepped out into the chilly March sunshine and headed towards Fork. They were meeting there and then heading to a nearby pub. As he turned the corner and Fork came into view, he saw Sarah waiting for him. She was wearing a tailored white coat with black knee-high boots. Her hair was long and straight, stretching halfway down her back. She looked his way and smiled. He'd made the right decision. She was bound to cheer him up; he'd feel much better in a few hours.

But she never had the chance.

Jameson caught sight of the cyclist, riding low and

fast, his legs pumping hard, just as he lost control. He mounted the kerb and hit Jameson at full speed, head on, striking him to the floor and knocking him out.

33

'Are you comfortable?' said Dr Bloom. Her voice was softer than normal.

Seraphine wiggled around to find the best position. She was sitting in a large cushioned chair with her feet flat on the floor, her hands on her thighs and her eyes closed. She listened to Dr Bloom's voice and followed her instructions. Her body felt heavy as she began to relax. She was totally awake and fully aware, but things felt different. She noticed the weight of her hands on her legs, and as she concentrated on breathing in and out, she became more conscious of her own body and less aware of the room around her.

'The first thing I'd like you to do, Seraphine, is imagine a place where you feel safe and happy. It might be a house or a park or a beach. The choice is yours. But it's a place you can go to when you need space and peace. I want you to pick the place, real or imagined, and study it. What can you see, hear and smell?'

Seraphine picked the children's playground she'd visited as a child, because she never felt different there, only excited and happy. She pictured herself standing at its centre, turning to see the large red slide built into a train, the yellow roundabout that she'd clung to, and the swings, two for babies, two for older kids. She remembered how the chains on the big swings could be wound around each other, so that you were high off the ground and could spin, wobbling, as they unravelled.

'When you're happy in your place, raise your little finger,' said Dr Bloom in her soft, distant voice.

Seraphine concentrated on the weather in the park. It was warm and sunny. She could smell chips. She remembered the ice creams from the cafe with their multicoloured sauces: red, yellow, blue and even black. There was not another soul in sight. The park was hers and hers alone. She raised her little finger.

'Good,' said Dr Bloom. 'Now I'd like you to think deeply about what makes you different and how that makes you feel.'

Seraphine pictured herself sitting on the roundabout.

'You may sometimes find it hard to identify your feelings, Seraphine, but that doesn't mean they aren't there. The volume of them is simply turned down. So here in your safe place you can practise turning the volume up and exploring how it feels to be sad, or afraid, or lonely.'

Seraphine recalled the first few weeks at secondary school when she realized that everyone else had moved on. They were having conversations that she couldn't follow. There were dramas, romances, and stupid fights over stupid things. She pictured standing with her back to the wall of the corridor, watching these laughing, squealing, screaming beings rushing by as she stood rooted to the spot. She had assumed she'd catch up. When she was more mature, she'd be just like them. But as the years went by she remained standing at that wall, watching and losing patience. Not with herself. Their dramas and romances and fights were nonsense. There was no logic, no gain and therefore no point in them. She didn't want to be like them. It was more important to them to be *seen* to win an argument than to actually win.

She thought of Mr Potts, the History teacher. He was a bully. He thought nothing of ripping up someone's homework, or keeping the whole class in at lunchtime to punish one disruptive boy. And if you were talking in his lesson he'd come up behind you and squeeze your shoulder very tightly. He wasn't supposed to, but no one dared say anything. Until Jamie Parker and Lucas Kane decided to turn the tables. They spoke louder and louder in his classes, becoming more disruptive, failing to turn up to detention, and not doing their homework. Jamie even walked up behind Mr Potts and squeezed his shoulder tightly one morning. They became the class heroes because they were seen to be fighting back, but ultimately they lost. Their parents were summoned, they were punished for their bad behaviour, and Mr Potts carried on as before.

So one morning, when Mr Potts had gone to the staffroom for his usual coffee, Seraphine sneaked into his classroom and placed a pair of girl's pants in the zip pocket of his work bag. She had bought the underwear specially. Then she went to the computer room, set up an anonymous Yahoo account and wrote an email: *I am a Year 7 pupil in Mr Potts' class and he kept me in detention and asked me to remove my knickers and give them to him. I knew it was wrong but I was scared and didn't know what to do.* She sent it to the headmaster and to Mr Potts's wife, who was one of the PE teachers. And that was the end of Mr Potts.

'There are many advantages to your condition, Seraphine,' said Dr Bloom's distant voice. 'You are unlikely to feel fear the way other people do and unlikely to panic in the face of danger. Which can make you brave and capable. But it can also make you reckless and unaware of possible dangers. There are people who will want to take advantage of you, manipulate you, or goad you into competition. But you should remember to keep your head. Logic and intellect are your strengths, so you must endeavour to use them wisely.'

Seraphine wanted to laugh. She knew that no one could manipulate her. They simply weren't clever enough.

Dr Bloom continued, 'You may hear it said that people like you cannot feel emotions, but you can feel happiness and sadness, pride and anger. What you may struggle with is feeling shame or guilt for the things you do, things that affect others negatively. But again, this does not mean you cannot understand, rationally, that such actions are wrong. Just because you can't feel it doesn't mean you don't know it. And this is where you get to choose.'

Dr Bloom would probably think that what she'd done to Mr Potts was wrong. But was it? The man was a tyrant. He clearly didn't like or understand teenagers. Is the means to an end ever justified?

And while she was contemplating her treatment of Mr Potts, Seraphine felt the strangest thing. She focused on it. She tried to turn up the volume. It felt warm and she struggled to put a word to it . . . *safe*, maybe? No, that wasn't right. It felt . . . she felt . . . *accepted*. For the first time in her life, she was sitting in the company of another person who knew exactly how she differed but didn't judge or fear her. Seraphine smiled.

34

'Marcus? Marcus, can you hear me?' The voice was distant, far away, as though he were hidden at the bottom of a well. 'He's been unconscious for the last four minutes,' said the same voice. 'His name's Marcus.'

'Marcus, I'm John,' said a second voice from the top of the well. 'Can you hear me?'

'A cyclist hit him and he banged his head on the kerb.'

Sarah. The first voice belonged to Sarah.

'He's coming round,' said John. 'OK, Marcus, I'm just going to check your vitals, mate. Where's the cyclist? Are they hurt?'

'He left.' Sarah's voice was shaky but a little clearer now, as if she'd been lowered towards him.

Jameson felt John's hands on his neck and tried to speak.

'I'm putting a neck brace on you, Marcus. It's just a precaution, because you hit the ground hard,' said John.

Jameson opened his eyes. The bright light hurt and he felt a piercing pain at the back of his head.

'Hey, you're OK.' Sarah's face came into view, her hair hanging over him.

He tried to speak again but there was no sound.

A hand took hold of his and squeezed tightly. 'Don't worry. I'll come with you. Not the ideal first date, but at least I get to show off a little.'

Jameson tried to smile.

35

Visiting hours had only just begun so there was no one else around. Jameson's injuries did not justify a private room but due to a full ward he'd been lucky enough to get one. Bloom entered and found him asleep on his back with his arms above the covers. His left arm was badly bruised and he had cuts and bruises on the left side of his face. His head was bandaged. Claire said there was a closed fracture to the back of his skull but, thankfully, no internal bleeding. Bloom pulled up a chair.

Jameson's eyes flickered open and he stared at the ceiling before looking her way.

'I've brought grapes and Lucozade,' she said.

'I love Lucozade.' His voice was hoarse but it did not mask his sarcasm. He frowned and rubbed his head. 'Can you find someone to get me something for this headache?'

Bloom returned a few minutes later with a nurse called Lucy who checked his chart and administered some more pain relief.

'So what happened?' asked Bloom.

'Some cyclist lost control and took me out.'

'You're sure it was an accident?'

'Yeah, yeah. The guy took the corner too fast and

I was in the wrong place at the wrong time.' He huffed a half-laugh. 'I nearly didn't go, too.'

'But Claire said the cyclist didn't stop.'

Jameson closed his eyes. 'He probably panicked.'

'When did you become so magnanimous?'

'It was an accident, Augusta. It happens.'

She didn't push it, but she knew they were thinking the same thing. 'So what have the doctors said?'

He turned his face to her and opened his eyes again. 'You mean when are they letting me out so I can get back to work?'

'Actually, I was planning to bring your work in.'

He smiled and then winced.

'But, really, what've they said?'

'It's a moderate head injury – I was lucky.'

'But you have a fractured skull?'

'Another war wound. It'll heal. I'll be out in the next day or so. You know how desperate they are for beds.'

'Well, don't rush to get out. And don't be getting all stroppy and bossy with them. Try to be patient.'

'Yes, Mum.' He faced the ceiling and closed his eyes again.

Bloom noticed the Fork deli logo on the two take-out cups on the table. 'Have you been sending Claire to get your fancy coffee? I'm happy to bring it in for you.'

'I'd be lucky if Claire went to Costa for me. Sarah bought them.'

'Sarah is your date lady?'

Jameson looked her way. 'Yeah, she's my date lady. You do have a way with words, Augusta.'

Bloom ignored his teasing and patted his hand as gently as she could. 'I'll let you rest.'

'What's happening with the case? With Jane?'

Bloom stood. 'We have it all in hand, Marcus. Just you get yourself better.'

The train to Bristol took an hour and a half. Bloom sat in the quiet coach, on a table of four, beside a businessman annotating a printout of a PowerPoint presentation. She looked out of the window. Something wasn't right. Her professional reputation was the most important thing in her life and Jameson's physical fitness was a source of great pride to him. Both had come under attack in the space of twenty-four hours. It couldn't be a coincidence. Jameson's accident and her investigation must have been engineered. Psychopaths were incredibly adept when it came to identifying and playing on an opponent's weaknesses. Bloom couldn't help but think of Seraphine.

Two hours later, Bloom arrived at Bristol's Central Police Station. They'd agreed to meet there instead of Portishead. She headed towards Chief Superintendent Barker's office, where the team were assembled.

'Sorry to hear about Mr Jameson,' said Barker. 'How is he?'

Bloom placed her coat on the back of the only spare chair and took her iPad and notes from her bag. 'In quite a bad way, actually. He thinks he'll be out in a few days, but I saw him this morning and I'm not so sure.' She sat down and looked around at the team. 'Quick question, before we begin. Has anyone else had bad news or a bad experience in the past day or so?'

The group looked at one other, shaking their heads and mumbling low 'no's.

'Why do you ask?' said DC Akhtar.

'I had a call from my professional body yesterday. They said a serious complaint has been made against me.'

'Are you thinking Jameson was targeted?' asked DS Green.

'Possibly. Whoever's collecting these psychopaths is clever. I'd be surprised if they didn't suspect they were being traced.'

'You think they know it's us?' said Barker.

'I'm not one for gut feelings, Steve, but I think we should all be on our guard, just in case.'

'I might be able to help there,' said DC Logan. 'It turns out that as well as one hundred and nine players still active, there are a few who've returned home.'

'And attacked their loved ones?' Barker's words were full of dread.

Logan shook his head. 'No. I've had one person contact me to say their father received one of these cards, disappeared for a bit, and then just came back.'

'What? Really?' said DS Green. 'As if nothing had happened?'

'Yep,' said Logan.

Everyone looked at Bloom.

'How does that fit with Faye Graham?' said Barker.

Bloom thought about it. 'We need to speak to the returned player. Can you arrange that?' she said to Logan.

He nodded. 'I don't see why not. I know who he is.'

'Good,' said Bloom. 'We need to find out what this game is really about.'

36

Jameson woke up hungry – ravenous, in fact, which he figured was a good sign. And his headache felt dull enough to ignore. He climbed out of bed, put on socks and a blue jumper that had been brought in by Claire, and went to collect breakfast from a room at the end of the corridor. It was a sad little collection of cereals, yogurts and toast, but he was too hungry to care. He selected a strawberry yogurt, three slices of toast and a pot of blackcurrant jam. Then he requested a mug of tea from the woman behind the counter, who had an impressive tattoo of roses that covered her left arm.

Back in his room, he watched the morning news as he ate. By the time he'd finished, his headache had picked up steam again. He put his headphones in and listened to the audiobook of Professor Kevin Dutton's *The Wisdom of Psychopaths*. It was all about how useful psychopathic traits can be. How it can be advantageous for surgeons or bomb-disposal experts, for instance, to suppress their emotions and operate in a calm and calculated fashion. And for spies and serial killers to be able to charm their target and mask their true motives. In his concluding remarks, Dutton described a common psychopathic blueprint: that whether such people are saints, spies or sinners, they are bound by their ceaseless quest for new heightened experiences.

What might that mean for how these people lived their lives? Jameson had experienced his own fair share of risk and he loved adrenaline-fuelled sports – that intoxicating combination of danger and endorphins – but he wasn't always looking for new highs.

For the first time, he was thinking about psychopaths as simply 'other' rather than 'wrong'.

'Christ,' he said to the empty room. This was what Bloom had been banging on about. Psychopaths were unavoidable. If it was advantageous for humans to be fearless, adventurous, calm, unfeeling or selfish, it made sense that some people would be dealt all these cards. That was evolution.

'All right, sleepyhead. Wake up.'

Something soft but heavy hit him in the face. Jameson opened his eyes and picked up the roll of fresh socks from his chest. 'Subtle, as always,' he said to his scowling sister.

'What's going on, Marcus?'

Jameson sat up. He checked the clock: 12.15pm. 'Give me a clue, sis.'

'Jane has been missing for four days.'

Jameson waited for Claire to expand, but she didn't. 'What do you want me to say?'

'I want you to say you're doing something, not just lying here listening to your stupid music.' She gestured to the headphones still plugged into his ears.

He removed the ear buds. 'I'm not the police, Claire. And I'm actually in hospital with a head injury.'

'Oh, man up. You're fine.'

Jameson knew better than to take on Claire when she was angry. He'd lost many fruitless battles over the years. So he waited, saying nothing and letting her pace the room.

'We have to find her. We can't sit around waiting. We have to do something. *I* have to do something.' Deep lines of anxiety creased her forehead. 'I've been calling the police every hour and they just say the same thing every time. No news, no news, no news. They think I'm crazy. And they keep pointing out that they don't need to update me because I'm not a relative. You can imagine what I said to that, the cheeky bastards.'

Jameson smiled. He wouldn't want to be on the wrong side of his sister. Was anger her most psychopathic trait?

'What are you smiling at? What the fuck is there to smile about?'

'Keep your voice down, potty mouth. There are kids around.' Claire frowned. 'The room next door has a young son who comes in every day.'

'Who gives a—'

Jameson threw the socks at her. He rubbed his aching head. 'Augusta says they're planning a TV appeal for Jane. There's stuff on social media already and posters are up at King's Cross and St Pancras, as well as around the school. But until someone comes forward with a sighting, it's a needle in a haystack.'

'I'll never forgive you if something happens to her.'

173

'Me? What did I do?'

'She came to you for help. I told her you'd sort it.'

'Well, that's on you then.'

Claire teared up and he immediately regretted saying it.

'Look,' he added, 'Lana may have been a crappy mother, but she never hurt Jane or put her in harm's way, did she? So let's just hope that's still the case and that they're together somewhere.'

Claire sat down in the seat beside him, her fight gone, and put her head in her hands and cried.

37

In the south-west corner of Surrey, not far from Hasle-mere, Bloom and DC Logan were driving up a private road that belonged to the Llewellyn family.

Freya Llewellyn had contacted DC Logan's online alter ego, Craig Hogan, to say that her father, Clive, had disappeared eight months ago after receiving the birth-day card, only to return six weeks later. She was more than happy for Craig to pop by for a chat with Clive. She said she hoped it would put his mind at rest; she was confident his sister would be home soon.

And so, here they were.

'Wow,' said DC Logan beneath his breath as a large stately home came into view through the trees. Its arched front door was framed by ivy that climbed the full height of the building. 'Being a corporate lawyer clearly pays,' he said, as the car tyres crunched on the gravel driveway. He parked and turned off the engine.

A woman in her early twenties opened the front door and came out to greet them. She had shiny, salon-styled hair and perfect make-up. Her skinny jeans and striped T-shirt were casual but clearly expensive and her nails were painted bright pink.

'Remember what I said,' whispered Bloom. 'Tread carefully and if in doubt follow my lead.'

'Freya?' Craig walked up to the young woman and shook her hand. He was wearing jeans and a faded T-shirt with a photo of a band on the front. Bloom guessed he thought it was cool but it made him look like the ultimate nerd. And that was no bad thing.

Freya Llewellyn flashed her bright white teeth. 'So nice to meet you, Craig. And this must be your aunt?'

'Alice,' said Bloom.

'I didn't want to raise my mum's hopes by bringing her,' said Logan, sticking to the pre-agreed back story, 'but Aunt Alice wanted to be here for some moral support.'

'Certainly. Do come on in. I'll take you straight through to Daddy. He's been in New York for the past week, but he came home early this morning and I know he'll be able to reassure you.' She led them through the grand hallway, past a sweeping staircase that led up to a balcony that circled the hall below. 'He said it was a life-affirming experience, actually. A time out that enabled him to reassess his priorities.'

'And he's happy to talk to us about it?' asked Bloom.

They reached a closed oak door with an elaborate doorknob in the shape of a dragon, with rubies for eyes.

'I find seeking forgiveness rather than permission is the best strategy with Daddy.' Freya opened the door and led Bloom and Logan inside.

Freya skipped to the large desk at the far end of the room. 'Daddy, I have some friends who desperately need a little chat with you.'

Bloom and Logan hovered in the doorway. The man

sitting in the chair looking out of the window turned at the sound of his daughter's greeting. He was a big man with thick black hair, broad shoulders and cobalt eyes. His daughter kissed him on the cheek and he smiled warmly at her before turning to his guests.

'This is Craig and his Aunt Alice. Craig's sister went missing to do that game thing that you did. I told them you came back fine and they shouldn't worry, but I hoped seeing and speaking to you might reassure them.'

Bloom was alarmed by Freya's naivety. She clearly didn't know about her father's real nature; she didn't understand the game. Clive Llewellyn was evidently a true master of disguise. Without missing a beat, he rose from his seat and beckoned Bloom and Logan forward.

'Of course. Of course. Come in. Take a seat. Freya, ask Mrs Burns to make us some tea and bring up some of that lovely ginger cake.'

Bloom and Logan sat in the two chairs facing the large desk. Llewellyn shook Logan's hand and gave him a firm shoulder-pat, and then placed both hands around Bloom's in an act of warm reassurance. His whole demeanour said, *Relax, you're with friends.*

'How old is your sister, Craig?' asked Llewellyn as he returned to his chair on the other side of the desk.

'Twenty-three.'

Llewellyn shook his head and tutted. 'Your poor mother must be going spare.' He looked at Bloom. 'Are you Mum's sister, Alice?'

'Yes,' said Bloom. Llewellyn used their first names with the familiarity of a lifelong friend.

'I can't imagine what we'd do if Freya disappeared off on a little jaunt like that.'

'A little jaunt?' repeated Bloom.

Llewellyn leaned back in his chair and smiled. He had the same sparkling teeth as his daughter. 'A jaunt, an exploration, a journey of self-discovery. Everyone needs some time out now and again to recharge the batteries and regain the old focus, don't you think?'

'Maybe at our age,' said Bloom. 'But my niece is just a child.'

Llewellyn nodded as if he agreed, but then said, 'Some of us are old souls even at a young age.'

'Do you know where my sister is?' Logan asked with a fairly convincing tone of desperation.

'Wherever she wants to be, I should expect.'

'Are you saying she chose to go off like this?' said Bloom. 'Nobody is forcing her?'

Llewellyn placed his hands behind his head. 'Let me tell you a little story. I'm a rich man, as you can probably tell, because I'm a bloody good lawyer. If you want your business sold for millions, I'm your man. If you want to fight the power-grabbing market-leaders looking to gobble up your company, I'm your man. If you want to gobble up the little guys stealing your customers, I'm your man. Up against me, no one wins – never have, never will. But what do I get out of it?'

Bloom fought the urge to wave her arms around the room and say, 'A massive house, a pampered, privately educated daughter, a trophy wife somewhere and a stable full of fast cars.'

'I get ungrateful little people complaining. *I wanted more, Llewellyn. You need to do it for less, Llewellyn.* When they haven't got the brains or balls to do it themselves. You see?'

'What's that got to do with my sister?'

Llewellyn looked at Logan for a moment, then said, 'Nothing.'

The silence was broken by a middle-aged woman in a maid's outfit, complete with white pinny and crisp white headdress, entering the room. She was pushing a silver trolley with a china teapot, matching cups and three plates topped with huge slices of cake. The maid – Mrs Burns, presumably – poured tea into all three cups and placed them in front of Llewellyn, Logan and Bloom, then positioned the plates beside the cups and put a jug of milk and bowl of sugar in the centre of the desk. Bloom and Logan thanked her, Llewellyn did not. She left without uttering a word.

'Why would my niece disappear to play some game without telling her family where she was going or if she's all right?' said Bloom. 'I'm sorry, but that just doesn't make any sense to me.'

'Is it a game or just an alternate reality?' said Llewellyn, in an airy, philosophical tone.

'We don't know,' said Bloom with a good dose of exasperation. She looked at Logan, then back at Llewellyn, 'But you do. You know exactly what the game – the alternate reality – is. So please . . . Please tell us what's going on and where she is.'

'Is your sister a smart girl?' Llewellyn asked Logan.

'I suppose.'

'Well, smart people are always fine, no matter what the challenges.'

Bloom sat up straighter at that. 'What sort of challenges?'

Llewellyn removed his hands from behind his head. 'Life. Love. Loss.'

'Is she in danger?' asked Logan.

'Craig, my dear boy, we are all in danger all of the time. It's an illusion to think otherwise.'

'OK, OK. But specifically – does this game make you do dangerous things? Could she get hurt?'

Llewellyn leaned forward and rested his arms on the desk. 'Nobody can make you do anything you don't wish to do, now can they, Alice?' He flashed a smile at Bloom and winked as if the two of them were in a secret alliance.

Bloom took the opportunity to make an appeal. 'Look. We just want to know that Sally is safe, that she isn't doing anything risky or getting into trouble.' She added her own touch of desperation. 'Surely as a father you can appreciate that?'

'One man's risk is another's daily task. One man's trouble is another's fair play.'

'How about real crime, though?' said Logan. 'You're a lawyer. If my sister's disappeared of her own free will, then what's she doing? Is she breaking the law?'

Llewellyn smiled and Bloom imagined a huge computer embedded in his brain working to calculate the appropriate response.

'You said the experience helped you,' said Bloom. She hoped that encouraging him to talk about himself would hold his focus. 'How did it do that?'

'It didn't help me. It helped me to help myself.'

'But a woman in Bristol killed her husband after playing this game for three months,' said Logan. 'So please, is my sister in danger of being coerced into criminal behaviour?'

Logan's words gave too much away. Not only were they too 'police speak', but the fact that Faye had murdered Harry was not yet public knowledge. Llewellyn stayed perfectly motionless, a smile still glued to his face, but something changed in his eyes. He stared at Logan with an intense, cold glare. DC Logan pushed himself back into his chair. His eyes flickered from Llewellyn to the floor and then back again.

'Who the hell are you?' Llewellyn demanded, his charm abating quickly.

'Detective Constable Logan, Avon and Somerset Police. We're investigating the death of Harry Graham.'

Llewellyn's stare slowly moved from Logan to Bloom. 'And you?'

Bloom set her expression to neutral and held his gaze.

'You're really the aunt of this Sally? No. Of course not. There is no girl, is there?' He looked back at Logan. 'Let me see your warrant card.'

That was a bad idea. Llewellyn might have already registered and remembered Logan's name and the police force, but Bloom hoped not. She interjected, 'How did you get selected? People are invited by name, so how did they know you were a suitable and willing candidate?'

'My dear lady,' said Llewellyn, 'we live in a world of constant and complete surveillance.'

'But how were you specifically selected?' Bloom couldn't imagine Llewellyn completing questionnaires on Facebook.

'Imagine that in a beach of pebbles and stones there's a handful of precious jewels. How would you find them?'

'You don't know,' said Bloom. 'I see.' She looked at Logan. 'I think Mr Llewellyn has outlived his usefulness to us.' She stood up and Logan followed.

'A good attempt to rile me, Alice, or whatever your name is, but it won't work, I'm afraid.'

'I'm not trying to rile you. I'm just disappointed. Based on your job, your house, your obvious intellect, we'd hoped to meet one of the masterminds, maybe even *the* mastermind, behind the game, but it's clear that you know nothing.'

There was the smallest of twitches on Llewellyn's forehead. Psychopaths might be immune to fear and empathy, but anger and ego were a whole different story.

Suddenly the door burst open and in strode Chief Superintendent Barker with DS Green behind him. They'd been parked down the road, listening, and had promised to stay put unless Bloom and Logan were in immediate danger – which they categorically were not. Bloom saw Llewellyn smile. He'd seen her disappointment before she could mask it.

'You have no idea who you're dealing with, do you?' he whispered.

Freya Llewellyn cried and apologized to her father as he climbed into the back of Superintendent Barker's car. He'd reluctantly agreed to accompany the police to the station to assist with their enquiries.

'I told you not to come unless we were in danger,' Bloom said to Barker, who was looking frustratingly pleased with himself.

'He blew your cover. We had to get in quick. We'll get to the bottom of this now.'

'You have no idea who you're dealing with, do you?' said Bloom, repeating Llewellyn's words. Barker frowned. He looked at Llewellyn sitting in the back seat of the car calmly flicking through photos on his iPhone screen and ignoring his crying daughter. 'These people are not pit bulls. They don't bite when you poke them with a stick because they don't have any buttons. They're alligators waiting just beneath the surface. They wait until you're vulnerable and then they strike. You blew it, Steve. You won't get a single thing out of him now. He knows how badly we want what he knows, so he'll talk a lot, but I guarantee he'll say very little.'

Barker shifted his jaw from side to side. 'So why have you wasted valuable police resources leading us on this merry dance?' Barker was clearly more pit bull than alligator.

'Because, despite his talents for subterfuge, he's still

human, and humans slip up when you catch them off guard.'

'But he didn't slip up.'

'He revealed that he's one of the most dangerous psychopaths around, that he's in total control of himself and those around him.'

Barker rubbed his chin with his right hand and watched DC Logan sternly reprimand Freya Llewellyn for inviting strangers from the internet into her home.

'But this wasn't a waste of resources, Steve,' Bloom continued. 'I may be frustrated that you cut our time with him short, but Llewellyn did slip up, and more than once.'

38

Jameson was sleeping fully dressed in the big armchair in the corner of his room. The TV was muted, subtitles flashing up on the screen.

'Jameson?'

He opened his eyes.

'How are you doing?'

'Missing out, clearly.'

Bloom smiled and placed the takeout latte she had purchased at Fork next to her partner. Then she sat in the plastic seat beside the bed. 'Did you listen to the file I sent over?'

'You know, I thought you were joking when you said you were going to bring my work in.' He picked up the cup. 'For me?'

She nodded. 'Tell me what you heard.' She'd emailed him a recording of the meeting with Clive Llewellyn.

'Thanks,' he said, taking a sip, then reached for the spiral-bound notebook on his bedside cabinet. 'He's a slippery old fish, that's for sure. He didn't answer a single question with a straight answer. He was all philosophical shit and metaphor, but my research suggests that's to be expected.'

Bloom nodded. 'Most psychopaths love playing conversational games in order to control and manipulate.'

'But he took your concern for your missing niece at face value, at least for a while. I think he gave a few things away early on.'

She knew Jameson would notice the slip-ups, but it was always good to have her high expectations confirmed. 'Go on,' she said.

'He didn't dispute having played the game. He's a self-obsessed narcissist with an ego the size of his bank balance. And coupled with the charm offensive and question-dodging, that makes it look like he's a psychopath.'

'You almost sound like a psychologist.'

Jameson looked up from his pad with a raised eyebrow. 'Was that a joke, Dr Bloom?'

She waved his comment away. 'He was completely calm throughout. He treated us like old friends, and then he simply switched it off. And when these people look at you with that stare, it's cold and empty. It spooked Craig.'

Jameson nodded. 'So no more doubts. The game targets psychopaths.'

'I'd say so. Although why he returned home after six weeks while others have been missing for months is strange . . .'

'OK. So it's a game for psychopaths. Or budding psychopaths, people with psychopathic traits. And whatever it entails, they enjoy it. That's the other big thing he revealed.'

'Indeed. In rather flowery language.'

Jameson read from his pad. *Jaunt, exploration, journey of self-discovery, recharging the batteries, regaining focus.* He said it was about life, love and loss. And that the smarter you are, the easier the game.'

'"Smart people are always fine, no matter what the challenges,"' said Bloom. 'I think the challenges are a crucial component.'

'So they're set a series of challenges?'

Bloom thought about it. 'For this type of person to want to compete, there'd need to be a real sense of achievement at the end. The game would need to be highly competitive ... So players either feel they're winning against other people or there are substantial rewards. There needs to be a kick-back.'

'Any word from Barker?' asked Jameson.

'They didn't get anything else from Llewellyn. Barker wants to try again with one of the other returned players, but my guess is that as soon as Llewellyn left that police station he alerted everyone. The shutters will be down. We aren't going to be able to infiltrate the game. There's no way to get you in.'

'Look,' said Jameson, turning up the volume of the TV.

'Police are very concerned about the whereabouts of sixteen-year-old Jane Reid,' said the newsreader. 'She was last seen leaving her school in Wembley on Friday at lunchtime. She was on foot and wearing her school uniform. Anyone who has seen or heard from Jane in the past few days is asked to contact the police immediately.' The contact details hovered on screen for a few moments beneath a picture of Jane. Then the newsreader moved on to a story about strike action on the London Underground.

39

'They're discharging you today,' said Sarah as she walked into Jameson's room. 'Your consultant says your head is healing well and they've been able to reduce your pain medication.'

The last few times she'd visited, he had been in bed and in a hospital gown, so it felt good to be dressed and sitting in a chair.

'Who's the coffee from?' asked Sarah, pointing at the Fork cup on the bedside table.

'My business partner.'

'I thought you were freelance?'

'We are. There are two of us.'

'And is he a researcher too?'

'In a way, yes, she is.'

Sarah smiled and sat on the end of the bed. 'You don't like talking about what you do, do you?' Her dress had a slit in the front and as she sat down it revealed a small section of thigh.

'I've learned it's best not to share too much too soon.'

'Why's that?'

Jameson smiled.

'What's the big secret? It doesn't fit.'

'With what?'

'With your character. You're so friendly and easy-going. But if that's just a big con I'd rather know now. Because I have no secrets.'

'Oh, I don't buy that.'

'No, really. What you see is what you get. I'm a middle-class girl from Yorkshire. I'm an only child. My mum was a book-keeper, my dad a company director, and I'm a doctor. I lived my whole life in one county until this recent secondment. I went to church every Sunday. I'm a good girl. That's it. That's all there is to know.'

'You telling me you're one of those waiting-for-marriage types of good girls?'

Sarah narrowed her eyes and a small smile reached her lips. 'Not that good a girl,' she said.

'Thank the Lord.'

'And what makes you think that information is in any way useful to you?'

Jameson held up a hand. 'Sorry, you're quite right. I was thinking out loud.'

Sarah nodded. 'So what about you? Where did you grow up?'

'Berkshire – not far from Ascot. My father was in the forces and my mother is a psychiatrist. I have one younger sister, Claire, who lives in Wembley – if you hang around long enough you'll probably meet her. She comes in every lunchtime.'

'I'd like that.'

'Don't be so sure. If she finds I'm seeing someone she'll have you at every family function and talking babies before you can say second date.'

Sarah raised her eyebrows. 'OK.'

Jameson mentally kicked himself. Why did this woman make him say such stupid things? 'Anyway, talking of second dates, would you like to have one? Without the drama of paramedics and ambulances.'

Sarah nodded. 'I thought we could take a picnic to Hyde Park on Saturday. The weather's meant to be nice. Do you think you'll be able to get into the city? I'm not sure they'll let you drive yet.'

'I never drive in the city.'

'Is that a yes?'

'That is a yes.'

The room suddenly felt smaller, as if a bubble was tightening around them, pushing them closer together.

'OK, you win the staring competition,' Sarah eventually said as she looked away.

Jameson laughed. 'What you lack is a sibling, you see. I was the unbeaten family champion for three years running, ages twelve through to fifteen.'

'And then what happened?'

'Claire found boys and make-up and refused to play stupid games with her stupid brother.'

Sarah looked amused. 'Fair enough.'

'It must have been boring growing up without a playmate.'

'I had lots of friends; I didn't really notice.' She checked her watch. 'I should go. I have a meeting at eleven.' She stood, leaned forward and kissed him on the cheek. He caught her wrist and she hovered, her face above his.

Then the door swung open. 'Right then, young man. Time to get you washed and brushed and ready for the road.' Nurse Janet had a shock of red hair and a twinkle in her eye. She was oblivious to the tension in the room.

Sarah stood up straight. 'Saturday then. Midday at the Serpentine Gallery?'

Jameson kissed the back of her hand and then released her wrist. 'See you there.'

40

The initial meeting with the Health and Care Professions Tribunal Service was wholly frustrating.

'So you deny any wrongdoing in relation to the interactions you had with twelve-year-old Amy Jones in the period between 12 October 2016 and 4 December 2016?' said Keith Timms, the badly suited, balding official tasked with briefing Bloom on the misconduct case.

'Absolutely,' she replied.

Keith turned his tablet around so that Bloom could see the screen. 'Can you tell me if you recognize this residence, Dr Bloom?'

'Of course. It's my house.'

He flicked to the next photograph. 'And who is this outside your house?'

'That's me. But who took these photographs and when?'

Keith flicked to the next photograph. 'Some time between 12 October and 4 December 2016.'

Bloom stared at the third photograph. It didn't make sense.

'Can you tell me who is in this image?' asked Keith. 'The two people walking up the pathway to the door of a residence you previously confirmed to be your own home.'

'I can, but the photograph isn't real. Amy Jones has never been to my house. I have never met her outside the consulting room.'

'But you can confirm that the people photographed here are you and Amy Jones?'

Bloom nodded. It was so realistic. She could see herself mid-stride in black trousers and her winter coat, and then just a couple of steps behind her was the unmistakable image of Amy in jeans, pink trainers and her grey duffle coat. Bloom recognized Amy's coat and trainers. She had worn them to their sessions, taking the coat off as she arrived, putting it back on when she left.

'How do you explain this then?' said Keith.

Bloom looked him in the eye. 'I suggest you ask a photography expert to look at this forensically. Someone has faked this to frame me.'

'And that is your defence.' It wasn't a question. Keith sighed as though he'd heard the same tired excuse a million times before. He turned his tablet away and folded up his papers. The meeting was done.

After the meeting, Bloom went to meet Professor Mark Layton at a nearby cafe. He was sitting at a table by the window when she arrived. He'd been her psychology professor at Sheffield University and then her mentor as she worked through her professional qualifications. He was an expert in criminal profiling and one of the first psychologists to provide assistance to the police. Layton had championed Bloom even as a student whose ambition lacked real direction.

'How are you doing?' he said to Bloom.

'My main reaction is one of disbelief. Have you decided?'

Professor Layton nodded, and Bloom waved at the waiter.

'I'll have whatever he's having with a glass of tap water, please.' She closed the menu and handed it to the waiter.

'Eggs Benedict and an Americano with hot milk for me, thanks.'

'Thank you for meeting me,' said Bloom. 'I didn't want to take a lawyer with me as that would have felt too much like I was guilty of something. But I'm glad to debrief with someone I trust.'

They talked about the investigation. They reviewed the original case. They discussed Professor Layton's latest group of undergraduate students, who he described as lazy and rude (which was nothing new – he always described the undergraduates that way).

'As I have you here, I wanted to pick your brains on another matter, if that's OK?' said Bloom as they came towards the end of their lunch.

Professor Layton nodded. 'Of course.'

'If you were to design a set of challenges that would appeal to psychopaths – a game, of sorts – where would you start?'

'Why would I do that?' He wiped his mouth with his napkin.

'To recruit them for something.'

'So I want to test how psychopathic they are?'

'Probably.'

'And what type of psychopath? Criminal or functional?'

'Functional, in the main. You'd need to attract them from the general population and inspire them to walk away from their lives in order to play.'

Mark wrinkled his nose, a sign that he was deliberating. 'Why are you asking, Augusta?'

'It's just a project. Theoretical in the main.'

'And it has to be a game, does it?'

'As opposed to?'

'A simple incentive or bet.'

'Like a dare?'

'Psychopaths tend to be attracted to high-risk activities with high potential gains,' said Professor Layton. 'Think about studies into psychopaths and gambling. They live in the moment, so they treat each bet as an isolated event. Non-psychopaths might start out with a nothing-to-lose attitude, but once we've won or lost a few rounds we become protective and cautious. Our past experience affects our future decisions. But psychopaths simply carry on betting high as if every round is the first. It's a good strategy, too; they win more often.'

'The risk is high – leaving their lives and so on – so there needs to be some truly impressive gain too?'

Mark nodded. He looked out of the cafe window. It had started to rain and passers-by were putting up umbrellas and hoods, or sheltering under newspapers held above their heads. 'Or perhaps you'd need a series of continual wins. Just like gambling. Psychopaths need more and more stimulation to experience that feel-good factor, which is why they go to such extremes, but an on-going stream of quick wins would work just as well as one larger deferred win. Better in most cases, I'd expect.'

'Like Scientologists and their levels of initiation. Their followers are always hungry for more because they're constantly working towards the next level of member-ship.' Bloom was finally getting some traction on what such a game might look like.

'And like all the best video games.' Layton stacked his coffee cup and saucer on top of his plate and placed his knife and fork next to them.

'I was also thinking that to select such people in the first place you would plant profiling questionnaires on social media,' Bloom said.

Layton wrinkled his nose again. 'Well, that would give you a sample of psychopaths who like to engage in social media. But I expect you'd need more data for a psychopathic diagnosis.'

'Exactly. You would use their whole online profile.'

'People reveal too much online. And if they're on Facebook and Twitter, we get two sides of their person-ality. Facebook reveals their idealized self – "me as I wish the world to see me".'

'The facade?'

'Indeed,' said Layton. 'And then Twitter provides a more anonymous forum where they can express their truth, whether it be anger, bitterness, prejudice or joy.'

'The private self.'

'It would be tricky to avoid attracting non-psychopaths.

A lot of people have dark inner lives for all sorts of other reasons.'

'The abused, the angry or the downtrodden might all exhibit similar profiles.'

Layton leaned forward and gestured as he spoke. 'But our psychopaths would lack the emotional context. Their language would be different and their behaviour more rational.'

'So you would filter for that?'

He sat back and exhaled. 'It's a big job, Augusta. A sophisticated process and certainly not one your average university department could handle, if that's what you're getting at.'

Bloom shook her head. 'And not something an individual could pull off alone either.'

Layton frowned. 'You're not thinking of doing this, are you? For what possible purpose?'

'Goodness, no. I'm just conducting a feasibility study. Like I say, this is theoretical.'

Layton insisted on paying. 'You get the next one,' he said, inserting his card into the machine and tapping in his pin. Bloom left a tip on the table and they collected their coats from the stand by the door. The rain was falling heavily on the pavement.

'Seeking out functional psychopaths is one thing, Augusta,' said Layton as they stepped outside, 'but what on earth do you do with them once you've found them?'

You read my mind, thought Bloom.

41

'Are you sure you're up to this?' Bloom said as she arrived in the office for the daily conference call.

'Stop fussing.' Jameson sat at his desk with an untouched sandwich and drink in front of him. Even his freckles looked pale today. 'Tell me again what Barker said yesterday.'

'Just that he'd be taking up the Assistant Chief Constable post a little earlier than expected, so he might not be as available going forwards.'

'And what did you say?'

'I told him that it seemed a bit of a coincidence that he was suddenly needed elsewhere. And he said it was just one of those things.'

'Like your professional conduct coming into question and me being hospitalized by a rogue cyclist.'

'You've changed your tune.'

'I've had time to think.'

'If the person running this game didn't know about us before Llewellyn, they certainly do now. So it's not paranoia to question why our most senior officer is suddenly needed elsewhere. He says that police can't be influenced by an outside party, but look at DCI Warren Beardsley.'

'The police officer who's playing the game? You think he's influencing the investigation?'

'Maybe not directly. But the game has identified at least one potential psychopath within the police force, and I'm pretty sure there'll be others. It's an obvious career choice for people drawn to power.'

Jameson swivelled his chair to face her.

'Whoever's running this thing wanted to be noticed,' she went on. 'Like you said, they could have carried out the whole recruitment process in secret, but they didn't. I don't think the dare-to-play invitation was meant exclusively for the psychopaths. I think it's also meant for us and for the police.'

'So we're playing too?'

'We're part of it somehow, no doubt about it. I was talking to Professor Layton.' Bloom saw Jameson nod his recognition. He and Layton had met a handful of times. 'We talked, and to design this game would be a phenomenal undertaking. It would need lots of money and lots of time. And technical skill. I'd be amazed if it's the work of one individual.'

'Do psychopaths do working together? Aren't they just self-centred egotists out for themselves?'

'That's been the predominant theory. But what if it's wrong? Or something's changed?'

'They've evolved into pack animals?'

Bloom gave him a dismissive look. 'Evolution is not that quick. This is motivated by something more human.'

She dialled in to Barker's conference call and put the phone on speaker so Jameson could listen too. After a few moments the music stopped and DS Phil Green's voice filtered through.

'Afternoon, both. It's just me, Kaye and Raj today. The others have all been called to an incident in town.'

Jameson raised his eyebrows at Bloom. It seemed their investigation was no longer the top priority.

'Hello, everyone,' said Bloom. 'So here's what we know so far. One hundred and nine people have received a birthday card and taken up the dare. Craig tells me he has now identified four players who have returned home after a month or so, including Clive Llewellyn and Faye Graham, although after killing her husband Faye has disappeared again. All the others have been missing for anything from a few weeks to over a year. We've had no one come forward to say they received a card but didn't take up the dare.'

Bloom paused to see if anyone would dispute that. They didn't.

'We're bringing in the other two returned players for interview,' said DS Green.

'Good,' said Bloom. 'Although I expect they'll be as slippery and uncooperative as Llewellyn was.'

'Don't underestimate us.' DS Green sounded offended.

Bloom didn't rise to it and continued her briefing. 'Then last Friday, Jane Reid – the daughter of one of our missing players, Lana Reid – also went missing, near her school. She was caught on CCTV at King's Cross station on Saturday morning, but no one has seen or heard from her since then.'

'That reminds me,' interrupted DC Raj Akhtar. 'A Thomas Lake was in touch yesterday. He'd seen the appeals for Jane Reid. I'll email over his number. It sounds legit, but he's not a criminal. He's a dentist in Manchester.'

'What?' Jameson looked up from the desk.

Bloom turned to him and spoke quietly so that only he would hear. 'Are you still under the impression that Lana's a trustworthy source, Marcus?' Then she said, 'Thanks, Raj, we'll look into that.'

'A few more things to add in,' said Jameson. 'Augusta is facing a tribunal case for fictitious professional misconduct and I was hospitalized by a mystery cyclist. Both in the last week. Then yesterday, the most senior member of our task force was promoted and suddenly half the team are too busy to attend this call.'

'You think that's all related, do you?' said Green's droll voice.

'I'm just stating the facts.'

Bloom continued with her summary. 'Our primary theory is that this game is targeting functional psychopaths. This is based on evidence from interviews with those who knew Lana, Faye, Stuart and Grayson, and from our meeting with Clive Llewellyn too.'

'We didn't see anything other than a pretentious prick, did we?' said Green.

Jameson responded, 'I analysed the recording and Llewellyn's manner suggests psychopathic tendencies, such as superficial charm, manipulation and deceptiveness.'

'Like I said before, just your typical criminal,' said Green.

'Psychopaths do make very good criminals, you're right,' said Bloom, 'and I take your point. If this game is not targeting out-and-out psychopaths, at the very least it's targeting people with a potential for committing crime and evading capture.'

'On that point,' said Jameson, 'while I was relaxing at the NHS's expense I kept an eye on crimes reported locally and nationally. Even if we ignore all possible terrorist activity, there's arson, burglary, harassment, intimidation – there's a lot of noise. And plenty of fraud. People being defrauded of their life savings, online bank accounts hacked. And most have yet to result in an arrest.'

'Well, yeah, that's the nature of crime. What are you suggesting?' said Green.

'That our players could be out there committing crimes without being detected.'

'Why are you dismissing terrorist activities? What if ISIS has decided to radicalize natural-born killers?' said Kaye Willis.

Bloom and Jameson looked at each other.

'Don't tell me you've not thought of that?' said Green in response to their silence.

'No, we have,' said Jameson. 'But radicalized terrorism is highly emotive, based on a sense of injustice, or a response towards core religious principles.'

Bloom added, 'Your average psychopath just doesn't care enough about other people. Everything is about them. If they're getting what they want, all is good. It's highly unlikely they'd be interested in a cause, let alone be willing to sacrifice themselves for it.'

'What about organized crime then?' said Akhtar.

'Now you're talking,' said Jameson.

'This comes right to the core of what we need to know,' said Bloom. 'Why is someone doing this? Creating this game would require huge resources, so the pay-off needs to be worth it. So who would benefit from having one hundred con artists, manipulators and morally bankrupt operators without a conscience sitting in their pocket?'

'I can think of a few answers to that,' said Green with a laugh.

'Me too,' said Jameson, but he was frighteningly serious.

42

Thomas Lake lived in a large detached house in Dids-
bury, Manchester, with his wife Suzanne and their twin
boys, Lucas and Jacob. As Jameson and Bloom walked
towards the front door, Jameson braced himself for disappointment. This couldn't be the same Thomas Lake
described by Jane.

A tall man with fair hair and a tanned complexion
opened the door. He wore jeans with a checked short-
sleeved shirt and Dennis the Menace slippers. Bloom
explained they were following up on his call about Jane,
and he invited them in.

Lake sat on the edge of a turquoise love seat. Bloom
and Jameson sat opposite on a deep-blue velvet sofa.
'Lana? She was my wife. And Jane is my daughter.'

'Your wife?' Jameson couldn't hide his surprise.

'For eighteen months. What's happened to Jane? It was
on the news and the policewoman I spoke to said someone would be in touch. Can you tell me where she is?'

'I'm afraid not, Mr Lake,' said Bloom.

'Thomas, please.'

'We think she might be with Lana. Lana went missing
a few weeks ago. But other than the sighting of Jane at
King's Cross station on Saturday morning, we have no
further information.'

Suzanne Lake came into the lounge carrying a cafetière and a plate of biscuits and placed them on the glass coffee table. She was pretty, with long red hair and kind eyes. She squeezed her husband's arm before excusing herself.

'We think Lana might have been recruited by someone,' said Bloom.

'Run that by me again?'

'When was the last time you saw Jane?' said Jameson.

Thomas Lake looked down. 'Too long ago.'

'Why? Why haven't you made more effort?' Jameson knew not to look at Bloom; he didn't want to see the warning on her face.

'Things between Lana and me were very complicated. She made some pretty horrific accusations.'

'That you were a violent drug-user who harmed his own child?' Jameson hadn't intended to sound quite so judgemental.

'I beg your pardon?' Lake looked from Bloom to Jameson. 'Is that what Jane thinks of me?'

Jameson didn't respond.

'I'm afraid so,' said Bloom. 'Is that not the case?'

'I would never hurt Jane – or any child, for that matter – and I have never taken drugs.'

Jameson didn't buy it. 'So what did you mean when you said things were complicated between you and Lana?'

Lake exhaled and looked down at his hands in his lap. 'I was young and naive when I met Lana. I thought . . . I thought that she was all I'd ever need. She liked the things I liked, enjoyed the same sports, liked the same clubs, the same music and films. I thought I'd met my soulmate. My parents were livid when they found out we were engaged. They said I was rushing things – but I was in love. Or I thought I was in love. I was infatuated. And within a few months she was pregnant. We married in the town hall when she was four months gone. I thought we were set for life.'

'But?' said Bloom.

Lake looked at the ceiling and then at Bloom. 'None of it was real. She was . . . I can't describe it. She was sort of empty.' He reached for a biscuit and broke it in half. 'She just tuned out. I couldn't get any response. She couldn't have a conversation without hurling abuse at me. I thought it was pregnancy hormones, but she just got worse after Jane was born. As far as Lana was concerned, the baby was hers. I had no say and no rights. All she wanted was my money. She kept pushing me to get a better job. She wanted a better house, nicer clothes, foreign holidays. She was killing me. And when I couldn't keep up, she . . .' Thomas looked at the broken biscuit in his hands. He placed both halves back on the plate and brushed the crumbs from his palms. He looked at Jameson. 'Do you know Jane?'

Jameson nodded. How had Lake clocked that?

'Is she OK? I mean, other than going missing . . . has she been happy?'

'She's a great kid, very mature and capable, probably because she's had to mother her mother.'

Thomas frowned.

'We think Lana might be a psychopath,' said Jameson.

The stunned look on Thomas Lake's face was mirrored on Bloom's. She clearly didn't approve of Jameson's blunt pronouncement, but Jameson wanted the man to know what a bloody awful decision leaving his daughter with Lana had been.

'I'm sorry, Thomas,' said Bloom, leaning forward in her chair. 'What Marcus means is that we think Lana may have an extreme personality type. We don't think she's necessarily dangerous, we simply believe—'

'No, I agree.' Lake looked at Bloom and then at Jameson. 'I've never said it out loud to anyone, not even Suzanne, but I've always thought my first wife was a psychopath. It's a relief to hear you say that.'

Jameson clenched his fists, trying to get a handle on his temper. Then he spoke as calmly as he could. 'And yet you left Jane with her?'

'Good God, no. I would never, never have done that. But Lana took Jane with her when she left for the women's refuge. She said I'd beaten her. Obviously they believed her. They helped with a restraining order. I fought it for a year, but Lana was relentless and vicious. She'd be sweet and lovely in front of the social workers or in court, and then when it was just me and her she'd become this sneering monster. She scared me. And as soon as she had the court's approval for sole custody, she was gone. I never saw them after that day.' Lake looked at Jameson. 'But I have never stopped looking.'

'I know it's been a long time, Thomas,' said Bloom,

'but can you think of anywhere Lana might have taken Jane?'

'If I could, don't you think I'd have found them by now?'

They walked back to the car in silence. Jameson knew what was coming. He climbed into the passenger seat and fastened his seatbelt. Then he sat, eyes front, not looking at Bloom.

'What was that?' She turned in her seat to look at him. 'Marcus?' she said when he didn't respond. She faced the steering wheel again and started the engine. 'I know Jane is important to you and your family, but you can't go on the attack like that. That poor man is not responsible for Jane going missing.'

'No?' He could hear his own petulance.

'No.' Bloom pulled out of the parking space. 'He's as much Lana's victim as Jane is. He said he'd been looking for them all these years.'

'Well, he didn't look hard enough then.'

Bloom sighed. 'Even if he'd found them, Lana had sole custody. What could he have done?'

Jameson stared out of the window. He knew Bloom was right. And he knew it was a good thing that they'd found Jane's father and discovered such a good, kind, honest man. Would he really rather he'd turned out to be an addict? Only because he was so damn angry and desperate to vent his frustration on someone. God help Lana when he finally got his hands on her.

43

Jameson lay on his side and watched Sarah sleeping. He wanted to trace his finger down her cheek and across her lips. But she looked so peaceful. So he simply watched. Their date had been a huge success – obviously. They had met at the Serpentine Gallery as agreed. Sarah had brought a picnic rug and a bag full of Marks and Spencer goodies, and he'd brought a bottle of chilled Sancerre and freshly baked chocolate brownies. She'd been impressed. He'd explained that it was his grandma's recipe and usually reserved for his nieces, but that he'd made an exception for her.

'I'm honoured,' she'd said, taking a bite. 'Gorgeous.'

'Me or the brownies?' he'd replied.

She had been right about the weather. Almost. They'd enjoyed an hour or so of warm sunshine before the first drops of rain splattered on to their picnic. They'd packed up quickly and run for shelter. Sarah had giggled as they'd splashed through puddles of water. Jameson remembered taking her hand and feeling her lace her fingers through his.

They'd spent the afternoon in a bar and then, when he thought she'd make her excuses and leave, she'd suggested dinner, and then they were heading back to his. The rest, as they say, is history.

Sarah opened one eye and smiled. 'Hi.'

'Morning,' he replied. 'How are you?'

'Comfy.'

'Good. I like the women in my bed to feel comfy.'

Sarah closed her eyes. 'You make it sound like there've been dozens of women in here.'

'I realized something last night,' he said, knowing to ignore the silent question in her statement. 'You aren't a good girl at all.'

Sarah rolled on to her back and smiled. 'I don't know what you mean.'

Later, as they sat at the breakfast bar eating toasted crumpets with butter, Jane's appeal came on the radio. Jameson turned it up. There was nothing new, just the same request for information.

'She's a friend of the family,' Jameson explained as he turned the volume down again.

'I'm so sorry.' Sarah placed her mug down. 'What do they think happened?'

'We think her mum might have taken her. She's going through a rough patch. It's hard to explain.'

'Is she ill?'

'Well, she's not normal, that's for sure.' He clocked Sarah's expression and elaborated. 'She has a history of drink and drugs. She's not been the most responsible parent.'

'Well, at least with her mum it's better' – Sarah paused – 'than someone else taking her.'

'I really hope you're right.' Jameson kissed the top of

Sarah's head. 'Let's change the subject. I want to hear more about those secrets you don't have.'

'Is it related to your work? To your research?'

'Why would you think that?' he asked.

'You get this haunted look on your face when you talk about your job – or should I say, when you *don't* talk about your job – and you have it again now.'

He must be losing his touch. He used to be better than this. Or maybe it was Sarah. He found himself wanting to confide in her and that had never happened before.

'You're not trying one of those staring competitions again, are you? Because I should warn you, Marcus, I've been practising.'

The sound of his name on her lips made the muscles in his stomach clench.

'Practising with who?'

Her lips twitched. 'That would be telling.'

'So we both have secrets. I knew it.'

'You admit you're keeping secrets?'

He almost choked on his tea. 'You don't miss a beat, do you?'

'Would you want me to?'

She placed her hand on the back of his neck and pulled him closer. His phone started to vibrate on the table in front of them. She didn't let go. The tightening in his stomach travelled towards his groin and he pulled away while he still could.

'One minute,' he said.

It was Claire. There might be news.

He sat upright and answered. 'Hey, sis. Give me one sec.' He placed a hand over the microphone. 'Yes, Jane's disappearance is related to my research.' He felt strangely liberated speaking the truth.

'Sorry, Claire,' he said into the phone. 'Everything OK?'

'I've had a message from Jane.'

Jameson stood. 'What? When?'

'She sent me a private message on Facebook yesterday morning. I never go on so I didn't see it until today when Dan was showing me pictures of his cousin's new baby.' She sounded agitated.

'It's all right. Calm down. Don't beat yourself up. You've seen it now. What does it say?'

Jameson glanced at Sarah. She raised her eyebrows and mouthed, 'Bad news?' Jameson shook his head.

'It says, "Hi Claire. It's Jane. I'm with Mum. I'm OK but she has me locked in the attic of some house near Leeds—"'

'What? How did they get to Leeds?' said Jameson. The police said she hadn't boarded a train. Idiots.

Clare continued, '"We were in the taxi for about half an hour and came to a town. I don't know what it's called, but I remember a church. I think it was All Saints. And a Majestic Wine shop. Sorry. That's all I can remember. The house we are in is a three-storey terrace on a back street."'

Jameson scribbled notes on the back of an envelope: *30 minutes from Leeds, All Saints Church, Majestic Wine, three-storey terrace on back street.*

'Then she says,' Claire went on, '"I've only managed to get hold of Mum's phone because we had a fight this morning and she dropped it, so this might be my only message. She's acting weird and I want to come home. Please ask Marcus to find me."'

Jameson stopped writing and swallowed the lump in his throat. How were they supposed to find her? A house with no number, no road name, no idea which suburban town near Leeds.

'What does she mean, *they had a fight*?' said Claire. 'Lana won't hurt her, will she? Tell me she won't hurt her?'

Jameson knew he couldn't do that. 'Let me call Augusta.'

'You have to find her, Marcus.'

'We'll do our best, Claire. I promise.' He put the phone down.

'I'm going to head off and let you get on,' said Sarah. 'This sounds important.'

'I'm sorry.'

'Don't be.' She came over and kissed him softly.

He instinctively covered the notes with his hand.

Sarah stepped back and narrowed her eyes. 'Wow. You really do have trust issues, don't you?'

It wasn't the first time a woman had said something like that. 'Force of habit. Sorry. I used to work for the Secret Service.' He blinked a couple of times. Why had he said that?

'Oh,' said Sarah. 'I see.' She ran a hand through her hair and pulled it over one shoulder, smoothing it over her left breast. 'That explains a lot.' She stood still for a moment, as though taking it in, and then burst back to life. 'Oh, I forgot,' she said, 'I have something for you.' She walked through to his bedroom, returning a moment later with her coat and handbag. She placed the latter on the table and reached inside to remove a paper bag.

'Here,' she said.

'A book?' he said, opening the bag.

'I have a friend at the publishers. It's an advance copy. I know you like cycling and I really liked it.'

'*The Hardmen: Legends of the Cycling Gods*,' Jameson read aloud. Then he looked at her. 'You've read this?'

Sarah nodded. 'It's about the craziest, bravest cyclists in history. I like my cycling too, you know. Maybe we could go for a ride some day?'

'I thought we already had?'

'All right, smutty mouth,' she said, putting one arm and then the other into her coat. 'Go be a hero, then. Call me when you're ready to mix with mere mortals again.'

Jameson took her face in his hands. 'I'm not a hero. And you're the one who saves lives.'

'Just a lowly researcher, you said.'

This woman was hot, intelligent, loved cycling and was more than a match for his wit. Could it get any better? For the first time in his life, he was in real danger of falling in love.

Bloom was back in her hometown of Harrogate, where the stresses of living and working in London simply ebbed away. She ran faster here, breathing in the fresh

214

Yorkshire air and feeling younger and freer than she had in months.

The sensation was short-lived.

Her music was interrupted by her phone.

'It's me,' said Jameson. 'Are you still in Yorkshire visiting your mum?'

'I am,' said Bloom, wiping the sweat from her face with her sleeve.

'Claire's received a message from Jane. She's locked in an attic somewhere near Leeds. I'm on my way to King's Cross now. I arrive in Leeds at two thirty. Can you meet me?'

'Jump on a train to Harrogate from Leeds. I'll meet you at the station. There's plenty of room at the house.'

'Are you sure? I'm happy in a hotel.'

'I'm rattling around this place. It'll be good to have the company and we can set up a proper base.'

Bloom jogged back to the house. It was a five-bedroom detached building in an upmarket part of Harrogate. Her father had been a lawyer and her mother a cardiac surgeon, and both had been totally obsessed with their work. They never travelled, they never ate out. The only thing they spent time or money on was their home.

Jameson would be surprised at the invite. He'd never been asked to her home in London, but this place was different. For a start, it wasn't hers. Well, not yet, anyway. Not with Mummy still alive. And she was different here, too. Her work made her paranoid and obsessive about privacy. She'd seen too many cases of people placing their trust in the goodness of others and paying the price. She recalled the stalker who'd gleefully explained to her how a running app made it so much easier to track the women he preyed on. 'I just need to run around an area for a few days and I can see all the women who run there and where they live. Most accounts include real names and a picture, too.' He would turn up at their home and claim to be an old work or school friend. And so it would begin. Bloom had switched off all location services on her phone and avoided social media. Big Brother was watching through cleverly designed surveillance tools that people opted in to.

She unlocked the front door, then removed her trainers before stepping on to the parquet floor. Her mother didn't allow shoes in the house. After a quick shower, she organized a hire car and called up an old friend from the West Yorkshire Police. Caroline would help. She had been there all those years ago when Bloom made her first mistake and the world came crashing down. She'd want to help.

44

Jameson walked out of Harrogate station and into an unexpectedly pretty town. Blossoming trees lined the pavements in all directions and an impressive building stood opposite, a crescent of caramel stone surrounding a large concourse and dotted with raised flower beds.

'Marcus?' Bloom walked towards him in a white cotton shirt and navy jeans. He'd never seen her in jeans before. On her, even denim looked pretty smart. 'We can walk back to the house,' she said. 'It isn't far.'

'Lead on,' he said and followed her down a street lined with smart boutiques and high-end chains. 'So this is where you grew up?'

'Yes. I had a bit of a rough start,' she said.

'Another joke, Augusta? This is starting to get a bit old.'

The road opened out on to a large junction. To the left, a wide grass verge fronted a long line of impressive Victorian buildings, and ahead, a needle-shaped cenotaph rose from the centre of a square roundabout swathed in spring flowers. Jameson spotted an expensive-looking cafe as they crossed the road towards a large green.

'Betty's,' he said. 'Have I heard of that?'

'Probably,' she replied. 'It's famous around here. Tourists queue for hours for a table.'

'Is it worth it?'

'My mother used to say, "It's only bloody tea," but it is actually very good.'

Bloom was more relaxed here. In London she rarely talked about her mother, except when mentioning an impending visit. Maybe he'd learn a bit more about her. He did respect her privacy – he knew it was important to her – but he was also dying to know what made a woman like Augusta Bloom.

Jameson whistled as they approached Bloom's family home. Set in its own grounds and surrounded by a low wall topped with a neatly manicured privet hedge was a stone building with large bay windows either side of the front door and actual turrets on the roof. 'I can see why your mum would want to stay here.'

Bloom unlocked the front door. 'She's in a home now.'

'Sorry. I didn't realize.'

'Dementia. You can pop your bag in the first room to the left at the top of the stairs. I'll get the kettle on and show you what I've found so far.'

Jameson nearly whistled again when he opened the door to his room. Decorated from floor to ceiling in floral fabrics and wallpaper, it had two large windows, one overlooking the green and the other with views across the driveway. He placed his bag on the mahogany sleigh bed and checked out the en-suite. It was like being in a country-house hotel.

Downstairs, Bloom had laid out a china teapot and

matching cups on the oak kitchen table. Next to them was an open Ordnance Survey map with a large red circle drawn in the centre.

'Thirty minutes in all directions. That's from Knaresborough, near here, to Tadcaster and Sherburn in Elmet at three o'clock, Darton and Holmfirth at six o'clock, through to Hebden Bridge and Howarth at nine o'clock. And everywhere in between. It's huge.' She passed him his tea.

'Any have an All Saints Church and a Majestic Wine?'

'There are All Saints churches in Bradford, Kirkby Overblow, Ilkley, Sherburn, Batley and Bingley.'

'Majestic Wine?'

'Five stores in West Yorkshire: Leeds, Huddersfield, Wakefield, Harrogate and Ilkley.'

'So Jane's in Ilkley.' Jameson's phone vibrated once.

'Jane's in Ilkley,' agreed Bloom.

'In a house with no known number, in a road with no known name. How big is Ilkley?'

'Too big. We're going to need help. I've a contact in the West Yorkshire Police and she's arranged for the Ilkley officers to make some enquiries. I've sent them pictures of Jane and Lana.'

'You've been very busy.' Jameson fished his phone out of his pocket. 'Thanks, Augusta. If I have to knock on every door in that place, I will.'

'Shall we drive over?'

'Yes, let's.' Jameson looked at his message. It was a traffic alert from Google. More spam.

*

Bloom drove and Jameson called Claire. She'd wanted to come along, but he'd managed to talk her out of it.

She answered after the first ring, sounding more than a little frantic. She kept telling him to hurry up and find Jane – as though he wasn't doing everything he could. He managed to keep a lid on his irritation. He knew she felt helpless.

'Is there a tourist information centre in Ilkley?' Jameson placed his phone beside Bloom's in the tray behind the gear stick.

'I haven't visited for a while, but I think there's one opposite the station.'

'Let's head there first. If they have a town map, we can split it into quadrants, then search section by section.' They stopped at traffic lights near a BMW dealership. 'Do you know where the police are making enquiries?'

Bloom pulled on the handbrake and looked his way. 'Caroline said they'd check with the train and bus stations first, then the taxi rank, then some of the banks and the supermarkets.'

'So they're not going door to door?'

The lights changed. 'I don't expect so. I left a message for Barker asking him to contact Caroline's boss and stress the importance of our search, but I've not heard back yet from him.'

'He knows what's going on here. He needs to stop poncing around in the world of police politics and pull his bloody finger out.'

At the roundabout, Bloom turned right on to a road that curved through fields and quaint villages. As they passed a pub next to a farm shop, her phone buzzed. 'It might be Caroline with an update. Check it.'

Jameson picked up Bloom's iPhone and entered her PIN as she said it. 'That's weird,' he said, on reading the message in full.

'What?'

'That traffic alert on my phone. It had the shortest route to a place I'd never heard of. I figured it was junk. But you've just got a message from Trainline mentioning the same place.'

'What place?'

'South Milford. Do you know it?'

Bloom slammed on the brakes so hard Jameson's seat-belt locked, yanking him back into his seat. She swerved through the smallest gap in the oncoming traffic and into a petrol station.

'Let me see.' She took her phone. She looked strange, pale but with flushed cheeks.

'Augusta?'

She looked up at him, her mouth slightly open, her eyes panicked.

'Talk to me,' he said.

She tapped at the screen and then held the phone to her ear.

After a few seconds, she cursed under her breath and then said, 'Caroline, it's Augusta. I think we have a situation at South Milford station.' She checked her watch. 'It's three thirty-five. Call me as soon as you can.' She ended the call and handed the phone to Jameson. 'Go on to the Trainline website. I need to know when the next express train from Leeds to Hull passes through South Milford.' She put the car in gear and pulled out on to the road again.

Jameson did as instructed. 'Augusta? What's going on? Where's this South Milford?'

Were there tears in Bloom's eyes? He'd never seen that before.

'Augusta?'

'It's the place where my life fell apart.'

45

Jameson had questions – of course he did – but he knew better than to quiz Bloom now. Her demeanour told him that this was serious. He typed 'Leeds to Hull' into the journey planner and then looked through the calling points for each service until he found South Milford. 'We have a 15.52 train leaving Leeds and calling at South Milford at 16.15.'

Bloom shook her head. 'Not the trains that stop there. We need the express trains that go straight through.'

Jameson looked up. 'You mean . . . ?'

Bloom checked her mirrors and pulled out to over-take the transit van in front. 'I mean a train you can jump in front of.'

'Shit. What do you . . . ? Who . . . ?' He didn't need to finish that question. 'Lana,' he said under his breath. 'Right, there's a train that left Leeds at 15.38 and gets to Selby at 15.58 with only one stop.'

'South Milford is just under ten minutes from Selby.'

Jameson looked at his watch: 15.42. 'That's six minutes.'

Bloom nodded once. 'Call 999.'

He did as requested. Bloom stopped in front of a gate to a field and took the phone from him.

'This is Dr Augusta Bloom. I'm a psychologist and

have it on good authority that someone is going to jump in front of a train at South Milford station this afternoon. The next express travels through in five or six minutes.' Bloom listened. 'A sixteen-year-old girl called Jane Reid and her mother Lana Reid.' She listened again. 'Maybe just one of them, maybe both. I don't know. And no, I don't know which train. I simply received a message that leads me to believe that is their intention. I'm twenty minutes away.' Bloom listened once more, then gave her contact details. 'If you speak to Inspector Caroline Watkins at Weetwood station, she's aware of the situation.' Bloom thanked the operator and hung up. 'She's dispatched a car to South Milford.'

'Will they make it before the train?'

Bloom pulled out on to the road. 'She seemed to think so.'

Jameson watched the clock on the dashboard. It clicked from 15.46 to 15.47. The car shunted him left then right then left again as Bloom threw them around the country bends. Would Lana really hurt Jane? He had no idea. But Bloom was driving as if her life depended on it. And Bloom knew psychopaths. The clock clicked to 15.48. The train would pass through South Milford any minute now. He watched Bloom's phone. It didn't ring. The clock clicked on to 15.50.

'Should I call back?' he said.

They jumped at the sound of Bloom's ringtone. Jameson grabbed it. 'Dr Bloom's phone.'

'Is she there? It's Caroline.'

'She's driving. Hold on, I'm putting you on speaker.'

'Caroline,' said Bloom. 'Can you hear me? I'm in a rental car so no hands-free.'

'I can hear you. There's a patrol heading to South Milford for a jumper. Are you OK?'

Caroline's tone softened for the last question. Caroline clearly knew something.

'Fine,' said Bloom, in a manner that indicated quite the opposite. 'Is there any news?'

'The site is clear. No one there except our officers.'

'Keep them there . . . please.'

'The express trains to and from Hull have been through and it's an hour until the next one. We'll go back at four thirty.'

'OK. We'll be there soon.'

'Is that wise, Augusta?'

'It's a station, Caroline. I'll cope. It's not like I was there last time, is it?'

'I know, but . . .'

The line fell quiet and Jameson glanced at Bloom. Her jaw was locked and her eyes fixed on the road.

'I've a meeting this afternoon,' said Caroline, 'but I can get out of it if you want me there too.'

'That won't be necessary.'

'I'll see what I can do,' said Caroline and then hung up.

'She's protective of you.' Jameson placed Bloom's phone beside his. Bloom said nothing. 'Who jumped?'

Bloom kept her eyes on the road and her hands tight on the steering wheel. 'Someone very important to me . . . Someone I cared about. I was supposed to . . .'

She came to a junction and turned left. 'I let them down and I'll never forgive myself.'

'When?'

'Fifteen years ago.'

Jameson did the maths. She'd have been in her late twenties. Had she had a lover? Had she broken some-one's heart? He looked at Bloom. Was this why she was so resolutely single? It would make sense.

46

South Milford contained nothing more than a petrol station and a couple of pubs. Bloom parked the rented Seat in the station's small car park. There were only four other cars there. The station had two platforms and was deserted. Jameson checked the four cars: all were empty.

'So what now?' he said.

'Let's walk down to the main street in case they've parked there.'

But there were only more empty cars and more empty streets. They walked back to the station as a police car pulled in. A female officer climbed out of the passenger seat and walked towards them. She introduced herself as PC Fisher. She explained that two express trains passed every hour and within a few minutes of each other. She suggested that Bloom stay on the eastbound platform with her male colleague, and that Jameson accompany her to the opposite side.

'Who is it you think might jump?' asked PC Fisher as they walked through the underpass to the westbound platform. She clearly thought they were wasting her time.

Jameson was tempted to use an old Secret Service line about those in the know, but instead said, 'A young girl and her mother. The mother, Lana, is unstable.'

'Dispatch said you're her psychologist?'

'Dr Bloom's a psychologist,' Jameson said. He heard the grumble of the first train approaching. He looked to his right and saw the train in the distance. If it were him, and he really wanted to do this, and he thought someone would be trying to stop him, he would hide until the train was closer and then make a run for it. He scanned the platform again. The train was closer now, louder. The car park was clear. The path behind him was clear. The train rumbled louder and louder and then it blew its horn. He looked back. Jesus, it was coming fast. He stepped away from the platform edge as the train flew past. Each carriage sent a blast of air towards him, pushing the hair from his forehead and rippling the fabric of his sleeves.

He watched it speed away and finally exhaled. His eyes met Bloom's across the train tracks and her face reflected his own sense of relief. And then, before there was time to appreciate that feeling, he heard the second train approaching.

Jameson saw the lights of the Hull-bound express in the distance. He scanned the car park and the fields either side of the platforms. If Lana was here, wouldn't she have jumped in front of the first train? Or was she watching to see what they and their police companions would do? It would make sense. She'd have seen him walking down the platform, scanning, ready, and she'd have seen the police officers standing at their chosen midway points. They would not stop someone who was running at speed. They weren't here to perform heroics. And how about Augusta? If she tried to intercept Lana, would she be strong enough or would she just get dragged along too?

If Lana was watching and calculating, she would head for the far end of the other platform. As far as possible from the person most likely to intervene. He looked back at the train speeding along the opposite tracks. He didn't have time to run to that side. The only way to the other platform was across the tracks and that would be stupid. There was no real reason to suspect that Lana and Jane were here.

And then he saw it. A flash of something at the far end of the opposite platform, exactly where he would jump from in Lana's shoes. He began running, shouting to Bloom and the male officer, pointing to where the movement had been. Bloom ran, but the officer didn't.

She can only stop one, Jameson thought.

He passed PC Fisher. 'I saw something down there!' he shouted. The train was getting closer and closer. He could see the purple and blue TransPennine livery on the front carriage, but he was pretty sure he had time.

He saw the movement again, a flash of red in between the trees. He heard Bloom shout. He couldn't make out her words. He glanced back at the train one more time. He was nearly at the end of his platform now. *Do it*, he told himself.

Bloom shouted again. 'Stay there! Stay there!' Her voice was shrill.

She can only stop one, he repeated like a mantra. The train blew its horn and without hesitation Jameson launched himself across the track towards Bloom's platform.

Lana Reid paced back and forth in the ankle-high grass. The last message had said they were on their way, but now she was in the middle of bloody nowhere with no signal, no idea what was going on and no clue how long she'd have to wait. All because she'd wanted Jane's help. They told her she'd be disqualified – help wasn't allowed – unless she did as she was told. She glanced back at the trees, at the figure huddled in the shadows. No going back now. She had to sit it out until the job was done. She'd enjoy seeing the expression on Marcus's stupid fucking face.

47

They were sitting side by side in the car in silence. Bloom had never shouted at Marcus before, but he'd really bloody scared her. As soon as he'd made it up from the tracks on to her platform, she'd lost it. She'd been scream-ing at him – that he was an idiot, what the hell was he thinking, did he have no respect for his own life?

He'd ignored her, of course. He'd been totally focused on his goal and oblivious to her yelling and the express train thundering behind him, its horn blaring. He'd pushed his way through the large shrubs lining the platform and found a discarded plastic bag attached to a branch; then, finally, he'd sunk to his knees. Was it relief or the realiza-tion that he'd risked his life for a TK Maxx carrier that had brought him to the ground? She hadn't much cared at that point. She'd run towards him and shoved him hard.

'Don't *ever* do anything so stupid again,' she'd hissed. Then she'd walked away and left him to receive some even sterner words from the police.

'Thank you,' she whispered now.

Jameson turned towards her. He'd picked up dinner from the petrol station but his vacuum-packed sandwich sat untouched in his lap. 'Huh?'

'I know you want to go to Ilkley, but I need to stay here until the last train passes.'

The police had said they had more pressing issues to deal with.

'It's the least I can do.' He picked at the packaging. 'What happened, Augusta? Was it a boyfriend?'

'It was a child,' she said, then added quickly, 'Not mine. But I had a duty of care.'

Bloom could remember her mother standing at the open door of their home as the woman screamed, *'Where is she? Tell me where she is!'*

'Augusta?' Jameson rested his hand on her arm.

She forced the memory away. 'Sorry. This is hard to talk about.' She took a breath. 'Hard to remember.'

Jameson removed his hand and she knew he was telling her to take her time.

She took a minute to compose herself. 'My mother had a friend. Her name was Penny. They'd known each other since primary school. Her daughter . . .' She needed to keep the images at bay and focus on the facts. 'Her daughter was twelve years younger than me. Penny had struggled to have children.' She paused. Was that relevant? Of course it was. To desperately hope for a child, then lose them, only made the tragedy worse. 'Penny's daughter had been in trouble at school and Penny asked if I would speak to her.' A small, strangled laugh escaped her throat. 'I thought I could practise my new skills, show off to my mother, who frankly thought my becoming a psychologist was one step away from hypnotizing partygoers to bark like dogs.'

Jameson made an appreciative hum in response to her attempt at humour.

'I had no idea the damage I could do.'

They were silent. Then Jameson said, 'The first blood on my hands was a young farm labourer in the Ukraine. We suspected a criminal organization was using the farm he worked at to hide weapons. I knew the organization was ruthless and dangerous, but I convinced this kid to spy for me. I told him it wouldn't go unrewarded. I knew he had a sister. She was hoping for British Citizenship and I implied that I could help. They shot him in the head and hung his body on a fence in the local village so that everyone would see it. I didn't sleep well again for . . . well, for ever really.' He looked at Bloom. 'None of us know the damage we can do when we're young and inexperienced, Augusta.'

She looked at him through her tears. He'd left MI6 after one trauma too many, but he'd never shared any of this before. It made her feel braver. 'I thought I was helping. I thought we were making progress. The morning it happened, I was planning to ask permission to write the whole thing up as a case study . . . a success story.'

'You can't blame yourself for someone else's choices.'

'Oh, but I can. In this case, I really can.'

Bloom remembered Penny barging past her mother and barrelling up the stairs to where she herself stood. Their faces were just inches apart. Penny spoke low, almost hissing, her voice filled with hate. 'My baby threw herself in front of a train.' She remembered sitting heavily on the stair behind her, the strength knocked from her legs, the air knocked from her lungs. Penny kept

233

talking – shouting – but she only heard a high-pitched whistling, no words. *My baby threw herself in front of a train.* She remembered looking at her hands. She couldn't feel her fingers. She tried to move them but they stayed splayed out on her knees.

Her mother was standing beside them. She had an arm around Penny. 'Come on, Pen. Come with me.'

But Penny wouldn't leave. She kept waving a piece of paper. Bloom remembered staring as it oscillated back and forth in front of her. 'I will never forgive you,' Penny said.

'This is not Augusta's fault, Penny. Come on now.' Her mother's voice was calm, as though she were talking about the weather.

Penny turned to Bloom's mother. 'Really?' she said, handing over the piece of paper. 'Not her fault?'

She watched her mother take it. It was an envelope. Her mother removed the paper inside, looked at it for a moment, and then said, 'Oh dear.'

She looked at Augusta and her eyes expressed everything she would never actually say: *I am disappointed. I am embarrassed. I am ashamed.*

Bloom remembered taking the piece of paper from her mother, who then led Penny back down the stairs and into the kitchen.

Eventually she looked down. There were only two lines, but they would haunt her for the rest of her life.

I can't be normal. And I don't want to be a monster.
You told me to choose. I've chosen.

48

Bloom hadn't allowed herself to think about that day for years. The details had become foggy and vague over time. But as she ran through the events in her mind, her memory cleared and something came back to her.

She grabbed her phone, opened Google maps, zoomed in on South Milford, found the train line and tracked it first towards Selby and then towards Leeds. Where the train line crossed a road, she converted to a satellite image, looking for something specific. When she finally found it, she double-checked the location, handed her phone to Jameson and started the engine.

'But the last train isn't for another twenty minutes,' said Jameson.

Bloom pulled out of the now empty car park. 'The pathologist said that if the gods were kind, the fall would have knocked her out before the train hit her. *The fall.*'

Jameson looked down at the phone and zoomed in on the image. 'She jumped from a bridge?'

'That's the only one near South Milford.'

'It looks like a farm-access road.'

Bloom nodded. 'Can you direct me?'

Darkness had fallen and the lack of street lighting made it hard to see. Bloom switched her lights to full beam as they passed open fields and dense woodland.

'Slow down,' said Jameson. 'Train lines often have wooded embankments.'

He was right. There it was. Bloom pulled over to park on the grass. They climbed out and walked back to the bridge.

Bloom could just about make out the parallel train tracks below. So this was it. The place where it happened. The place she'd jumped from. There was no way a drop this short would have knocked her out. The pathologist was just being kind.

'Augusta?' Jameson's voice was urgent.

There was a woman standing at the edge of the bridge. She was walking slowly towards them. And when her face came into view, Bloom put a hand on Jameson's forearm. His muscles tensed and she knew he'd clenched his fists.

Bloom stepped forward. 'Lana?'

Lana stopped. 'What took you so long?'

'Who told you about this place?' Bloom said. Who would know to bring her here? The pathologist? The police? Penny?

Lana smiled.

'Where's Jane?' said Jameson, his rage barely contained.

Lana stepped towards them. 'With a friend.'

'With what friend? Where?' Jameson took a step forward.

'On a bridge,' said Lana, her eyes fixed on Jameson.

Fear sliced through Bloom's chest. 'Which bridge?'

'Above a train track,' said Lana, her voice almost robotic.

Jameson lunged at Lana. He was too quick – Bloom couldn't stop him. He grabbed her shoulders and pulled her face right up to his own.

'Tell me exactly where she is, you crazy bitch, or I'll throw you in front of the next train myself.'

'Oh, Marcus,' she trilled. 'How manly you are!'

'Marcus?' Bloom placed a hand on his back.

'Don't think I won't do it,' Jameson said. 'Jane and the world would be better off without you. Now where the hell is she?' When Lana failed to respond, he dragged her into the middle of the bridge, his knuckles white on her shoulders. He pushed her to the edge and checked his watch. 'You've got two minutes.'

Bloom watched her partner. She was ninety-nine per cent sure he wouldn't do it. He was a good man, a law-abiding man. But he'd just told her about the *first* death he was responsible for. There were more.

'Marcus?' she said again. If he was bluffing, he wouldn't thank her for ruining it. But if she showed just enough fear . . . 'Don't do anything stupid, Marcus.'

'Where is she?' Jameson's voice was low and menacing. She'd never heard him like this before.

'How do you expect to find her if you throw me over?' Lana's voice was still completely calm.

'She's right, Marcus,' said Bloom. 'Don't let your hatred cloud your judgement. I know you've struggled with those who've died at your hand before.' Lana responded with a hint of panic and Bloom felt a small surge of satisfaction. The woman strained against Jameson's arm for the first time. She didn't want to die. 'If Lana is killed by this train, what will we have gained? She won't be here any more, breathing, thinking, talking. She'll be nothing.'

Jameson tightened his grip against Lana's attempts to wriggle free. 'Tell me where she is and I'll let you go. It's that simple.'

He was playing along. He was still thinking clearly.

Lana stopped squirming. In the distance Bloom heard the low murmur of the next train approaching.

'Decision time, Lana,' said Jameson, pushing her further over the edge.

'You know, I never did like you.' Lana craned her neck to see his face. 'And neither does Jane.'

Bloom could see the train's headlights. 'Why would you wind him up right now, Lana?'

Lana looked at her and smiled.

And then Bloom saw it. The reason they'd been lured to this spot. The reason Lana had waited all afternoon and into the night for them. This was a demonstration of power. They had somehow discovered Bloom's biggest weakness and this elaborate theatre was designed to exploit it. They had manipulated technology to lure her here. They had sent Lana alone. They had made it seem like Bloom and Jameson might actually have the upper hand. But it was all an illusion.

The train bore down on them, fast and loud, pushing gusts of air on to the bridge where they stood.

'She'll never tell us where Jane is, Marcus,' said Bloom. 'Do it.'

Lana's eyes widened as Jameson's head snapped right

and his eyes met Bloom's. The train was here. Bloom could see the driver in the brightly lit cab. She held Jameson's gaze and said again, 'Do it.'

Lana's hands grasped the barrier as Jameson lifted her feet from the ground. She wasn't screaming, but Bloom hadn't expected her to. She was a psychopath – she wouldn't feel fear the way they would.

The train's loud rumbling vibrated in her ears, but Bloom heard another sound, another engine.

The dirt bike skidded off the field from behind their parked Seat and headed straight for Bloom. She jumped backwards – as the rider no doubt expected – as its front wheel stopped a millimetre from the bridge wall. Its back wheel skidded in an arc as the express train thundered underneath them.

Either Jameson had let go of Lana or Lana had broken free, because when Bloom's vision cleared, Lana was sitting on the back of the bike. She patted the rider's shoulder and the bike roared into action, sending dirt into the air, then reversing past Bloom, spinning 180 degrees and speeding down the road.

'I'll drive!' shouted Jameson, already running back to their car.

Bloom didn't argue. She climbed into the passenger seat and fastened her seatbelt as the car swerved off the grass and over the bridge. She could just see the rear lights of the bike in the distance. Jameson accelerated and Bloom hoped his memory of the road was better than hers.

'We'll never catch a bike,' he said, 'but let's try to keep it in view.'

The road was straight for a few hundred yards. Then the small red bike light began to blink in and out of view as the road curved away and then straightened again.

'You had me going for a second there.' Jameson didn't take his eyes off the road or his foot off the accelerator.

'As did you.' Bloom braced herself against the dashboard with her outstretched hand.

'How did you know to call their bluff?' They reached a T-junction and Jameson threw the car round to the right.

Bloom lurched towards Jameson and then back again. Fumes filled the air as Jameson burned through their fuel. 'Instinct.'

Jameson raised his eyebrows. 'Did you follow your gut, Dr Bloom?'

Only a person whose life had always been full of risk would try humour at a time like this. 'Would you have done it if I'd been wrong?'

For the first time, Jameson's eyes left the road and he glanced at her. It was enough.

'Sorry,' she said quickly. 'I shouldn't have asked that.'

They passed a level-crossing. Bloom looked down the tracks, checking for trains.

'Shit,' said Jameson, under his breath.

'They're in the field.' Bloom picked up her phone, but there was no service. She scanned the horizon, looking for a possible route. Jameson turned left and accelerated along the road that ran parallel to the field, but it quickly began to veer away. They were losing them. Bloom craned her neck, looking back to try and find the bike. There was nothing but empty fields.

The car slowed. 'It's a dead end,' Jameson said, as they reached the entrance to a factory. 'They knew what they were doing.'

49

It was after midnight when Jameson and Bloom arrived back at the house.

Jameson headed to his room and took a shower. He turned the heat up high to wash away the frustration. What the hell had that been about? What had Lana gained? Bloom said the game's creators had been manipulating her emotions, that they'd have got a kick out of it, but Jameson didn't buy it. There had to be something else, some practical reason, some fundamental gain. When he could take no more, he wrapped the large bath towel from the radiator around his waist. It was soft and warm. He reached for his phone and replied to Sarah. She'd texted earlier to check that he'd arrived safely and to ask how things were. He said he was fine and that he'd call tomorrow.

He found Bloom in front of an empty fireplace in a wing-backed leather Chesterfield chair. He sat in the matching one opposite and she handed him a heavy tumbler. From the colour and smell, he guessed it was a rather nice Scottish malt. He wondered if Bloom had bought it herself. He couldn't imagine her buying spirits; a good red wine or a crisp white, maybe, but whisky? He took a sip. It tasted peaty and warm and was very much needed.

'Whose is this glass of old tat then, yours or your father's?'

'My mother's, actually.' Bloom looked up. 'She liked a stiff whisky after a difficult operation.'

'A cardiac surgeon, right?'

Bloom nodded and watched the whisky spin as she rotated her glass. 'We'll head over to Ilkley first thing tomorrow.'

'I expect they'll be long gone by now, don't you?' That was it. Of course. That was the tangible gain. Lana had bought herself time to move Jane.

Bloom didn't reply.

Jameson's phone buzzed in his pocket. 'Just a second,' he said, walking through to the kitchen to answer.

Sarah's voice came down the line, a splash of normality in an otherwise crazy night.

'Hey you,' she said.

'I thought you'd be asleep or I'd have called,' he said.

'Any luck finding your young friend?'

Jameson took a large swig of the malt. It stung the back of his throat.

'Marcus?'

'Sorry. No. No luck.'

'Are you OK? You sound . . .'

Jameson closed his eyes. He'd really thought they'd find Jane today. Even when they were with Lana, he'd believed that she'd tell them where Jane was. And when it became clear that she had no intention of doing anything of the sort, he had been truly tempted to throw her

243

over that bridge. He hadn't come face to face with his dark side for quite a while and it didn't feel good.

'I don't know that we'll ever find her.'

Sarah was quiet for a moment. 'Why? What happened?'

He didn't respond.

'Look,' she said, 'if you don't want to talk about it, I get it. But if you need me, I'm here, OK? Just call.'

He thanked her and promised to keep in touch. When he rejoined Bloom her glass was empty. 'Tough night,' he said. He'd never seen his partner this affected. He wanted to know why she blamed herself for that girl's suicide, but he couldn't think of the right words. So instead he simply sat and waited, on the slim chance she might want to talk.

'She was this beautiful little thing,' Bloom said eventually. 'With long curly hair and angelic features. Looking at her, you'd think she was the sweetest child.'

'But?'

'Let's just say I've been thinking about her a lot lately. This case has brought it all back. She was magnetic and intelligent and so inquisitive about how and why she was different. I wanted to be the person who harnessed all that potential and moulded it into something good.'

'She was a psychopath?' Another piece of the Augusta Bloom jigsaw clicked into place. This explained her life-long obsession.

'I was naive. She was more vulnerable than I thought. I'd viewed psychopaths as another species, a sort of giant mutation. Then I did what so many of us do. I generalized.

I expected her to be exactly the same as these tough, cold characters, but at the end of the day she was just a young girl who knew she was different, who wanted to fit in.'

He really felt for Bloom. There was no guilt as grim as someone's blood on your hands.

'What was her name?'

'Seraphine. Seraphine Walker.'

50

Bloom heard footsteps on the landing outside her room. She'd been dreaming about trains and bridges and smashed-up bodies. She sat up and blinked at the clock beside her bed. The small white cube her grandfather had given to her for her tenth birthday. 5.13am. The footsteps came closer and she sat up, scanning her childhood bedroom for a weapon. A rarely played guitar leaned against the wall in the far corner. There was a letter opener still in the drawer of her dressing table. Look at the damage Seraphine Walker had achieved with a sharpened pencil. She'd been a quick thinker with an exceptional knowledge of human anatomy and the sort of dispassionate ruthlessness that chilled Bloom to the bone. The idea that there were hundreds of Seraphines playing games with other people's lives, games like the one they had played last night, made Bloom both anxious and furious.

She paused for a second as an idea began to form.

There was a gentle rap on her door. 'Augusta?'

She'd forgotten that Marcus was staying.

'Come in,' she called. She could see from the light in the hall that he was wearing only a T-shirt and his boxers.

'Have you seen your WhatsApp?' he said.

She reached for her phone. She always set it on silent when she went to bed.

Jameson took a few steps into the room and then paused. Bloom flicked on the bedside light and he looked deftly around the space, taking it in, no doubt revelling in the insight into her youth. She expected him to make some sarcastic remark about the girly decor, but he didn't. Which meant that whatever was in the WhatsApp message was not good.

She clicked on the icon and saw only one new message in a newly created group consisting of her, Jameson and one blocked number. The title of the group was 'Dare to Play?' She looked at Jameson briefly before reading the message.

Blocked

Dear Dr Bloom and Mr Jameson. You are clearly intrigued by our activities and we have been impressed with your tenacious deductions.

So we wanted to afford you the courtesy of an invite.

Dare to Play?

5:00am

'What do we say?' said Jameson.

'I take it you want to reply with a yes?'

Jameson shrugged. 'I thought *bring it on* had a nice ring to it.'

'Of course you did.' Bloom clicked on the text box and typed a reply.

Bloom

I thought we were already playing.

5:17am

Jameson read it. 'Or that could work.'
Bloom looked down at the screen, waiting for a reply.

Blocked
Whatever would give you that impression, Dr Bloom?

5:18am

Let me show you what it's really like to play.

5:18am

Bloom and Jameson looked at each other. Then Jameson began to type his own message.

Jameson
And who is 'we'?

5:19am

Blocked
That, Mr Jameson, is for me to know, and you to find out . . .
if you can . . .

5:20am

'I need coffee for this,' said Jameson, and left the room.

What was motivating this invite? There must be a reason for it. Clive Llewellyn had been sent home, presumably because he'd passed the challenges. He was successful, self-controlled and perfectly immersed in the real world. Not even his daughter suspected anything. Perhaps the game searched for psychopathic personalities who knew how to hide? But then what? What were they being asked to do?

Bloom thought about the key motivators for those

with a high degree of psychopathy: excitement, self-aggrandisement and manipulating others for personal gain. On a grander scale, what would that mean? How might that convert to a collective goal? She reached for her jumper and typed one more message before heading downstairs to join Jameson.

Bloom

Why would we play? What would we gain? How can we compete when we don't have the basic characteristics required?

5:26pm

In the kitchen, Jameson was dressed and pouring coffee into two mugs. He'd turned on the main light, flooding the space bright white. Bloom turned it off again and switched on the wall lights instead, which shone a soft yellow.

'Coffee OK?' Jameson said.

'Yes, please.' She sat at the table and took the mug. Jameson pushed the milk her way and she shook her head.

'I saw your last message. Was that the best idea?' He sat opposite her. 'I thought we wanted to play. That's why I did all that reading, isn't it?'

'That was when we wanted to insert you as a stooge. They won't be inviting us to play for real.'

'So what do you think they're up to?' He checked his phone. He smiled and typed a response.

'What does it say?'

'It's Sarah. A message I missed last night.'

249

Bloom sipped the coffee. 'You like her, don't you?'

'She's not bad.' Jameson's smile gave him away. 'What?' he said.

'Nothing, Marcus. Nothing at all.' She wished she was as good as Claire at winding him up. This felt like a prime opportunity.

He shook his head. 'What are they up to then?'

'Why us? What do we gain?'

'Jane. That's what we stand to gain. We need to cut a deal. Get them to let her go.'

'Easier said than done.'

'But that's what we want. I couldn't give a . . . whatever, about Lana or Stuart or that kid in Sheffield.'

'Grayson.'

'Let them play. I couldn't care less what they're doing. It's not our problem and we can't fight them or stop them on our own.' He ran his hands through his hair. 'But we can get Jane.'

'I know.'

'But we'll have to play.'

Bloom nodded. 'They can't control us through a network or an infrastructure as they can with the police. We're independent and that makes us harder to pressurize. Which is why they'll attack us personally . . . and those we care about.'

'You mean Jane . . . or Claire?' Jameson sounded worried.

Bloom nodded slowly. 'And Sarah.'

'But they don't know about that.'

'How do you know?'

Jameson's phone beeped. Another message. He read it aloud.

Blocked

What would you gain? I'm disappointed that you haven't worked this out for yourself, Dr Bloom. Do you really think it's a coincidence that a family friend of Mr Jameson's is one of our players? Lana Reid is not exactly the calibre we normally require, but I have persevered with her because she provides something I want.

5:30pm

'What the hell?' said Jameson.
Bloom grabbed her phone and typed a reply.

Bloom

Which is?

5.32pm

She had a horrible feeling she knew the answer, and when it came a second later, the knot in her stomach tightened.

Blocked

YOU.

5.33pm

51

Jameson was on the train from Harrogate to Leeds, sitting opposite a teenage boy with earrings that opened vast holes in his lobes. What did it look like when he took the earrings out? How would he secure a decent job with saggy lobes? Jameson felt tired and old. This boy's generation would be different; their world would be full of saggy earlobes.

In Leeds, he followed the map on his phone past the queuing taxis towards Laynes Espresso on the opposite side of the road. The terracotta-coloured cafe reportedly sold some of the best coffee in Leeds. Jameson entered and scanned the small space. Sarah was sitting at a table for two.

'I ordered you a latte,' she said as the waitress delivered two coffees with perfect rosetta designs in the milk.

'Are you here for work or family?' said Jameson.

'Neither.'

'Oh?'

'It sounded like my boyfriend needed me, so I came.'

Jameson tossed the word 'boyfriend' around his mind for a few seconds and decided he rather liked the sound of it. 'Really? I assumed you'd be visiting family. Don't they live nearby?'

Sarah shook her head and a strand of hair fell in front of her face. She pushed it behind her ear. 'They're way up in North Yorkshire. It's the largest county, you know.'

'I had heard that. You didn't need to come up here for me, though.' He absolutely didn't mean it, but it felt like the right thing to say.

'Don't worry. I have a meeting with the Chief Executive of Leeds Hospital Trust later today.'

Jameson did his best to mask his disappointment. She was here, having coffee with him, resting her calf against his leg, and that was all that mattered. After spending a futile fourteen hours knocking on doors in Ilkley yesterday, this was exactly what he needed.

'Well thank you, Mr Chief Executive.'

'*Mrs* Chief Executive,' said Sarah from behind her coffee cup.

Damn it. 'Wow. They have a professional doing the job. Good for them.'

Sarah placed her cup in its saucer. 'Nice recovery.'

He grinned. 'Thank you very much.'

'I missed you.'

He hadn't expected that and he knew he'd failed to hide his surprise. Sarah dropped her eyes and he wasn't sure what to say next. In a simple world, he'd say, *I missed you too*, and in an ideal world he'd say, *I'm so glad you said that because I want to spend every minute of every day with you.* But his world was neither simple nor ideal, so he said, 'I'm afraid that's not going to get any better.'

She shuffled in her chair. Her leg was no longer touching his. 'I see.'

He took one of her hands in both of his. 'No, you don't. It's complicated. This case is twisted and bad and I can't have you anywhere near it.'

Sarah frowned at their hands.

'The research Augusta and I do is for the justice system, or for the victims of crimes. Sometimes it involves meeting unsavoury characters. And in this case, with Jane, I don't even know who we're up against. But what I do know is that they're playing games with Augusta's life, and with mine too.'

'Why?'

'Because they don't want us interfering in whatever the hell they're up to. But we can't stop. We have to get Jane back, so things might get hairy.'

Sarah squeezed his hand. 'Are you in danger?'

'I'm always in danger, babe. I live on the edge.'

She kicked him underneath the table. 'That's neither impressive nor funny.'

'Sorry.'

'And it was downright cheesy.'

He laughed. It felt good to break the tension.

'How are they messing with your lives?'

Jameson recalled Bloom's cautionary words as he left to catch the train: *Be careful what you share.* He knew she was right. Telling Sarah the whole story would make her vulnerable. But he wanted to be as honest as possible. 'It turns out Jane and her mother may have been targeted deliberately because they know me, and because I know Dr Bloom.'

'Dr Bloom?'

'Augusta. She's a psychologist.'

'Your partner?' Jameson nodded. 'Why are they targeting her?'

'We're not sure, but she has a history of working with these kinds of people, so maybe she pissed someone off.'

Sarah fiddled with her teaspoon. 'What kind of people?'

Jameson selected his words carefully. 'Well, she's a forensic psychologist, so she's dealt with a range of challenging characters.'

'Bad people?'

'Some of them.'

'And the ones after her now – do you think they're bad people?'

Jameson shrugged.

'Are they dangerous? Have they done anything to harm her . . . or you?'

He took a breath and tried to think of a way to change the subject.

'Marcus! Tell me. Do you think these people are trying to hurt you?'

'Not physically, no.' He thought about the cyclist who'd knocked him over.

'What does that mean, "not physically"?'

'Look, Sarah, I said I don't want you involved in this. I can't tell you any more.'

She nodded solemnly. They talked instead about her medical research, something to do with DNA profiling, but neither was concentrating fully.

'I have an hour or so before my meeting,' Sarah said after the waitress had cleared their cups. 'And my hotel is just around the corner.'

An hour and fifteen minutes later, Jameson walked back through the lobby of the Malmaison Hotel feeling pretty damn good. He smiled at the well-dressed businessman still working on his laptop. He'd noticed him when they'd arrived – or rather he'd noticed his Breitling watch. He waved a cheery goodbye to the receptionist and headed to the station. He had three messages from Bloom.

Today 11:15am
I've been summoned back to London by the HCPC. My tribunal has been set for tomorrow. They had a cancellation. Bit convenient! Call me when you can. A

Today 11:35am
DS Green called. There's been an unconfirmed sighting of Jane in Manchester. He wants to know if you can go and help the officers there?

Today 12:00pm
The games are most definitely on, Marcus. I've just heard from Libby Goodman. Stuart sent her a text message this morning. CALL ME!

'Sorry,' he said. 'My phone was on silent.'
'I do not need the details, thank you.' She sounded annoyed. 'I'm on the two p.m. train back to London, so

I need you to speak to Libby and then go to Manchester. Can you manage that?'

He fought the urge to apologize again; it would only irritate her. He had acted irresponsibly; he knew it and she knew it. All so he could have the enjoyment of Sarah.

'Of course. Who's the witness for Jane?'

'A security guard at Piccadilly station. He tried to speak to her, but apparently she ran away. DS Green will fill you in.'

'Why would she run? Her message to Claire said she wanted us to come and get her. That doesn't sound like Jane.'

'Maybe not. Maybe it wasn't Jane. But if it was and she really is travelling to Manchester alone, she is doing so for one of two reasons. Either she's escaped, in which case she'll be trying to contact you and Claire, or . . .'

'She's out on condition.'

'Yes. And who knows what they've threatened her with if she talks or gets caught.'

Jameson passed through the ticket barriers and walked towards Platform 1c for the Harrogate train. He'd pick up the rental car, drive to Manchester and call Libby Goodman on the way. He squeezed on-board and into a seat beside a large lady with five big shopping bags. She shuffled her significant backside and nearly pushed him off the seat.

'Sorry,' Jameson said as he pushed himself back on. Why was he apologizing? And that was when it hit him. The thing he had missed. The type of thing he'd been trained to spot. *Shit*. He was losing his touch. He stood and moved to the end of the carriage. The train wobbled and he almost fell, grabbing the handrail above to steady himself. Sarah's phone went straight to voicemail. He checked his watch. She would be in her meeting with the Chief Executive. He googled Leeds Hospital and found a number, but halfway through the instructions for selecting a specific department, his phone lost signal.

'Shit!' he said loudly, and the people standing nearest looked his way.

No reception.

Jameson closed his eyes and took three very deep breaths. Now was not the time to panic. He'd been an idiot. Bloom had warned him and he had dismissed her concerns. But she'd been right: they knew about Sarah. That businessman in the designer suit and the Breitling watch was Stuart Rose-Butler. He remembered him from the photograph on Libby Goodman's mantelpiece.

One bar of reception. He dialled the hospital again.

'Good afternoon. Chief Executive's office.'

'This is Dr Jameson from the BMA. I need to get an urgent message to my colleague Dr Sarah Mendax. I believe she's in a meeting with your CEO.'

Getting past the gatekeepers was all about the right credentials.

'I'm sorry, Sir, Dr Mendax isn't here.'

Jameson felt panic rising and suppressed it. 'Is that because she failed to turn up?'

'The meeting is off-site. Have you tried Dr Mendax's mobile?'

Gosh, no, I hadn't thought of that. 'It's turned off. Could you tell me where the meeting is, please?'

The PA fell silent for a few moments. 'I don't know.'

'You don't know where your boss is having a business meeting? What sort of PA are you?' The words were out of his mouth before he could stop them.

'I'm sorry, Sir. I cannot help you.' Her tone was clipped and frosty.

'This is very urgent. Can you call your boss and find out where they are, please?'

'Can I take your name again?'

He'd lost control of this. This woman knew where her boss was and was refusing to say out of some elevated sense of duty. 'It's of utmost importance that I find Dr Mendax. Can you help me or not?'

His next call was to DS Green in Bristol. 'Green, it's Jameson. I need a favour.' He hopped off the train and on to the platform of a station called Horsforth.

As Jameson waited for his Uber, DS Green called back. 'You were right,' he said. 'The PA did know where the meeting was. She was very apologetic. It's a lunch meeting in a restaurant called Browns which she told me is in The Light, a shopping centre at the top of town. I called but the woman said they were busy and it was impossible to check who was there.'

'I'll head there now. And thank you. I owe you one.'

'What the hell's going on up there? Why the panic?'

'I saw Stuart Rose-Butler this morning in a hotel. My girlfriend's staying there. I think he was waiting for her.'

'Why didn't you approach him?'

'He looked nothing like his photograph. He was clean-shaven and well-dressed. I didn't realize it was him at the time.' The Uber arrived and Jameson waved to the driver and climbed in the back seat.

'But you're sure now?' Green's tone had its typical air of suspicion.

'Positive.'

'After that Faye Graham business, I hope for your sake you're wrong.'

Me too, thought Jameson as he hung up. *Me too.*

52

Bloom was on the train to Leeds when Jameson called from a taxi. It took a lot of willpower not to say, *I told you so*. When Sarah had called yesterday to say she'd be in Leeds, Bloom had told him not to go. But he had brushed off her concerns.

She'd replied to the last WhatsApp message with a very specific question – *Why me?* – but there'd been no response. As they'd canvassed Ilkley, Bloom had kept an eye on her phone. Was this someone who knew her? Or a family member of someone she'd helped convict? How could she know when these functional psychopaths were all hiding in plain sight?

Bloom watched Leeds come into view, Bridgewater Tower rising above the other buildings like a ship's sail. For every step forward, they fell back five. She made a list of all the things they knew. Someone, probably a well-funded group or organization, had designed a way to identify psychopaths. They had then invited them to play a game, probably with a range of challenges, for some unknown purpose. Most of the hundred or so players were still playing, but a handful – three to be exact – had returned home and resumed their lives as if nothing had happened. As Bloom had anticipated, DS Green had elicited no further insight from interviewing the other two returnees. Llewellyn was bound to have tipped them off, making them more than capable of running rings around the police. But where were the rest? Some had been missing for over a year. Were they still playing or . . . ? How long would the game hold their attention? A few weeks, maybe months – but a year? Surely not.

Bloom stepped on to Platform 1b and wheeled her case to the ticket barriers. She'd abandoned her trip to London. The tribunal would have to wait. She'd call later and invent a family emergency. They wouldn't buy it, and it would make things worse, but that was the least of her worries.

She abandoned her suitcase in Left Luggage and headed towards Browns. The old bank had a dark bar, floor-to-ceiling windows and wooden table sets straight out of a Paris cafe. There were business diners and ladies lunching, chatting and clinking cutlery. It reminded Bloom of her days as a waitress. Jameson sat at the far end of the bar on his phone. He didn't look surprised to see her. He was leaving a message for Sarah, asking her to call him as soon as she could.

'I take it they're not here?' said Bloom, shaking her head at the barman coming their way.

'I've walked round the place twice and waited near the ladies' just in case. No sign.'

'And the PA at the hospital can't get hold of her boss?'

Jameson shook his head. 'They either have their phones off or are out of signal or . . .' He scanned the room again.

Bloom's phone buzzed in her jacket pocket as Jameson's vibrated against the bar. Their eyes met, then they both checked their screens: there was a new message in the 'Dare to Play?' WhatsApp group.

Blocked

Dr Bloom, how are you enjoying the game so far? I want to see what you're made of, so here is your first challenge. A choice.

1:32pm

They stood motionless in the midst of all the laughter and conversation, both staring at their phones. The next message arrived a few seconds later.

Blocked

Would you like me to return Mr Jameson's girlfriend?
Or . . .

1:33pm

'Yes,' said Jameson. 'Crap! Yes . . . whatever the *or* is, we want Sarah back.'

Bloom placed a hand on her partner's arm. 'Wait,' she said quietly. A few seconds later the next message arrived.

Blocked

Or would you like Grayson's father to have his son back, Libby's child to have his father back and Mr Jameson to have his family friend and her daughter Jane back?

1:33pm

'Oh, Christ.'

Very clever, thought Bloom. She was in Marcus's bad

books whichever option she chose. It was a lose-lose scenario, one that would wreck life as she knew it.

'What do we do?' asked Jameson. 'I mean I couldn't give a crap about the psychopaths and their families. I expect everyone would be better off without them. But Sarah and Jane aren't part of this.'

'It's a moral dilemma.'

'You think?'

'No, I mean, it's a famous thought experiment in ethics. One life for four lives. It's the Trolley Problem.'

Jameson stared at her.

'There's a trolley speeding down a railway track and ahead are four people tied up and unable to move. The trolley is heading straight for them, but you are standing by a lever which, if you pull it, will divert the trolley to a separate set of tracks. However, there is one person standing on that second track. Do you sacrifice the one to save the four?'

'Well . . . probably.'

'And what if the one was your partner, or your child?'

'Then I wouldn't flick it.'

'Why?'

'Survival of the fittest. Protecting my genes and all that.'

'OK, so try it this way . . . You're a doctor. You have four patients who will die in the next few hours without organ transplants. There is no chance of any organs arriving. Then a lone traveller comes into the hospital for a check-up and you find he is a match for all four sick patients. Do you sacrifice the healthy man to save the four?'

'Of course not.'

'Which is exactly what most people say. It is a core human moral.'

'Don't tell me. The average psychopath kills the one.'

'Of course they do. It's the most logical solution. To them, it's the same as the trolley problem. Four lives have to be more valuable than one.'

'I'm getting pretty sick of train shit,' said Jameson.

Tell me about it, thought Bloom.

'But don't you see?' she said. 'This whole thing has been orchestrated from the start, right down to the people Jane found. The people they're offering to send back are the people we've been looking for.'

'So they're observing us, listening in on our calls.'

'Or . . .' What if the whole thing had been a game? A game to get at her? The cards, Jane's request for help, South Milford. Bloom typed out a response and showed it to Jameson before hitting Send. He nodded. His complexion was grey.

Bloom
What happens to the person, or persons, I do not pick?

                                              1:35pm

The barman came over. 'Can I get you guys something?'

'We're just waiting for some colleagues,' said Bloom.

'Can I get you something while you wait? We do coffee as well as cold drinks.'

265

'We'll tell you when we want a drink,' said Jameson.

The barman shrank at Jameson's tone, but continued to smile. Here was a man used to dealing with dismissive comments from people who thought they were more important.

'Thank you,' said Bloom. The barman walked back down the bar as her phone vibrated again.

Blocked
Choose and you'll find out.

1:36pm

'You can't choose,' Jameson said.

Bloom thought about that. Could she do nothing? Let them choose? She could see Jameson fighting to keep a lid on his temper. 'What if they keep them both?' she asked.

'They can't make you choose. You can't choose. You wouldn't be able to live with it.'

He was right. She wouldn't be able to live with herself if something happened to either Jane or Sarah. Which was the point of the challenge.

'Wait,' she said. She scanned back through the WhatsApp messages, reading each one carefully, then typed a quick response.

Bloom
How long do I have to decide?

1:39pm

'That's him!' Jameson pointed towards a man walking

past outside and then sprinted to the door and out into the street without glancing back.

Bloom's phone beeped and she checked the response.

Blocked

Until 3pm.

1:40pm

53

Lunchtime pedestrians filled the pavement outside Browns. Jameson craned his neck as he rushed along, trying to find Stuart Rose-Butler. He was half a block away, strolling casually. Jameson reached him in a matter of seconds and slammed him into the wall. Rose-Butler barely reacted.

'Where is she? Where's Sarah?' His hand was around Rose-Butler's throat. Most pedestrians sped up to avoid the drama, but a few slowed to watch.

'I've no idea what you're talking about.' Rose-Butler's crisp accent bore the clear marks of a public-school education.

'Don't fuck with me, Stuart. I know who you are. I saw you in the hotel.'

A smug smile crossed Rose-Butler's face. He moved his head from side to side against the pressure of Jameson's hand. 'I don't know who you think I am, but I'm not Stuart,' he lied. 'And I have no idea who Sarah is.'

Jameson tightened his grip around the creep's throat. 'Are you denying you were in the lobby of the Malmaison this morning? Because I saw you. You were watching us.'

'Let me breathe.'

Jameson released his hold slightly, then continued:

'Were you in the Malmaison this morning? Were you watching us?'

Rose-Butler held his hands up and spoke calmly. 'Yes. I was in the Malmaison this morning. I had a meeting there. But I wasn't watching you. I don't even know you.'

'Liar!'

'Leave the guy alone,' said a male voice on Jameson's left. Jameson looked up at two large businessmen just a few feet away. Further down the road a woman was speaking to a police officer and pointing in his direction. The smaller of the two businessmen stepped forward and spoke again. 'He clearly doesn't know what you're talking about.'

'Stay out of it,' Jameson said to him, holding eye contact for longer than was polite. He turned back to Rose-Butler. 'I know you people are masters of disguise and all that shit, but I know who and what you are.'

Rose-Butler sniggered. 'Look, Sir, I'm not who you think I am.'

'Are you laughing? Do you think this is funny?'

'Just calm down, mate,' said the businessman.

'I told you to stay out of it,' Jameson said without looking over. He tightened his grip around Rose-Butler's throat. 'I'm only going to ask you one more time. Where is Sarah?'

'Let go of the gentleman, please,' said a policeman as he walked into Jameson's eyeline. 'Sir?'

'Fine.' Jameson released Rose-Butler's neck. He didn't want to get arrested.

The policeman hooked his thumbs into the arm holes

of his body armour. 'Would you please tell me what's going on here?'

Rose-Butler beat Jameson to a response. 'This gentleman appears to have a problem with my kind.' He held out his hand to the police officer. 'Stuart Lord, QC.' The officer didn't move.

'He's no QC,' said Jameson. 'He's a low-life, shelf-stacking psychopath playing games with people's lives.'

'Let's keep this calm, please,' said the officer.

'His name is Stuart Rose-Butler. He left the scene of an accident two months ago, walking away from his heavily pregnant partner to play a sick psychopathic game. He's on your missing-persons list.'

'I'm not who this gentleman thinks I am. I tried to explain, but he became very aggressive.' Rose-Butler managed to look both annoyed and concerned simultaneously.

'Marcus?'

Jameson turned to see Bloom approaching them.

'And your name, Sir?' the officer said to Jameson. He took out his pocketbook and a pen.

'Marcus?' Bloom said again. 'I'm very sorry,' she said to Rose-Butler and the police officer. 'My colleague has been under a lot of strain.'

Jameson looked at her with astonishment. 'What are you doing?'

'This is not Stuart, Marcus.'

Jameson turned back to look at him again. His hair was short and neat, his clothes tailored and expensive, and his five-grand Breitling watch poked out from beneath his shirt sleeve, but this was definitely Rose-Butler. Jameson had an uncanny ability to recognize faces; he could remember people he hadn't seen for decades. In his MI6 tests, he'd been flagged by the examiners as a 'super recognizer'.

'Your name, Sir?' the policeman insisted.

'Marcus Jameson.'

Bloom took hold of Jameson's arm. 'Come on. Let's go. We've got more important things to do.'

'More important than getting the truth out of this piece of shit?'

'Sir, I am going to have to ask you to calm down.' The policeman blocked Jameson's access to Rose-Butler with his body.

'Am I able to go back to work now, Officer? I have clients waiting in chambers.' Rose-Butler adjusted his suit jacket.

'Let's go,' insisted Bloom. 'This won't get us anywhere good.'

Jameson met his partner's eyes and the red mist gave way to logic. Stuart hadn't been at the doorway to Browns by accident. They were up to something. And he was playing right into their hands.

'Fine,' he said. 'My apologies, Officer.' He held his hands up in a show of restraint as the policeman warned him about keeping his temper, then let Bloom lead him away.

In the lobby of the Malmaison Hotel, Jameson sat in a plush armchair trying to steady his breathing. A headache radiated from the injury at the back of his skull.

'You requested some water, Sir?' A barmaid in a smart black shirt placed a glass in front of him.

'Cheers.' He took a large gulp. Bloom was heading back to her mother's house. There were some files in the loft she wanted to consult. He was waiting to view the hotel's CCTV footage. DS Green had been rather persuasive, but the manager had insisted that a local officer should attend too. A few minutes later a young – rather attractive – police officer joined him in reception and introduced herself as PC Hussain. She had a clear remit from her boss's boss's boss to gain access to the hotel's CCTV for Jameson. Soon they were both sitting in the manager's office watching the morning's footage alongside the Head of Security, who was a slick-haired muscular man, no doubt ex-military.

'There's Rose-Butler.' Jameson watched as Stuart took his seat in reception and removed a small laptop from his briefcase. The security man fast-forwarded the image. 'OK. Stop. There's Sarah and me coming in.' Jameson watched himself walk across the lobby with his hand on the small of Sarah's back. As they waited for the lift she looked up at him and smiled, as he ran his fingers slowly up and down her spine. He remembered her smile and closed his eyes. Why hadn't he been paying more attention? Why hadn't he seen Rose-Butler then?

He knew why, of course, but it was no excuse.

The Head of Security fast-forwarded the footage again. Rose-Butler didn't move and no one joined him. Jameson watched himself retrace his steps across the lobby. Rose-Butler had looked up and brazenly met his eye. Had he wanted Jameson to recognize him? Expected him to?

'What does he do now?' said Jameson. He watched as Rose-Butler stood and walked to the lifts. The Head of Security fast-forwarded the footage once more. There were no cameras in the bedroom corridors, only in the main public areas, so this was all they had. The lifts opened and closed and strangers got in and out, but neither Rose-Butler nor Sarah appeared.

'Her room. I need to see it.' Jameson turned to the security man. 'Now!'

54

Bloom got off the train and checked her watch: 2.34pm. She had less than half an hour to get to the house, into the loft and find the file she wanted. It was going to be tight. Really tight. She'd left her case at Leeds station, knowing it would only slow her down. She wished she'd had time to collect her iPad, but she'd have to rely on good old-fashioned memory.

At the house she checked her watch again: 2.42pm. She'd made good time. Her feet hurt from running in her court shoes and it took a moment for her breathing to steady. She kicked her shoes off, not caring if they scratched the parquet floor, and ran barefoot to the landing and the loft hatch. Her mother kept the pole to open the hatch in the corner of the master bedroom and Bloom knew exactly where her old boxes were. This shouldn't take more than a few minutes. There was only one document she needed to see.

But the pole wasn't there.

'Dammit!' Her mother's final few months before moving to the home had been clouded by dementia. It had turned a once-capable and routine-orientated woman into a paranoid shell of herself. A person who hid her jewellery in the freezer because she thought her daughter might steal it. Bloom scanned the rest of the room and then checked her own room, the spare room, the box room and the bathroom. Then she checked her watch: 2.48pm.

No time.

She dragged the linen basket from the bathroom and placed it under the hatch. It was about half her height. She might be able to reach. She lifted one knee up and then the other, found her balance and then shifted her weight, making sure the basket could hold her. It wobbled and she steadied herself. She reached up and hooked her middle finger through the loop, then leaned away from the hatch and pulled as hard as she could. It opened just a sliver. She leaned further back and pulled harder. This time it opened enough for her to fold her hand around the edge and pull the hatch fully open.

Then it swung back, pushing her off the linen basket. She landed heavily on her left arm outside the spare room. The hatch had split her skin on three fingers. Little droplets of blood began to bubble. She climbed back on to the basket, reached up with both hands and pulled herself into the loft.

The boxes were exactly where she'd left them. 2.56pm. Less than four minutes to respond to the challenge. She opened the first of six square storage boxes and quickly set it aside. The second and third weren't it either. But there in the fourth was the blue file she needed.

She rested it on her knee. The name on the front was written in very neat handwriting. It was the first file she had ever produced. She'd prepared it with the care of a new mother. *Seraphine Walker.*

Bloom riffled through the pages for the pathologist's

report. She skimmed the page. How had they identified Seraphine's teenage body? Bloom had assumed they'd looked at her dental records. Trains at speed do unspeakable things to the human body. But they hadn't checked. Seraphine had left a note for her mother telling her what she was planning to do and where. The body had been wearing Seraphine's clothes, a watch engraved with her name and a necklace borrowed that very day from her mother. This had been deemed sufficient evidence.

Bloom stared into the dark recesses of her parents' loft. This was crazy. How could a fourteen-year-old girl find another girl of similar height, weight and hair colour, convince her to swap clothes and jewellery, take a bus to a random town, walk a mile and a half to a farm road and then . . . ? But this was Seraphine. She had the ability to fool people, to lure them into her web.

I can't be normal. And I don't want to be a monster.

Her challenge was more than just the Trolley Problem. It was very specific. She was being asked to choose between the life of one normal person, Sarah, or the lives of three psychopaths, Grayson, Stuart and Lana. Jane was a red herring. She came with Lana.

When working with Seraphine, Bloom had stressed that the young girl could choose who she wanted to be. That she didn't need to be defined by a label. That a psychopath's life was just as valuable as any other. This challenge was predicated on that very principle.

The alarm on her phone began to jingle. It was 2.59pm.

55

Jameson stood at the doorway to Sarah's room, one hand on the frame. He'd been here just a few hours ago. He remembered purple velvet curtains, a damask chaise longue at the end of the bed, a neatly organized wooden desk and bedside tables, the smart king-sized bed. The room he saw now bore no resemblance to this memory.

'Was this how you left the room?' said PC Hussain from behind him.

Jameson looked around. The desk chair lay halfway across the floor on its side. The contents of the desk – the information pack, the tea and coffee sachets, the phone and the kettle – were strewn across the floor. The bed sheets were crumpled and hanging from the bed.

'No,' said Jameson. 'No. It wasn't like this. Everything was . . . where it should be.' He stepped into the room. The bed sheets covered the chaise longue. Sarah's bag had been there.

'This might be a crime scene,' said PC Hussain, before she radioed for assistance.

Jameson's head pounded and his vision narrowed as a migraine took hold. He lifted his chin and forced himself to take deep breaths. He'd been in many dangerous, disturbing situations in the past and he'd coped with them with the calm disposition of a well-trained professional. But this was different. This was Sarah. *His* Sarah. Everything about their short relationship had been astonishing. He finally understood the connection he saw between his sister and brother-in-law. He got it. He saw with total clarity that he would never quite get over living his life without Sarah. He should have listened to Bloom.

His phone rang. *Sarah?*

Claire's voice sounded loud and urgent in his ear. 'Marcus, where are you and why the hell are you not in Manchester?'

'It's Sarah. They've taken Sarah.'

'Who is Sarah? Oh, for fuck's sake, are you kidding me? You're fretting over your latest bit of skirt? We have a chance to get Jane back. I'm telling you now, Marcus, I'll never forgive you if anything happens to her.'

'Sarah is not my latest bit of skirt.' A look passed between PC Hussain and the Head of Security.

'I don't care if she's your frickin' soul mate, Marcus. Jane is a child.'

'And you'd just leave Dan to the whim of some twisted psycho, would you?'

'Dan would never expect me to pick him over his child.'

'Jane is not my child.'

'Oh, I can't believe . . . What sort of a man are you? I thought my brother had principles; he fought to protect people.'

'Claire . . .'

'No. Forget it. I'll go to Manchester myself.'

278

Claire hung up. Jameson looked at his phone. Bloom had one minute to make her choice.

PC Hussain moved past him and into the room. 'I'm going to make a brief assessment of the scene and check the bathroom. Could you both step into the corridor, please?'

The bathroom. Jameson looked at the closed door to the en-suite and felt his heart quicken. He knew there was a bath, shower, toilet and basin inside that black and white room, but what else would Hussain find? He knew from bitter experience that there were some things you could never unsee.

As he stood in the hallway, his phone buzzed. He checked the message. Bloom had made her choice. She'd have thought through every angle – he knew that – so why did he feel so sick?

Because whatever Hussain found behind the bathroom door was irrelevant. Sarah's fate was sealed. He looked down at his phone and squeezed his eyes shut to hold in the tears.

Bloom
I choose Stuart, Grayson, Lana and Jane.

3:00pm

56

Bloom let her phone slide on to the floor of the loft. She hoped this gamble would pay off.

She removed a familiar white envelope from the file and took the note from inside. The paper felt thick and when Bloom held it up to the bare light bulb it shimmered. She read it for the first time in fifteen years.

I can't be normal. And I don't want to be a monster.
You told me to choose. I've chosen.

What did you choose, Seraphine? If Seraphine really had orchestrated her own fake suicide, it would not have been in a fit of teenage pique. It would have been logical, a rational decision, carefully planned for a specific purpose.

Bloom reached back into the expandable blue file and pulled out an A5 black notebook. It had arrived in the post the day after Seraphine's mother had visited. There had been nothing with it, no explanation, but Bloom had always assumed it held some significance. Seraphine rarely acted without motive. And so she had studied it for hours and hours, looking for the message, trying to learn where she'd gone wrong, what she'd said to cause such drastic action.

Bloom opened it now and flicked through until she

reached the final entry. It was longer than the others. Most of the entries were short paragraphs expressing anger at someone's actions or smugly recording vengeance. But this one was more like a letter, and even though it began, as all the entries did, with Dear Diary, Bloom felt sure Seraphine had meant this one for her.

Dear Diary

I did it on purpose.

I made sure Dreary Darren would come to the sports hall. I looked for the carotid artery in my biology textbook. I found out which was the toughest pencil – H6 – and I got Mr Richards to sharpen it for me on his fancy sharpener.

You want to know why?

It's not what you think. It wasn't to get some kick. And I didn't enjoy it. But neither did I feel bad about it. But you probably guessed that. I did it because I knew that creep had raped Claudia. On the day of the summer fair, I heard him bragging about it and telling her that if she told anyone he'd hurt her mum. They were behind the cricket pavilion. I'd gone there to get some peace and quiet from all the stupids. It's exhausting hanging around with normals all the time. Claudia and Dreary didn't see me and she never said anything to any of us. But I figured someone needed to teach him a lesson.

He was a typical stupid too. He never suspected I was flirting with him for any particular reason. I wore my shortest skirt and my tightest top and I'd walk past his shed slowly until I caught his eye and then I'd smile. He started making comments and asking me to come inside. But I always kept walking without saying a word. So he was gagging for it by the time I walked by that morning and said, 'Sports hall after registration.' I knew he'd come. And Claudia was supposed to be my alibi. I was doing this for her and she was supposed to say he'd attacked me, like he had attacked her. But I'd forgotten what a needy bitch she can be. As soon as she saw the chance to push me out of the group, she took it. She hated how popular I was. It was the only bit I got wrong — misjudging her. If I'd waited a few seconds longer, let him grope me a bit, she probably wouldn't have had any reason to suspect me, but you live and learn.

No one at school looks at me the same way now. My blabbermouth mother couldn't keep quiet about sending me to speak to a psychologist so the whole school got to hear about that too. So even though the police have dropped charges, I'm still the school weirdo. Parents move their kids away from me and the teachers watch me with this look of fear and disgust. Dr Bloom told me to avoid labelling myself as a psychopath because I'm just Seraphine with as much right as anyone else to choose how to live and what to do. But everyone else is labelling me: my parents, my teachers, my so-called friends. And it makes me want to get back at them. I want to hurt them all. I want them to know exactly who I am and to teach them that there are some people you really shouldn't mess with.

But mostly I just don't want to feel so alone.

Bloom read the last line again. Was that the orchestrator's motive? To find more of their own kind. Could that be the reason for this game? Not a crime or a menacing plot, but simply the basic human need – as true for a psychopath as for anyone else – to avoid loneliness?

57

Jameson sat in the hallway outside Sarah's hotel room with his back to the wall and his eyes closed. The migraine battered his brain with splinters of pain and the only way he could handle it was to remain very still. He should be on a train to Manchester. He should be trying to find Jane. If they released her, he should be there to meet her. Who knew what kind of trauma she'd experienced over the past week? She'd want a familiar face and he could be there in half the time it would take Claire. But he couldn't move. He felt physically and emotionally incapable.

It took him a few seconds to distinguish the vibrating of his phone in his pocket from the pulsating throb in his head.

'Jameson,' he answered, keeping his head still and his eyes firmly shut.

'It's me.' Bloom sounded anxious.

'I'm banking on you knowing what you're doing, Augusta.'

She said nothing for a second and then muttered, 'Me too.'

'There's been no reply,' he said.

'No.'

'What does that mean?'

'I don't know.'

'Great.' He squeezed his eyes tighter, but somehow the daylight still seeped in.

'I think Seraphine's behind this.'

Jameson opened his eyes. 'What?'

'I had to select between a normal person and the psychopaths. I think Seraphine wants to know if I still believe a psychopath's life is worth as much as anyone else's.'

'That makes no sense. Jane's not a psychopath and she's in the group, and Seraphine Walker is dead.'

'No. Jane comes with Lana; she's part of the package.'

'Part of the package? Are you kidding me? And Seraphine Walker? You're gambling Sarah's life on the idea of a resurrected teen psychopath?' Jameson took a deep breath. This was making his migraine worse.

'I don't think she's dead, that's the thing.'

'I got that.' Jameson closed his eyes again. 'Shit, Augusta, that's one hell of a leap. I thought you said this was an organized group.'

'I know.'

'So you've just forgotten that because it doesn't fit your latest theory? I'm sorry. I can't talk about this any more.'

He hung up.

58

Jane walked along clutching the piece of paper with the address. She reached a large semi-detached house with a red-brick porch over its front door and a fancy car in the driveway. Why would her mum be here?

She had not seen her mum since Saturday afternoon, when she'd forced her into the back of a car driven by a woman called Denise. Denise had taken Jane to an impressive barn conversion for two nights and she had been allowed her own room with a real bed and a TV.

But a few hours ago, Denise had driven Jane to Leeds station and given her this piece of paper. She'd said, 'Go here and nowhere else. Don't speak to anyone. Don't call anyone. Because we'll be watching you, and if you do you'll never see your mother again.'

Jane had taken the paper and bought a ticket to Manchester. In Piccadilly station she'd spent too long studying the map of the city and a security guard had approached her. She had no idea who Denise meant by 'we', but she gave Jane the creeps. Something about the way she looked at you, sort of cold and distant.

Jane checked the number of the next house. Forty-one. There was a large vase of white lilies in the front window. Jane knocked on the door and waited, scrunching the piece of paper in her hand. A red-haired lady in a knee-length denim dress and Converse trainers answered.

'Can I help you?' she said.

'I'm Jane. I was told to come here to meet my mum.'

'Oh, my.' Jane couldn't read her expression. 'Come in. Come in.'

Jane stepped into the hallway.

'Thomas?' called the woman. 'Can you come here, please?'

'Is my mum here?' Jane said, as a tall man walked out of a room at the back of the house. 'Her name's Lana.'

The man stopped, the polite smile frozen on his face.

'Jane?' he whispered. He didn't look like the other men her mum usually spent time with. He had kind eyes. A phone started ringing and he reached into his pocket for his mobile.

'Lake,' he said, the polite smile still in place.

'Darling, is this the right time to . . .' The woman held her thumb and little finger out, mimicking answering a phone.

'Yes, she's here,' the man said.

'Is that Mum? Can I speak to her?' Jane stepped towards him.

He shook his head. 'I see . . . OK . . . And why?' He listened for a moment.

His eyes met Jane's and she was sure she saw tears.

'Has something happened to my mum?' she asked. 'I want to speak to her. Let me speak to her.' Jane lunged for the phone, grabbing it from his hand and holding it to her ear.

'Mum? I'm here. I came straight here, just like you said. I didn't go anywhere else or speak to anyone. I did just what you said. Hello? Hello?' They'd hung up. 'Was that my mum?'

Lake shook his head. 'A friend of hers.'

'Is she coming?'

Lake shook his head and then looked at the woman.

She placed an arm around Jane's shoulders. 'Come on into the kitchen. Let's get you a warm drink.'

Jane shrugged her away. 'No. Not until you tell me where she is.'

Jane had lost her temper on Saturday morning and Lana had lashed out and hit her. After that, things changed quickly. Jane knew that her mother could turn her anger on and off, but when she returned to Jane's attic room that evening, something was different. Jane expected her mum to lose it again when she discovered she'd left her phone behind, but she just put it in her pocket without a word. And then on Sunday, her mum told her the same story three times. Something about a bridge and a motorbike. It didn't make sense. And then she'd gone on and on about how much she hated Marcus. Jane worried that her mum was having some sort of breakdown.

'Jane, do you know who I am?' said the man. 'My name is Thomas Lake. I was married to Lana . . . to your mum . . . sixteen years ago.'

Jane felt the ground shift beneath her feet. That was impossible. Her mother had never been married. And sixteen years ago her mum would have been living in

287

London with Jane's druggie dad. Jane studied Thomas Lake. He looked athletic and healthy, like some of her friends' dads: men with jobs in the City who spent their weekends cycling and camping with their families.

'Mum was never married,' she said, but her words didn't sound convincing, not even to her. Her mum's career had been a lie, so how could she be sure of anything?

'Come to the kitchen. I'll explain everything, I promise. I just need to make a very quick call.' Lake held an arm out to direct her to the back of the house. 'And Jane, you're safe here. Suzanne and I will take care of you.'

59

Bloom still sat in her mother's attic with her papers on Seraphine spread around her. Jameson's reaction had been as expected. But if she was right and Seraphine really was behind this, she felt sure that the situation was salvageable. This had been a test for Bloom, not a punishment for Jameson.

Her phone rang; it was forever ringing. She didn't recognize the number.

'Dr Bloom,' she said.

'This is Thomas Lake,' said the caller. He dropped his volume. 'I'm Lana's ex-husband.'

Bloom closed her eyes. He wanted an update on Jane; she couldn't tell him anything. Not yet. 'Hello, Mr Lake,' she replied. 'I'm afraid I have no news about Jane.'

'She's here,' he said, in the same whispered voice.

'She's what?' This didn't make sense. She'd been released already? 'With you? Where?'

'At my house. She arrived five minutes ago.'

'And is she OK?'

'I think so ... She's confused ... I don't think she knows who I am. She thought Lana would be here.'

'How did she find you?'

'She was sent. By the same person who called me.'

'Who called you?' Things were moving incredibly

quickly; it was impossible to keep up with this damn game.

'A woman. She didn't give a name. She said that Lana was unable to look after Jane any more and that it was my turn to step up. Then she said I should call you.'

'She told you to call me? What *exactly* did this woman say?'

'She said that before I did anything else, I had to call you and tell you that you did the right thing, that Jane is safe now.'

Bloom felt a surge of hope. Maybe she'd been right. 'Can I speak to Jane, please? Just quickly. She knows me.'

'Would you? That would be great. I'm not sure what to say. I don't want her to freak out. If she believes all those things about me that Lana said . . .'

'I'll explain.'

'And one more thing. The woman who rang – she said something strange about someone called Carl Rogers and positive regard.'

'Unconditional positive regard?'

'That's it. What's that?'

'Carl Rogers was a psychologist. He developed a therapy for his patients founded on the principle that we only need unconditional support from one person in order to recover from psychological abuse.'

'Why would she mention that?'

Bloom thought about it. 'I think she's saying that Jane needs a different kind of parenting, someone who will love and respect her unconditionally.'

'Because Lana doesn't?'

'Possibly. I don't know enough about their relationship to comment.'

'OK.'

'Do you think you can do that?'

The line fell quiet for a moment. 'Be her father, you mean?'

'Yes.'

'It's all I've ever wanted.'

Bloom asked again to speak to Jane and was relieved to hear her voice, clear and confident, down the line.

'Are you OK?' she asked.

'I don't know,' replied Jane. 'Who are these people? Why is he calling you? Where is my mum?'

'Jane, I need you to listen to me carefully. Marcus and I met Thomas earlier this week, because we'd discovered that your father was nothing at all like your mother had described. He wasn't a drug user or a child abuser. When you were born, he was a newly qualified dentist who loved you and your mum very much. He's spent most of your life trying to find out where your mum took you.'

'This man is my father?'

'Yes, and he's a good man with a loving wife, and you've two step-brothers who you can get to know now. I know this is a shock, but you're safe there.'

'That's what he said.'

'I'm going to call Marcus. He'll want to know that you're safe. We've all been so worried about you. He or Claire will come and get you soon. But, in the meantime, talk to Thomas. Get to know him.'

'And my mum?'

291

'I'm not sure yet, Jane. When did you last see her?'

'She left me with a woman called Denise two days ago.'

'What was Denise like?'

'Sort of plump, with short dark hair. I think she was mixed race.'

Not Seraphine. She'd been very fair. 'Anyone else?'

'There was a man at the house one day. Mum brought him to the attic. I don't know why. He didn't speak to me. He just looked around the room, nodded at Mum and then left.'

'Did you get his name?'

'No. But he was skinny and sort of creepy. Denise said that if I came here, I'd see Mum again. She'll be OK now, won't she?'

Bloom wasn't surprised by Jane's concern for Lana. She knew as well as anyone that your mum is always your mum, no matter how flawed she might be. Jane had never known any parent other than Lana – she might have been inadequate and irresponsible, but she'd been the only constant in Jane's life.

'She's with these people voluntarily, so yes, I hope she'll be OK.'

60

Half an hour had passed and Jameson was still sitting
against the wall of the hotel corridor. The phone buzzed
again in his hand.

Jameson stood in one smooth motion, his migraine a
fading memory. He so wanted this to be over, but it was
only just beginning. He walked past Sarah's room and
away from the police officers. He needed to find Sarah.
He called Bloom's phone, but the line was engaged. He
swore under his breath and googled Q-Park Leeds. Five

bloody car parks. Of course there were. As the lift descended, he checked the capacity of each. Something told him to find the tallest. Two had a capacity of only 250 cars, so he focused on the other three. Wellington Street and The Light each had a 400-car capacity and Sovereign Square could hold 500 cars. He set the timer on his phone for eight minutes. Then he walked to the reception desk.

The woman behind the counter was speaking to a young colleague who looked nervous and new. She was concentrating hard on the screen in front of her. The older receptionist caught his eye and smiled, but continued to speak to the new girl. Jameson didn't have time for this.

'Sorry to interrupt,' he said, 'but I have an urgent matter. Can you tell me which is the tallest of these car parks: Wellington Street, The Light or Sovereign Square?'

'Well, The Light is underground,' she said. 'I'm not familiar with Wellington Street, but Sovereign Square is a high-rise.'

'I saw someone jump from the car park next to the market once. They were totally dead,' said the new receptionist. Her colleague glared at the young girl. Her cheeks turned pink and she looked away.

'Which car park was that? A Q-Park?' Jameson asked.

Both women looked at him curiously.

'Is someone jumping?' said the girl.

'The market car park isn't a Q-Park, as far as I'm aware,' said the older receptionist. 'Sovereign Square is the closest. It's just around the corner.'

'How long to walk?'

'A couple of minutes, tops. You can see it from the door.'

'And what about St John's?'

'That's further away. Ten minutes . . . maybe more?'

Would they choose a place that he couldn't get to within their time limit? Of course they would. *Catch a cab, man*, he thought. 'But Sovereign Square is higher?'

Jameson's phone rang. Bloom.

'Good news,' she said as he answered.

'Whatever it is, I don't want to hear it. Did you see the WhatsApp? They're threatening to throw Sarah off a car park in just over five minutes.'

The two women behind reception looked at each other, one shocked, the other excited.

'I've been on the phone to Jane. Wait.'

'Jane? Is she OK?'

There was no answer. Bloom was checking her messages. 'I see,' she said, when she came back on the line. 'What's the plan?'

'Is Jane OK?'

'She's with Thomas Lake. She's fine.'

How the hell . . . ? Jameson forced the thought aside. He didn't have time to dwell on that right now. The psychos had been true to their word: Jane had been returned.

But that news only made Sarah's situation worse.

'Give me a sec,' he said to Bloom. He needed to concentrate. People rarely picked a location at random. In MI6 he used to run sessions with new recruits in which he instructed them to select a location to meet a source

295

in a city they weren't familiar with. They could choose the city and the specific location. The only rule was it had to be somewhere they didn't know well. His job was to guess where in their given city they'd selected, to within a radius of one mile. They all went away to research their locations and then returned with a smugness that said: *You'll never guess this*. But he usually did, because people couldn't escape their own unconscious biases. If they preferred to travel by public transport, they'd pick somewhere within walking distance of the train station. If they preferred to drive, they'd go for somewhere near a car park – especially if they had a decent motor. If the recruit in question was a football fan, they'd pick a point within a mile of the stadium. The more Marcus knew about them, the easier it was to guess. It's surprisingly hard to pick something at random. He was banking on that being true for psychopaths, too.

He looked at the options again. St John was one of Jesus's disciples. Was religious symbolism likely for a psychopath? Sovereign signified royalty and independence, and Wellington, if you were talking the Duke of Wellington, was a master of war. Either of those could work. He thought about the message again. *The lovely Sarah will be taking a closer than usual look at the view.* What could be seen from the top?

'If you were standing on the top of each of these car parks, what would you see?' he asked the receptionists.

The older woman looked down as she thought about the question. 'From St John's, you'd see the top end of town, towards the university. Wellington Street goes out towards the ring road, so maybe you'd see all the business buildings along the waterfront. But like I said, I don't know exactly where that car park is. And from Sovereign Square, you'd see this hotel and the train station.'

'The train tracks?' said Bloom in Jameson's ear.

'The station or the tracks?' he asked, but he was already moving. Sovereign Square was the largest, so probably the highest, had a name that signified standing out from the crowd, and overlooked the train line. That was enough. His gut said it was the place.

'Both,' called the receptionist as he dashed towards the door.

'I'm going to Sovereign Square, Augusta. It's the largest, so probably the tallest. Why are they doing this? If this is your Seraphine girl, why is she after the people I care about?'

Bloom sighed. 'I expect because you're the person I most care about.'

'What?' he replied. He could see the Q-Park sign at the corner of the road. He broke into a run.

'You're not only my business partner, you're my closest friend. My mother's in a home, my father's dead and I don't have any other family. If someone wanted to hurt the people closest to me . . . well, it's you.'

'Great. I befriend some loser with no friends, and now I have to suffer.'

Bloom didn't reply.

'Well, I'll tell you what, they're not coming after you

or me without a bloody good fight. I'll call you back.'
He reached the pedestrian entrance to the car park. He
needed a ticket. Damn it. He ran towards the vehicle
entrance. One car was waiting to go in and two were
queuing to come out. As the car drove into the car park,
he sprinted up to the ticket machine and pressed the button. It emerged frustratingly slowly. When it finally came
out he ran back to the pedestrian entrance, inserted the
ticket, then took the stairs two at a time.

The open-air top floor had ten cars parked directly in
front of him, another dozen in the central parking bays,
and a couple more further away. Beyond them, he could
see the city and the train-station roof. But in front of
that, at the very edge, were two figures with their backs
to him, one behind the other, just as he'd held Lana over
the railway bridge.

Should he run at them? Or creep up quietly? Neither
had turned to look his way. As he was going through his
options, his phone began a jingle that indicated his eight
minutes were up. He silenced it, but it was too late. The
man holding Sarah turned and locked eyes with
Jameson.

Stuart Rose-Butler.

Rose-Butler smiled.

Jameson charged at them. It was the only option left.

Rose-Butler grabbed hold of a pole that supported a
narrow canopy running the circumference of the car
park and pulled himself up on to the perimeter wall. He
yanked Sarah up on to the wall beside him. She still had

her back to Jameson. He'd been expecting her to cry out or plead for her life, but she wasn't making a sound. He was in awe of her bravery.

'Rose-Butler,' he called. 'You psychopathic fuck! I made it in time. Let her go.' He was too far away. Even if he grabbed Sarah, at this speed he'd send her over the edge. Rose-Butler had the advantage.

'The challenge was to get here in time, Mr Jameson. But not in time to stop me – in time to watch.' Rose-Butler stared right at him. The fucker was enjoying himself.

'You've got a son now,' Jameson shouted. He was still five rows away. 'If you hurt her, I'll hurt him. You have my word.'

A flash of anger crossed Rose-Butler's face but disappeared as quickly as it had arrived. He still had Sarah by the arm. He winked at Jameson. He tugged Sarah around to face him.

'Sarah!' Jameson called.

Her wide eyes met his. 'Marcus?' she whispered.

And then they were falling backwards, both Rose-Butler and Sarah, toppling over the edge of the wall, her arms reaching out, her legs kicking.

He was too late.

61

Psychopaths never commit suicide.

When Bloom had sat on the stairs all those years ago, holding Seraphine's note, that had been the thought that dominated her mind. It was a simple truth. It was evidenced in all the research. Psychopaths were incapable of feeling anxiety or depression, guilt or shame. And they had an inflated sense of self-worth. They were immune to the main causes of suicide.

Only if there was a calculated benefit – such as avoiding jail – might a psychopath consider suicide.

And so she'd thought she must have been wrong. That Seraphine wasn't a psychopath, after all. Perhaps she'd had mild Asperger Syndrome. That might explain her lack of emotional sensitivity.

Bloom's guilt had intensified over the past fifteen years. She thought she'd seen a psychopath in Seraphine because that was what she'd wanted to see. And that the girl had paid the ultimate price.

But that was not the case. She'd been right. Seraphine Walker *was* a psychopath.

She looked at the file now spread across her mother's kitchen table: the session notes, Seraphine's diary, the pathologist's report, and a handful of press cuttings about the original stabbing and Seraphine's suicide.

She felt a strange sense of relief.

If Seraphine was the puppeteer and the game a means of gathering like-minded people, then they wouldn't harm Sarah. It was designed to test its players, and that was exactly what it was doing. Bloom had been set a moral challenge, based on her particular experiences and knowledge, and Jameson a tactical one based on his particular talents and background.

Bloom studied the suicide press cuttings again. Seraphine's pretty blue eyes stared out from the photographs. There was a statement from her parents saying that she'd never caused them any trouble and was the perfect daughter. Seraphine's kind words about her family had never seemed genuine, and Bloom doubted the veracity of their statement. There were no anecdotes or evidence to back up the rhetoric. Perhaps there'd been something going on that Seraphine had wanted to escape from. Bloom knew that Seraphine's mother, Penny, was overbearing and indulgent. And Bloom's own mother had described Penny's husband, Kevin, as a bully – and she rarely made such dramatic character assassinations. Any child would struggle with one parent who smothered them with emotional drama and another who attacked them. But a psychopath would quickly become intolerant of that level of irrationality. Seraphine's inner life would have lacked emotional depth. It would have been flat. She wouldn't have been able to understand her parents, because their behaviour had been completely devoid of calculated gain.

Bloom looked at the photograph of Seraphine again. What was she missing?

62

Sarah's scream was unbearable. Jameson froze a metre from the edge. He stared ahead, waiting for the impact. He knew what he was waiting for. He'd heard it before: the sound of a human body hitting the ground. It was always much louder than expected.

But the impact never came.

His phone buzzed. He couldn't look over the edge. He didn't want to see. He took the phone from his pocket.

Blocked

Be still my beating heart, Mr Jameson. You really came through for your sweetheart. You can look down now.

3:41pm

Jameson braced himself and peered over the wall. An abseiling rope hung loosely just above the ground. Rose-Butler stood beside it, looking up at him. His harness was discarded on the pavement. He gave a small salute then walked calmly away, one hand in the pocket of his designer suit trousers. Sarah's body was nowhere to be seen.

Jameson leaned further forward. A second rope secured to the base of the pole on his right stretched halfway down the building. At its end was Sarah. The relief made him feel drunk. She was tightly gripping the rope above her head.

'I'm coming down, babe. Hang on.' He ran back to the stairwell. *Hang on*, he'd said. Of course she was going to hang on. She would take the piss out of him later. Not that he would mind one bit.

He opened the stairwell door at the sixth floor. He could see the rope swinging, but not Sarah. He went down another floor. He saw Sarah's hands around the rope above the perimeter wall. He ran over and grasped her hands in his.

'Have you fallen for me, Sarah Something?' He was manic, so frickin' happy that she was alive that he'd become hysterical.

She looked up. Her cheeks were flushed, tear stains streaking her make-up.

'Too soon?' He tested the weight of the rope. She was at a bad angle. She'd be too heavy for him to pull her up. 'I'm going to get you off this thing, but you'll need to help me. OK?'

Sarah nodded. Her knuckles were white.

'I want you to give me one of your hands. Can you do that?'

She slowly unfurled her right hand from the rope and took his outstretched palm.

'Can you reach the wall with your feet?'

She looked down at her legs dangling below, then back up. She shook her head.

'I've got you, OK? And the harness won't let you fall any further than this. These nutters wanted to scare you, but they weren't interested in hurting you. Trust me. Find the wall with your feet and walk them up to meet me. I'll pull you over.'

'Marcus . . .' Her eyes were panicked; her face said, *I can't do it.*

'Listen to me, Sarah. Take a couple of deep breaths.' Nothing eased panic better than a good hit of oxygen. 'You've climbed plenty of walls in the past, I'm sure. This is no different. Look at the wall. It's three or four steps up, tops. I'll count them with you.'

Sarah lifted her left leg and placed her foot flat against the wall.

'Lean back against the rope. Don't worry. I've got you.' He squeezed her hand.

Her right foot slipped against the wall and she jerked backwards. Jameson locked his elbow and held her in place.

'See, I've got you. You'll be fine. Again,' he instructed.

This time Sarah placed her right foot firmly against the wall and quickly took three steps towards him with her body perfectly angled against the rope. As soon as her left foot reached the top, Jameson pulled her over. She fell into him and he lifted her down to safety. She grabbed him in a tight hug, her arms firmly around his neck.

'Let's get this thing off you,' he said, when she eventually released him. He undid the waist belt and the buckles on both her leg loops. The harness slid to the floor and Sarah stepped away from it. He placed both his hands on her shoulders and kept his voice low and calm. 'You're probably in shock. Just take a deep breath. You're safe now, Sarah. It's over. Take a few more deep breaths.' She did as requested. 'Are you OK?'

'Who are these people?'

'They're psychopaths.'

He expected Sarah to look shocked, but she just stared at him blankly. 'Psychopaths?' she repeated.

'Not the serial-killing crazies you hear about in the media . . .'

'Just the sort that throw people off buildings.'

'Yep,' he said. 'Just those ones.'

'He told me if I looked at you or said anything, he'd unclip the rope and let me fall for real.'

That explained her quiet bravery.

'It was all mind games.'

'But I did look at you and I did speak.'

'So when you fell, you thought that's what he'd done? I'm sorry.'

'It wasn't your fault,' she replied.

'No, but if I'd got here sooner, or stayed away from you in the first place, like Augusta said—'

Sarah stepped back. 'She told you to stay away from me?'

'Until this was over. She said they'd come after the people I cared about.'

Her eyes studied him. 'You told her you care about me?'

'I didn't need to. She's pretty good at reading people.'

Sarah held his gaze until he felt the tension building between them like electricity at the tips of his fingers.

'What the hell are you two idiots doing?' said a loud

male voice from behind them. Jameson and Sarah turned and saw a furious-looking car-park attendant heading their way. He was big, in his mid-to-late fifties with an impressive Magnum-style moustache. 'You can't play silly buggers with your ropes in here. I've called the police.'

'Good,' said Jameson. 'Because this wasn't us.'

The guy looked at the rope and harness on the floor beside them and then raised his eyebrows.

'Honestly,' said Sarah. 'We didn't do this. This was done to us.'

'We'll see what the police say.' He wouldn't be letting them go anywhere until the police had arrived.

'We're happy to speak to the police.' Jameson took his phone from his pocket. 'I just need to make a few calls while we wait.' He gave the car-park attendant his *Don't mess with me* look and it seemed to work.

'I've got Sarah and she's fine,' Jameson said when Bloom answered.

'Were they at Sovereign Square?'

'Yes. Bloody Rose-Butler had her. We're waiting for the police now. If I'd not walked away earlier—'

'They'd have used someone else,' said Bloom.

She was right. This had taken planning and a good deal of preparation. You can't abseil off a building on a whim. It needed equipment and accurate measurements.

'And Jane's OK?' he asked.

'I spoke to her. I said you or Claire would be in touch soon. Do you want me to call Claire?'

'I'll do it. And send me Lake's number. I want to talk to Jane. How did she sound?'

'She's an impressive young woman,' said Bloom. 'She took it in her stride.'

'And you? Have you gone off your suicide theory?'

Sarah watched him with intelligent eyes. The shock was beginning to dissipate and she was clearly full of questions.

'I'm trying to work out how sophisticated this thing is.'

'Well, let me know when you make a decision,' he said. 'Because I'm telling you, I'm done with this crap.'

He hung up and Sarah moved a little nearer. Maybe she didn't want the car-park attendant to overhear; maybe she simply wanted to be closer. 'Tell me what's going on. Now. And I mean everything. Or I'll . . . I could tell this nice man and the police that this was all you.' She waved her hand towards the rope and harness on the floor.

'There's no need for threats. I'll give you a full and frank explanation, but not here.' He nodded at the car-park attendant. 'We can't be sure who's listening.' She nodded. 'I don't know what I'd have done if something had happened to you.'

Sarah's mouth twitched at one corner. 'I'm sure you'd have coped.'

'I don't think so.'

Sarah looked away from him and across the car park. 'True. You'd have had to find someone else to stalk.'

He laughed. 'I think you'll find that I saw you in Fork by coincidence, and coincidentally enjoyed the coffee, so I returned regularly.'

'And is that why you loitered there most days even after you'd bought your coffee?'

'Oh God.' He looked down at the ground. What a loser. He was genuinely embarrassed, mortified even. He'd never before in his life done something like that. And he judged those who did.

Sarah put her arms around his neck. 'It's OK. I was flattered.'

He risked a quick look at her. He could smell her sweetly spiced perfume.

'But if I'd known how much trouble you'd be—' she continued.

Jameson cut her off with a kiss.

Sarah moved away. 'Don't you have calls you should be making?'

Shit.

Claire burst into tears as soon as she heard that Jane was OK. For several minutes, all he could hear were her muffled sobs. Eventually she spoke again. 'Is she with you?'

'She's with her father, Thomas Lake. He lives in Manchester. How far away are you?'

'I've only just got on the train. I'll be a couple of hours. Why with him?'

'That's where they sent her.'

'And she's OK? Have you spoken to her?'

'Augusta has. I'm going to call her now. I'll tell her you're on your way and send over the address.'

Claire hesitated. 'Are you nearer?'

'I can't get away. I'm waiting for the police.'

'And Sarah?' She sounded genuinely concerned, which was a step up from her earlier fury.

Jameson squeezed Sarah's hand. 'I'm with her now. We got her back, too.'

'So it's over? What about Lana?'

'I've no doubt Lana will be fine, but it won't be over until we find the sick bastards responsible.'

'Damn right,' said Claire. Sarah nodded at the stairwell where two police officers had just emerged. The car-park attendant was walking towards them, gesturing at the rope and harness.

'The police are here. I have to go.'

'What do we tell them?' said Sarah, as the three men walked their way.

'The truth.'

63

What had the message said? Bloom scrolled back through the conversation.

Lana Reid is not exactly the calibre we normally require.

Lana certainly seemed to be the most damaged and irresponsible member of the group: the drug use, the alcohol abuse, the sexual promiscuity. Her exact psychopathic profile might reveal more susceptibility to boredom and impulsivity than fearlessness. Bloom looked out on to her mother's once neatly landscaped, now overgrown garden.

There was one question she'd been asking herself since the very beginning, one that she still didn't have the answer to. Why would someone recruit psychopaths?

But perhaps that was the wrong question. What if she'd been looking at it from the wrong end of the lens the whole time?

She called Jameson, but he didn't answer. She hung up without leaving a message. He was probably with the police. She grabbed her coat and handbag, checked the back door was locked and left for the station. She'd head to Leeds and tell Jameson and Sarah her theory in person.

Parents and their children were crowded on to the green in front of the house, enjoying the warm spring evening. She remembered watching Penny cross it on that dreadful evening as she headed back to her empty home. How unlucky Penny had been. To struggle for so long for a child, and then to have Seraphine. She hadn't heard from Penny in years. Her mother had tried to keep in touch after the suicide, but Penny found it too hard to be around the family she blamed for pushing her daughter towards death. Did Penny have any idea that her daughter might still be alive? That she might have been out there since the age of fourteen, charming others, manipulating them into providing her with a new life?

Her phone rang. She was expecting Jameson, but it was DS Green.

'Here's a turn-up for the books,' Green said, in his usual dry tone. 'Grayson Taylor has been arrested in Peterborough, of all places. DC Logan has some fancy way to track arrest reports.'

Had whoever was controlling the game let him go? It was unlikely. They hadn't yet delivered on their promise to return Lana and Stuart. 'What was he arrested for?'

'Identity theft and fraud. He was using the details of a young woman he was living with to obtain money by deception. By all accounts she's some wealthy heiress whose daddy got suspicious.'

'Is he at the police station?'

'Peterborough, yeah.'

'You need to keep him there.'

'Well, he'll be interviewed and if he's guilty he'll be charged, then bailed to appear in court.'

'If Grayson's been arrested, that means he's failed the test. You need to keep him in custody until his father gets there. Does Geoff Taylor know?'

'I've no idea. Logan called me and I called you.'

'Call him. Get him to go to Peterborough station immediately. Then speak to the officer in charge and tell them it's critical they hold Grayson until his father arrives.'

'I can't do that. I've no authority. They'll tell me where to get off.'

'Like I said, if Grayson's been arrested, he's failed the test. Those people aren't seen again. If Grayson leaves that station alone, I guarantee he'll disappear for good.'

'Does that matter?'

'Oh come on, DS Green. He's a young man with his life ahead of him and a father who loves him very much. He could still have a positive future.'

'You really believe that crap? He's a flaming psycho. Better out of the way, in my book.'

Police officers dealt with the worst side of society. It changed their perception. 'It doesn't matter whether or not you share my views. We suspect he'll come to harm without intervention, so we have to act.'

'What makes you suspect he'll come to harm?' asked Green.

'You really think all one hundred and nine players are still participating in the game? No way. No game, no matter how clever, could hold a psychopath's attention for over a year. They simply don't have the patience.'

'So someone's doing away with them? That's a leap. Where's your evidence?'

It was a legitimate question. But the numbers simply didn't add up. 'If you need me to speak to Assistant Chief Constable Barker and get him to make the calls, I can.'

'No, leave it. I'll see what I can do. I'll tell them I need to interview him about a case here in Bristol and head over there myself.'

Mentioning Steve had had the desired effect. 'Thank you, Phil.'

She hung up and found a seat on the train. She checked her messages – one from Jameson: they were at a pub called The Lock – and then her phone rang again.

'Dr Bloom? It's Libby Goodman.'

'Libby.'

'I was expecting someone to come over, but—'

'I'm sorry. Circumstances have made it impossible today.' Bloom could hear a baby crying in the background.

'I needed to speak to you about the text I had this morning from Stuart.'

Bloom sat up straighter in her seat, holding the phone closer to her ear. 'What did it say?'

'It simply asked for the baby's name.'

'Can you read it to me, please, Libby?'

'"What did you call my baby?" That's all it said.'

My baby. That made Bloom nervous. Psychopaths were selfish and possessive. 'And what did you reply?'

An elderly gentleman sat down opposite Bloom. He was wearing cream slacks with a pale-blue shirt and had a coral jumper slung over his shoulders. The uniform of the well-to-do retired.

'I just said that if he wanted to know he should call me. But he hasn't. I rang the number a few times, but it just rings out. No voicemail. I didn't know whether to text again.'

Bloom didn't think Libby, now an exhausted new mum, would benefit from hearing the truth about Stuart over the phone. That was a face-to-face job. 'How about I call round tomorrow and we can discuss it?'

Libby agreed and said that late morning would work best, between naps and feeds. She hung up. Bloom caught the elderly gentleman's eye and smiled at him. He averted his gaze. Had he been listening? She looked out of the window at the city buildings drawing closer. The knot of fear in her stomach grew stronger and heavier. She looked at the old man, and again he looked away. She was paranoid. He was lonely, a man of a certain age enjoying a look at a younger woman on a train.

Or he was one of them and he'd been tasked with watching her.

Bloom made a point of leaning out of her seat and craning her neck to look at the doors at each end of the carriage. There was a sign for the toilet behind her. She stood and walked through to the previous carriage. She continued past the toilet cubicle and took a seat facing the way she had come. She scrolled through her phone, keeping an eye on the door. The elderly gentleman never appeared. Of course he didn't.

When the train arrived at Leeds, Bloom remained seated while everyone else disembarked. On the platform a woman in a red raincoat was struggling to strap a screaming, kicking child into his pushchair. Bloom stood – she should offer to help – but as she moved towards the door a man came to the mother's aid. Bloom waited in the doorway, watching. It was the elderly gentleman. He smiled warmly at the mother, then stooped a little and stuck his tongue out at the child, who paused his kicking for just long enough for his mother to weave his chubby arms through the straps and click the buckle shut. Her red face glistened with the effort. She smiled at the man, her expression revealing relief, gratitude and just a touch of embarrassment. The elderly gentleman said something to make her laugh and gave her arm a gentle squeeze. Then he straightened and looked directly at Bloom. She kept her face neutral, trying to read him. He was smiling, but his eyes were blank. And then he winked.

Bloom's heartbeat began to pound in her ears, a thud-thud pulsing far too quickly. She stepped off the train and when she looked up the man had disappeared. She checked back towards the rear of the train, but he wasn't there. Jameson was no more than five minutes away, maybe less if she walked quickly.

As she approached the front of the train, the driver climbed out and shut the door behind him. He was a young guy with pasty skin and far too much gel in his hair. He smiled at Bloom, then looked past her and, to her utter dismay, lifted his chin and gave another smile. She glanced at the train window's reflection to see who was walking behind her. It was the elderly gentleman. He must have stepped back on to the train and waited for her to pass. That's how he had disappeared. She didn't want to give him the satisfaction, or the advantage, of knowing she suspected him, so she concentrated on keeping her head up and her shoulders square. She climbed the escalator, but was blocked by a small Asian lady and her son. They were so engrossed in their conversation that they didn't hear her *excuse me*s.

Bloom placed a hand on the boy's shoulder and said, 'Sorry, can I get past?'

But by the time they'd looked at her, apologized and moved over, they were at the top anyway. She fought the urge to run. He might not be behind her; he could be stuck at the bottom of the escalator or behind some other slow family. She bolted past the Pasty Shop concession stand and around the back of Starbucks. The rear exit barriers were just ahead. She felt for her ticket in the left pocket of her coat. It wasn't there. She tried the other pocket. Also empty. She opened her bag and reached inside for her purse as she approached the barrier. The ticket inspector was resting against the gate post on the opposite side. There were no other passengers at this exit. She riffled through the receipts in her purse but it wasn't there. She knew it wouldn't be. Had she left it on the seat? Dropped it on the floor? She felt panic rising hot and acidic in her throat.

'You know you can get electronic tickets on your phone now,' said the inspector.

She always put her ticket in the left-hand pocket of her coat. She tried the pocket once more and there it was, a satisfyingly firm strip of card nestled against the outer fabric.

'Thanks,' she said to the inspector.

Once through the barrier, she risked a look behind her. The elderly gentleman was walking towards the barriers with his ticket in hand.

Keen to put as much distance as possible between them, Bloom walked swiftly down the escalator, glancing briefly back at the man behind her, who was sharing a smile and a few polite words with the ticket inspector. The inspector was standing straighter. He probably wasn't even aware of it. Most people unconsciously adjusted their behaviour in the presence of people they perceived as being more successful or powerful. And functional psychopaths had the uncanny ability to be both charming and intimidating at the same time, a combination that provided fertile ground for manipulation.

At the bottom of the escalator, Bloom walked to the Granary Wharf exit. She could see the entrance to the Hilton Hotel straight ahead and, housed in its ground floor, The Lock, where Jameson and Sarah were waiting. She broke into a jog. The elderly gentleman didn't look like the running type. As she ran out of the building and into the pedestrian area surrounding the fenced canal dock, a familiar face stepped into her path. She came to a swift halt. She heard footsteps behind her.

'Dr Bloom,' said Stuart Rose-Butler as he reached for her left bicep, 'perhaps you'd be kind enough to come with us.' The elderly gentleman took her right bicep, and she knew she had no choice but to do what they asked.

64

Jameson drained his pint and checked his watch. Augusta should be here by now. He scanned the large windows at the front and left side of the bar. There was only a handful of people heading home from work. Dusk had settled and they were all hunched over to keep out the chill.

'She'll be here,' said Sarah, folding slender fingers around the stem of her wine glass.

He'd told her the whole story – from Lana receiving the invitation, to his and Bloom's challenges.

'I feel rude for not having thanked you for coming to my rescue,' said Sarah.

'Of course I was going to come to your rescue,' he said.

'You've only known me a couple of weeks.'

'Sixteen days, but who's counting?'

Sarah sipped her drink, but he could see her smile behind the glass. 'You really think that's long enough to fall in love?'

Jameson smirked. He knew it was, but he was still a long way from being able to admit it. 'I wouldn't say fall in love, exactly.'

'They call it limerence, you know. The inability to concentrate, the increased heart rate, the acute longing for another person.'

'Limerence?' he repeated.

Sarah held his gaze. 'It's not love, but people mistake it for love. I'm not saying that's what you are doing . . .' She reached for his hand.

'I'm glad to hear it.' He rose from his seat, feeling more than a little awkward. 'Time for another drink.'

'Wait.' Sarah held his hand firmly. 'I did have a point. I read that psychopaths lack the capacity to experience limerence, because they don't produce enough oxytocin.'

'Isn't that the baby hormone?'

Sarah nodded. 'It's often referred to as the attachment hormone. We feel it when we bond with other people and even with animals. It's released when mums feed their babies, when we have sex and even when we stroke a dog.'

Jameson sat down again, intrigued. 'So psychopaths don't get attached because they can't feel that high?'

'It's just one hypothesis, but it might be why psychopathic partners can walk away from a relationship without looking back.'

'They really are wired differently.'

'Seems that way. Although whether it's in response to genetic factors or environmental conditioning . . . that's something Augusta would probably know.'

'I'll probably feel like a bit of a gooseberry when she gets here, with you two nattering on about psychopaths . . .' He checked his watch again. Her train had arrived fifteen minutes ago. 'I'll give her a call. Maybe she's gone to the wrong bar.' Before he could do so, a broad-shouldered man approached their table; his black suit, polished shoes and general demeanour screamed policeman.

'Mr Jameson, Dr Mendax – DCI Beardsley.' He flashed his warrant card, then placed it back in his jacket pocket. 'I believe you've just given a statement to my colleagues over in Sovereign Square car park. You mentioned a man called Stuart Rose-Butler? I've been looking for Mr Rose-Butler in connection with a case I'm working on. Could you spare me a moment of your time?'

Jameson felt a flicker of something, but he couldn't put his finger on it. But he and Sarah had indeed reported Stuart to the officers in the car park.

'Take a seat,' said Sarah, clearly happy to help.

'Could we discuss it at the police station?' The DCI looked from Sarah to Jameson. 'It's only a five-minute walk.'

'We're waiting for someone.' Jameson felt an echo of suspicion.

'You can text her and ask her to meet us there, can't you?' said Sarah.

'She should be here by now.' He stood, peered out of the window and scanned the concourse again. Four businessmen walked past and into the Brazilian restaurant on the opposite corner. There were three students in skinny jeans and trainers at the end of the dock, unlocking bikes from the railings. But no sign of Augusta.

He took out his phone and called her. It went to voicemail.

'It's me. Did you catch the four fifteen? We're still in

The Lock.' He looked at Sarah. She was standing with her jacket on and was chatting with the policeman. 'But we're heading to the police station to answer some questions about Stuart.' Sarah would do whatever it took to catch the perpetrators; he couldn't blame her.

'So what's this case you're working on?' Jameson asked, holding open the door for Sarah and DCI Beardsley.

Beardsley, he thought as the guy passed him. Why was that familiar?

'I'll fill you in when we get there, mate.'

Mate. There was a Liverpudlian undertone to his accent.

That was it. DCI Beardsley was the police officer in Liverpool who'd received a birthday card. He was one of them.

'Sarah?' Jameson held out his hand to her and she turned, confused by his tone. 'Come back inside.' At least there were witnesses in the pub.

Beardsley reacted quickly to Jameson's tone, reaching inside his jacket for a Taser gun and aiming it at Sarah.

'You're a man of the world, Jameson. You know what this is and what it will do to your little girlfriend here if I pull the trigger. Now, you wouldn't want that, would you?' Beardsley's smile failed to touch his eyes. 'On the other hand, if you're not bothered, I'm sure I'll enjoy seeing her pretty body writhing on the floor. Your call.'

Jameson couldn't disarm the guy. But it would be madness to go anywhere with the psycho.

'And if you're considering any heroics, bear in mind

that if this lovely lady has a heart condition, this thing *will* kill her.'

Jameson tried to read Sarah's eyes, tried to get her permission. They couldn't comply with these fruitcakes. Fighting back was the only option. But Sarah's gaze gave nothing away.

And then Beardsley said something that changed everything.

'We better get a move on. Dr Bloom is waiting for us.'

65

Bloom sat in a wooden chair. Her wrists were bound with a rope that was stretched in a taut line, binding her ankles too. Her feet were pinned together and her hands drawn flat on her lap. There were two other wooden chairs facing her, rope slung over their backs, and, surrounding this trio, six quite different chairs were set in a circle, with wide-cushioned seats upholstered in purple velvet. They were empty. Bloom was alone.

Stuart and his colleague had brought her to a derelict unit beneath the dark arches of Leeds station. They hadn't said a word. They'd ignored all of her questions. They'd taken her phone, tied her up and then left. Some of the arches facing out on to Granary Wharf had been converted into trendy bars and restaurants, but this was an internal arch, used only for parking. Its walls and ceiling were bare brick and there were sections missing from the concrete floor, revealing the cobblestones below. It was cold and the place smelled dank. To Bloom's left were six large window panes, cracked and with blackened glass from years of neglect. The sun setting behind created a mustard glow. The opening to her right, where cars entered and exited, bore wooden double doors, painted black and bolted shut. She had shouted for help, hoping a passer-by might hear, but no one had responded.

The door opened again now and Bloom locked eyes with Jameson. The fury on his face melted into concern as he scanned the rope that tied her to the chair. Behind him was a woman with long blonde hair – presumably his new girlfriend, Sarah. A man in a grey suit accompanied them and they were followed by Stuart, the elderly gentleman and a small plump lady of mixed race. Denise.

'Sit,' the grey-suited man said to Jameson. He pointed to the chair on Bloom's right.

Bloom thought he might refuse, but he did as instructed. Sarah was directed to the final wooden chair, where Stuart began to tie her wrists, just like Bloom's. Sarah avoided looking at Stuart, keeping her focus on Jameson. She didn't look scared. Bloom knew Jameson would be impressed by her bravery.

'You OK?' Jameson glanced briefly at Bloom.

'Yes. You?' she replied.

He didn't answer. His attention had moved on to Sarah. 'Don't worry,' he said. 'You're only here because they're using you to get at me. You'll be fine. I'll make sure of it.'

Jameson was speaking with such confidence.

Bloom felt a crushing sadness.

The grey-suited man secured Jameson and joined the others on the velvet chairs.

'Surrounded by a circle of psychos. Lucky us,' said Jameson. He glanced at the two empty seats, one behind Sarah and one behind Bloom. 'Someone can't keep time.'

Their observers didn't speak.

'Sarah, is it?' asked Bloom.

'You must be Augusta. Not the best circumstances in which to meet, but ... hello. Marcus tells me great things.'

Bloom smiled. 'We're something of a mutual appreciation society, aren't we, Marcus?' She was being childish, but she couldn't help it. Maybe it was because she was tied to a chair. Or perhaps it was the brutal reality of someone else receiving all of Jameson's attention.

Bloom looked around. She'd always understood why psychopaths existed. They were evolution's most uncomplicated human design. We are born alone, we die alone and the journey between is ours alone. So why not make it entirely about that single being?

She looked at Jameson looking at Sarah.

Love. That was why. And it was blatantly obvious that Marcus Jameson, her closest ally and dearest friend, was in love. A fact that broke her heart.

Bloom turned again to Sarah. 'Mendax is an unusual surname. Is it Latin?'

Sarah smiled, impressed. 'Actually yes. Do you know that you're the first person to ever ask that?'

'Why are we here and who are we waiting for?' Jameson craned his neck. 'OK, well, you can let her go.' Jameson nodded at Sarah. 'She has nothing to do with this.'

Bloom didn't miss the quick curl of a smile on Sarah's lips.

'They are not waiting for anyone else, Marcus,' she said. 'The two remaining chairs are for two of us.'

Jameson looked at her, his mind joining the dots, making the connections. 'A final challenge?'

'Not so much a challenge as an invitation, I think. Please do correct me if I'm wrong.' She addressed every other pair of eyes in the room.

'Not so much dare to play as dare to join?' Jameson's sarcastic delivery gave way to a deep frown as he absorbed Bloom's expression. 'Seriously. You think they're trying to recruit us?'

Bloom shook her head slowly. 'Not *us*.'

'You?' he asked. 'But there are two seats. Who's the other seat for?' He looked around the room again. 'Hey! Circle of psychos! How do you plan to fill seat number two? I'm not playing your games any more.' He looked back at Bloom. 'Why aren't they speaking? I thought you said these people were show-offs. Why are they sitting like timid mutes?'

'Because, despite their psychopathy, they are still human. They are primates. And they're waiting for their Alpha to speak. Isn't that right, Seraphine?'

Jameson twisted in his seat, the ropes straining against his skin, to face the plump olive-skinned woman sitting to his left. 'This is your teenage suicide girl? You were right?'

'Seraphine was always good at hiding what she was,' said Bloom. 'But no. Seraphine was fair-haired, pale-skinned and blue-eyed. Even she couldn't pull off that level of transformation.' Tears were stinging her eyes as Jameson swivelled back to face her. 'I'm sorry,' she said.

'What? I don't . . .'

'Mendax,' said Bloom. 'It's Latin for liar. A little joke of hers, I imagine.'

'I think you'll find it's noble liar,' said Sarah. Jameson spun to face her. She rubbed her left and right wrists together; the rope that had tied them now lay coiled at her feet. 'I thought you'd be pleased to discover that I'm alive. And that I've found a clear purpose.'

'This is not what I meant,' said Bloom.

'Did you really think I'd use all my talents and years of training as a doctor to become some brilliant but anonymous surgeon hidden away in a hospital theatre?' Sarah looked at Jameson. 'My kind have something of a knack for high-risk, high-pressure careers.'

'So you became a psychiatrist and collected psychopaths. Why?' Once Bloom had realized that they were missing a key component – the answer to *why* someone would bother to recruit psychopaths – she had been almost there. On the train, while hiding by the toilets, she'd finally found the courage to google 'experts in functional psychopathy' and she'd discovered, top of the list, revered psychiatrist Dr Sarah Mendax.

Sarah wrinkled her button nose. 'Oh, Augusta. You can do better than that.'

Jameson broke his silence. 'I'm sorry. What? You . . .' He looked at Bloom. 'She can't be Seraphine. I'd have known.'

'Seraphine Walker is a very high-functioning psychopath,' said Bloom.

'Fine. But Sarah is warm and . . . good. She's a doctor. She saves people's lives.' Jameson was staring at Sarah.

'Marcus,' said Bloom. 'Look at me. Look at me now. Seraphine ... will be whoever she needs to be ... Whoever *you* need her to be in order to get what she wants from you.'

The adult Seraphine stood and stretched her back. Her long, athletic limbs and attractive features were no doubt another great weapon in her armoury of manipulation. 'I prefer Sarah these days.' She cocked her head towards Jameson. 'I didn't really get why you worked with this guy before,' she said, walking over so that she could look down on him. 'Don't get me wrong,' she said. 'You're a treat in the sack.' She turned to Bloom. 'But I couldn't work out what he added to you. And now I see.' She placed a hand on Jameson's shoulder. 'He brings all the emotion. The stuff you lack nearly as much as I do; the humour, the trust ... the love.'

Jameson shrugged her away. 'Get your hands off me.'

'See? He's all reactive and passionate. It's gorgeous.' Seraphine moved into Jameson's eyeline. 'You really are gorgeous, Marcus. I'd love to let Augusta keep you.'

Bloom felt the room chill a few more degrees.

'Wait,' said Jameson. 'But what was all that about in the car park? Pretending to be thrown off?'

'Ah, bless. You're still catching up here, aren't you, sweetie?' Seraphine perched on the edge of her wooden chair. 'Augusta was taking too long to work out who your new girlfriend was, and quite frankly ... I was getting bored.'

'You were ... *bored*?' Jameson looked as if he might throw up. 'No. That doesn't follow. It would have taken

329

setting up. You'd have had to plan ahead, make measurements, acquire the equipment . . .'

Seraphine sat back in her seat and raised her eyebrows at Bloom. 'Brains *and* brawn. Why haven't you taken him for yourself, Augusta? Are you scared he might not go for your ageing-spinster vibe? You could be quite pretty, you know? If you made an effort.' Seraphine gave a little laugh and looked away. 'I think I may have touched a nerve.' Seraphine winked at Jameson. 'The truth is, Marcus, I was interested to know how strong your feelings were. You could say I'm quite fascinated with the love thing. I find it—'

'Fascinated?' said Jameson, repulsed.

'What's the word? Compelling. I find love compelling.' She spoke to Bloom. 'Like you say, we are more similar than we are different. And, like everybody else, we want the things we cannot have.'

Bloom met her gaze. 'Which includes me, by the way. Because the answer is no. You know that, don't you?'

'What do you want with Augusta anyway?' said Jameson. 'What can she give you that you can't take for yourself?' Anger dripped from every word.

Seraphine lifted her eyes to the cracked windows above Jameson's head. 'Augusta knew exactly what I was within just two meetings. No other psychiatrist or psychologist has ever worked it out and I've tested plenty. And I don't mean that it took them longer. They never suspected it at all. Because I'm really very good at hiding it.' She looked over at Bloom. 'She's the only person who ever worked it out, and I've had fifteen years to think about why that might be.'

'Because she's bloody good at what she does,' said Jameson.

'Maybe. Or maybe . . .' Seraphine narrowed her eyes. 'Once she'd made it clear to me what I was and that I wasn't going to grow out of it, I knew the only way to keep it secret was to start over. Over the years I made it my business to meet every expert on psychopaths that I could find. I even wrote a research paper with the world's leading authority and the man had no idea he was working with one. I came to two conclusions. That I am particularly talented. And that Dr Augusta Bloom must have had some extra insight.'

'What kind of extra insight?' said Jameson.

Seraphine folded her arms. 'Now, Augusta, what kind of insight could I possibly be talking about? Do you want to enlighten him or should I?'

'I don't know what on earth you're talking about,' said Bloom. 'And anyway, if all this is about me, why is Marcus here?'

'You know why Marcus is here.'

'Do I?'

'Of course you do, Augusta. Since your poor mother lost her grip on reality, you have had no one and nothing of meaning in your life . . . apart from him.' Seraphine looked at Jameson. 'I actually feel weirdly sad about this, but he's nothing more than leverage.'

Without warning, the man in the grey suit stood up

and fired a Taser gun directly at Jameson's back. Jameson's body flexed against the chair and the ropes that bound him, as if trying to flatten itself. He didn't make a sound as the jolt of electricity hit him, but the expression on his face screamed extreme pain. A second later his chair rocked on to its side and crashed to the floor. With his hands and feet tied, Jameson couldn't break the fall and his head hit the concrete with a loud thud. His body continued to tense as the volts circled his system, and then Grey-Suit released the trigger and Jameson was still.

'Marcus!' Bloom strained against her ropes. 'If you think hurting him is going to make me do what you want, you are bitterly mistaken, young lady.'

Seraphine chuckled, then picked up her chair and carried it close to Bloom's. 'I've always loved that tone you use when you're taking command. I copied that, you know, kind of made it my own.' She reached into the pocket of her jacket and removed a small yellow object which she placed in her lap. 'H6,' she said under her breath.

Bloom stared at the pencil. Its lead was pointed and sharp and, at the opposite end, a small cap of red paint prophesied what was to come.

'How did you know?' asked Seraphine. 'When did you know?'

'When did I know what?'

'That Sarah was really Seraphine. When did you figure it out?'

'I began to suspect you might still be alive, and maybe even involved, after the incident on the bridge. I knew that if you were, you'd want to get as close to our investigation as possible. I thought of all the women I knew and had spoken to over the past month and I realized there was only one I'd never met.'

'Marcus's lover.'

Bloom nodded. 'So I looked up experts in functional psychopathy. As soon as I saw your surname, I knew.'

Seraphine looked pleased. She rotated the pencil in her hand. 'If you join me, I'll make sure this goes nowhere near your gorgeous Marcus. But if you refuse, you should know, I have been practising . . . All those cadavers . . . All those hospital morgues.'

Jameson was lying motionless on the floor. How long until he recovered? Was he OK? How hard had he hit his head?

'What on earth could you need me for?' Bloom asked. 'Even if I did have some special insight – which as a matter of fact I do not – it couldn't match the sophistication of your game.'

'Really? You still don't know?'

'I have no idea whatsoever.'

'I don't need you for anything, Augusta. I don't need anyone for anything.'

Bloom frowned. If Seraphine didn't need her, then what the hell did she want? 'So?'

'So?' Seraphine's eyes were sparkling, playful.

Bloom laughed. Of course. It was obvious. 'You don't *need* me to join you. You *want* me to.'

Seraphine leaned forward, her elbows on her knees and her hands in a prayer position. 'You hide who you really are so very well. So well, in fact, that people use you to treat people like me. Do you know how awesome that is? But, you know, the thing I've always admired most is how you took us youngsters under your wing and steered us on to our path. That's what I'm doing now. I'm continuing your work. And you should absolutely be part of that.'

'I am not like you.'

'Really?' Seraphine gestured to Jameson lying motionless on the concrete. 'Look at him. What do you feel when you see that?'

She didn't know much about Tasers. But he should surely have regained muscle control by now. Why was he so still?

'What do you feel, Augusta? I know you don't want me to hurt him. You like his company, respect his judgement, etcetera, etcetera. But do you feel guilty that he's here?'

'I've got nothing to be guilty about. You did that to him, not me.'

'Ah, yes. But he's only here because of you. And he's only on the floor because of you. He only experienced all that pain and anguish because of you . . . And I'm not just referring to the volts. You saw how he was with me. How much he cared for me. And that is all because of you.'

Bloom stared at Seraphine and Seraphine stared back.

'What do you feel?' Seraphine asked, her tone urgent, bordering on excited. 'What do you feel?'

'I am not like you.'

334

'Are you sure?'

'Of course, I'm sure. You're a psychopath without any concern for the consequences of your actions. You can't understand how others care so deeply for their family and friends. Look at what you did to your poor parents. You think because you are logical and unbiased you're superior, but that doesn't make you a better person.'

'And you know what I say to that, Augusta?' Bloom strained her hands against the ropes. 'It takes one to know one.'

'It took you fifteen years to reach that conclusion? That I spotted the truth because I'm the same as you? You're smarter than that, Seraphine.'

'I bet if I studied your brain I'd see all the familiar patterns: the underactive amygdala, the reduced grey matter in the orbitofrontal cortex, all resulting in impaired social and emotional responses. I'd maybe even see a lack of oxytocin.' Seraphine took a purposeful glance at Jameson. 'Is it denial? Or have you just been hiding who you are for so long that you now believe your own propaganda? You're so distant and cool, clinical and incisive. Have you never wondered? Or been tested?'

'Do you know what projection is, Seraphine?'

Seraphine smiled. 'They wanted me to test you, like they were tested.' She looked around at the others in the room. 'But I told them, *She won't take on the dare. She's too in control.* When it comes to – what is it Professor Dutton calls it? – the mixing desk of psychopathy, your impulsive, risk-taking traits are turned way down low.

It's why you hide so well. I'm the same and I'd never have taken up the dare. I, like you, am too evolved, too perfected. So this was the only way to draw you in and show you what you can be part of. You started this because you knew we were outstanding. We are the master race. We control everything from politics to business. We pull the strings. We start the wars and end the wars. We are already in charge. Join us and you'll be free to be who you really are.'

Bloom watched Stuart take his phone from his jacket pocket, check the message on the screen and smile. It was the smug smile of a man who had obtained what he wanted and who knew he always would.

Seraphine continued talking. 'I know you're probably wondering why we've all gathered here. The truth is I wanted them to meet you. They've heard me talk about you so much and most of them have spent a good deal of time watching you. But I wanted them to see why you belong.' She turned towards Denise. 'Denise was the first to join me. When I saw her potential, I realized what you'd seen in me.'

Bloom took a look around the room again. 'This is not all of you, I take it.'

'Of course not. We are many strong, but those details are for later . . . and only if you join us.' Seraphine rotated the pencil between her thumb and forefinger. 'If you continue to deny the truth, I will be forced to take extra measures. I'll find another way to prove it to you. It was only when I saw all that blood spreading in a glistening pool across the floor that I realized just how different

I was. I wasn't horrified like everyone else. I was fascinated. Wanna see?'

Bloom stared at Jameson's body on the floor. She knew what she needed to do, but she didn't want to do it. He would wake up soon and hear everything and she wouldn't have a chance to explain. If this experience hadn't ruined things between them already, what happened next in this dank, dark room undoubtedly would.

Seraphine stood up. 'You'll see, I promise. Once I do this, you'll see.'

'There's no need,' Bloom said, meeting Seraphine's gaze.

The other woman studied Bloom and then a smile spread across her lips. 'You're admitting what you are?'

Bloom looked at Seraphine for a long moment, then gave the smallest of nods.

66

Lana opened her eyes. Her hands and feet were still tied, but she was no longer in a chair but lying on the floor. What had happened? She'd done everything they said. She'd completed their challenges and confronted Marcus Jameson and his mousy sidekick. She'd even given them Jane. Was her daughter tied up in the dark somewhere too?

She strained in fury against the ropes. The twine dug into her wrists and she pulled her legs against their restraints, but to no avail. She couldn't see anything, but she knew she was in a confined space. She used her feet to explore the walls around her. The boot of a car, maybe? She shouted at the top of her voice until her throat felt raw. No one answered. No one came.

Just a few hours ago, everything had looked so different. She'd received a call offering her the life she deserved and had made her way to the dark arches beneath Leeds station to meet the architect of the game, a woman called Sarah.

She'd caught the train from Ilkley. She'd wanted a drink, but she knew it was out of the question. How had they discovered what she'd done? No more than an hour after she'd picked up Jane outside the school, she'd received a call from a blocked number. The woman had said that Lana's actions were foolish. Lana had so much potential, she was truly special, and completing the challenges within the rules was the only way to get the life she deserved. They were prepared to give her one last chance to redeem herself. If she took Jane to an address in the Yorkshire town of Ilkley and kept her locked in the attic, she could continue. Lana didn't question their motives because she didn't care. She'd been sleeping rough for three days. Here was a place to stay, free of charge, and all she had to do was keep Jane out of sight.

A few days later, a skinny man had come by the house to check on them. Lana had taken him to the loft and he said she'd redeemed herself. He'd taken her to South Milford on the back of his motorbike to confront Jameson. Lana had enjoyed that. It felt good to show Marcus that she was strong and powerful. He had always looked down on her.

On her walk to the dark arches, Lana had wondered what her new life would be. She had potential. That was what they'd said. It was the sort of acknowledgement and praise she'd hungered for her whole life. She'd always known that she was better than most people, but the world around her couldn't always see it. It made her furious. Only the drinking and the drugs numbed her frustration. The only time she ever really saw the awe she craved was when she seduced a man away from his wife or girlfriend, and that never lasted long enough. They either became distracted by their own guilt or started to take her for granted.

She'd knocked on the large wooden door as instructed

and waited. It had opened to reveal four people on expensive-looking chairs in the middle of a bare brick cellar.

'Please, take a seat, Lana.' She'd recognized the voice from the phone calls.

'Sarah?' Lana had said as she walked to the wooden chair and sat down. Only then had she noticed the ropes on the floor. *What were they for?*

'We've been impressed with you, Lana.' The woman who spoke was attractive, with blonde hair and striking blue eyes. 'You handled the situation with Mr Jameson and Dr Bloom on the bridge particularly well and I thank you for that. It was a moment which held a degree of . . . importance for me personally.'

'What has impressed you?' Lana had said, desperate for praise.

Sarah had smiled. 'Do you know who we are?'

Lana had looked at each face in turn. 'That's Denise, who collected Jane. And that's the motorbike driver.'

'No. I mean, do you know who we are as a group? What we represent?'

Lana had shaken her head.

'I take it you know that you're a psychopath?'

Lana's temper had flared. It was not the first time someone had thrown that insult at her, but she hadn't expected it here. 'You think?' she had said with barely contained irritation.

'No, we don't think, Lana. We know. You are a psychopath. That's why we selected you and that's what we have been testing you on. The game is a means of analysing your choices and skills to determine if you truly are one of us. And I hope you feel proud, Lana Reid. Because I can confirm that you are.'

Lana had tried to process the information. Was this really something to feel proud of? Didn't it make her a freak or a monster? 'Are you all psychopaths?' She had looked at the five people around her and then at Sarah.

'Indeed we are. Albeit of a particular kind.'

'How do you mean?'

'Well, in the range of psychopathy, we have our out-and-out serial killers, those guys who can't keep a lid on their desires. And, yes, they are usually men. Then we have our general criminal psychopaths, whose impulsive and egocentric natures cause them to reject society's laws. And then we have the likes of you, Lana, the functional psychopaths. Personally, I prefer to think of you as the hidden psychopaths. You live and thrive within society, hold down jobs, have relationships, raise families, because you mimic what is required. I know that the normals can be incredibly frustrating and stupid at times, but you learn to cope. You find a way to escape through drink and drugs, or you hide for a time so that you can indulge your own needs. Sound familiar?'

Lana had nodded.

'And then, finally, you have us.' Sarah gestured around the circle. 'And we are the ones that the normals should really be scared of, because we don't just live within their society, we manipulate it. And we do it so well that they have no idea we're even doing it at all.'

Lana had thought of the bosses she'd worked for and

how easily she had manipulated them. 'You said I was special and had potential?'

'I did and you do.'

'How? For what?'

'Dr Bloom once told me that there's no such thing as normal. Everyone is unique. But, for me, there is a massive difference between those governed by their emotional attachments and those who operate in the realm of logic and reason. Psychopaths play to win and there is no bigger game than life. So I have a final challenge for you. It's a choice.' Sarah had picked up two metal boxes from the floor beside her chair. They were each the size of a standard glasses case and identical apart from the numbers etched on to their lids. She had held them out for Lana to see. 'You have a daughter and you have friends. If you select box zero, we will send you home, with our very best wishes, to continue hiding in plain sight.' Sarah had moved her head a little closer to Lana's. 'However, seeing as you have proven yourself to be a true psychopath, if you select box number one, we will enable you to have the life you truly deserve. The only condition is that you will never be able to go home.'

'Join you, you mean?' Was Lana hearing this right? Did they think she had the potential to be one of them, powerful enough to manipulate society from behind the scenes?

'Make your choice, Lana. And all will be revealed.'

And so she had.

67

Jameson lay with his right cheek pressed against the cold concrete. He'd been Tasered once before, in MI6, but two fellow trainees had been holding his arms to stop the inevitable fall, which is where the real injury can occur. He had felt nervous but safe. Experts were on hand and it would last no more than ten seconds. Ten seconds, it turned out, that felt like a lifetime.

This time, Beardsley must have held on for at least thirty seconds. Only now did he feel the heat of the injuries to his cheekbone and elbow. He hoped neither was broken.

But his physical pain paled against the shock of Sarah's deceit. He knew that somewhere in the world there were at least three women who would delight at the idea that when Marcus Jameson had finally fallen in love it was with an illusion, nothing more than a projection of his own fantasy. He also knew that the sick anger he felt now was only the beginning. The depression would follow. If he made it out of here alive.

There was movement above him. Chairs scraped the floor and shoes clipped against the concrete. He took a moment to check his body, flexing the muscles in his feet, ankles and legs, and, when all seemed well, repeated the process in his arms and torso. His right elbow sent a searing dagger of pain through his bicep and into his shoulder. He bit his tongue and counted to five. The heat dissipated. His elbow was probably broken. He lifted his head a fraction, releasing the pressure on his face. His cheekbone hurt, but his elbow was far worse.

There was something shiny nestled in a groove between the cobblestones in front of his face. It was a small silver L-shaped pendant. From a necklace. And not just any necklace. He was sure he had seen it around Lana's neck. Could that be right? There must be hundreds of similar silver necklaces, worn by hundreds of women, any one of whom could have dropped it here. Yet he was sure Lana had been in this room.

'Wakey, wakey, baby-facey.' He saw Seraphine's feet in their high heels. A few hours ago, those feet had been snaking up his thigh. And man, had he loved that. The disgust came again in a fresh wave of sickness. She stooped and her face came into view. 'Hey, baby. You OK?' The concern in her eyes looked so authentic that for a micro-second Jameson's brain read it as real.

'Back off,' he said as his senses recovered.

Seraphine tilted her head as if studying a cute puppy. 'You know that circle of psychos, as you so fondly christened us? Well, we just got one link stronger. So I'd be careful what you say.' She stood up straight before he could respond. 'Get him up.'

Beardsley and Rose-Butler lifted him and righted his chair. Jameson's elbow screamed at Beardsley's grip but he gritted his teeth and took the hit. Once upright, he noticed that Augusta had been untied and was now sitting in one of the velvet chairs, beside the older chap in cream slacks. She wouldn't look him in the eye.

'Augusta?' he said, but she didn't turn. *What was that? Shame? Embarrassment?* 'Augusta?' He kept his voice low and quiet, as if they were the only two people in the room. 'What are you doing?' Slowly she moved to face him, and for the first time since they'd arrived in this dungeon he felt a jolt of fear. 'Augusta?' he said again. Her eyes were dead.

'How much fun is this? Finding that *two* women have had you fooled all this time?' Seraphine was so gleeful and self-satisfied. 'So where were we?' she said to Bloom.

'This is not a game, is it?' said Bloom. 'It's a cull. A sterilization.'

Seraphine looked delighted. 'You see! The fact you clocked that just proves how much of an asset you'll be. The truth is, if we're going to convince the world that high-functioning psychopaths have every right to be here – more, even, because we're superior in all the ways that matter – we can't have those who let the side down muddying the water.'

'You can't play with people's lives like that,' Jameson said. Bloom and Seraphine both looked his way.

'Well, technically, they're the ones playing with their lives. Not me,' said Seraphine.

'A man died. Children lost their father,' said Jameson.

'Only one family.'

Jameson shook his head. 'No, not just one family. What about the families of the players who never return? What about Lana and Jane?'

345

'Jane is fine, as you well know.'

Jameson looked down at the silver pendant on the floor. 'But what about Lana? She wasn't up to your high standards, was she? You used her to get to us. So what happens to her?'

'Don't pretend you care about Lana. You told me she was an irresponsible parent.'

'That doesn't give you the right to take her from her child.' He'd never thought he'd be standing up for Lana.

Seraphine smiled at the rest of the group. 'Did you know that almost all of the world's secret societies, from the Illuminati to the Freemasons, have been dominated by people like us? You could say we like to steer things from behind the scenes.'

'So why all the theatrics?' asked Jameson. 'Why have us investigating Lana and Jane? Why have us doing your challenges? If your cause is so great, why not come directly to Augusta?'

'Because she needed to appreciate its scale and feel its elegance. I needed her to know how powerful it is.'

'You mean how powerful you are,' Jameson said, amazed at how his feelings towards this woman had changed so drastically in the space of one conversation. 'So why do you bring people in here? . . . Because you do, don't you?'

Jameson watched Seraphine's brow furrow and then relax. 'What makes you think that?'

He pondered the pros and cons of mentioning Lana's pendant.

Bloom responded for him. 'I expect he's referring to

the set-up. He's observant about that kind of thing.' She tapped the base of her chair with the palms of her hands. 'These are heavy oak. They were brought here for more than one gathering.'

'Some meetings require absolute privacy.'

'I've been in the sort of meetings that require absolute privacy,' said Jameson. 'What do you do to people in here?'

'Oh, we're people now, are we? Not psychos or monsters?'

He ignored her. 'You bring your players here? Players like Lana? Was Lana here?'

'This has been a lot of fun, Marcus, darling, but now I have what I need' – Seraphine gestured to Bloom – 'I no longer need you.'

'What are you planning to do with him?' asked Bloom. 'I take it you won't just let him go.'

Jameson tried to catch Bloom's eye, but she wouldn't look his way. Was she really going to sit there and let this crazy woman do whatever she wanted?

'Don't worry. It won't hurt,' said Seraphine.

Bloom nodded as if that made it all right. 'I am impressed with your game's elegance and its scale,' she said. 'But surely you can't have managed all this on your own?'

'I'm not on my own,' Seraphine said, looking around the room.

'But the technology alone must have cost a fortune.'

'You could say I'm independently wealthy. You know how easy it is for us to take their money, don't you, Augusta?'

The smile Bloom gave her protégée turned Jameson's stomach.

'Fascinating,' said Bloom. 'And you profile them by their online activity?'

'It couldn't be easier, what with the popularity of social media today. Everyone is so desperate to reveal themselves and to be seen. It's quite tragic, really. But that's just the beginning. We then have to test if they're worthy.'

'How do you test them? How do you find out who's worthy?' Jameson said. He figured it was incumbent on him to get some answers, even if the chances of walking out of here alive were looking slim.

Seraphine turned to him. 'First, we just test their character. Are they really impulsive? Are they prepared to walk away from their lives, even if they are about to become a father?' Seraphine glanced over at Stuart. 'Then we push a bit more. Are they willing to do something dangerous in order to beat the competition? Will they steal, speed, get a tattoo on a whim, or remodel themselves into someone new?'

'And if they do?' said Jameson.

'You know what comes next, don't you, Augusta?' Seraphine's voice was syrupy sweet.

Bloom answered without a beat. 'Once the traits of impulsivity, risk-taking and rule-breaking have been established, the next step would be the social traits. So you have to make them manipulate others, use them or even harm them.'

'Exactly.' Seraphine turned to Jameson. 'We test if you're good at playing with others.' She tilted her head and a patronizing smile touched her lips. 'You know. Like I did with you.'

'You total—' He stopped. It would be stupid to lose his temper. 'Is that why Faye killed her husband?' he asked instead.

'That was unfortunate. Their final challenge is to pick someone they know and destroy them. Most functional psychopaths read this as destroying their relationship or their career, but Faye took it a little more literally.' Seraphine shrugged. 'With our kind you're always going to get the odd one with violent tendencies.'

'You're sending these sickos out there to destroy innocent people's lives? For what possible purpose?'

'It's simple,' said Bloom. 'If she's designed a good enough test, it will show whether the players are truly worthy of the label.' Bloom looked impressed; she actually admired Seraphine.

Seraphine responded to Bloom's appreciation with increased confidence. 'If done well, it can not only identify the high-functioning psychopaths, like Bloom and myself, but also be used to remove the weaker strains.'

'Christ, you really are cold,' Jameson said. 'You're turning the country into a playground for psychos.'

'You do have a lovely turn of phrase, Marcus. But let's face it, society is already our playground.'

He ignored her self-satisfied smugness. 'And if they excel at your challenges, and prove to be high-functioning, what then?'

Seraphine turned back to Bloom.

'They re-enter society,' said Bloom. 'But working

349

alongside you. I met Clive Llewellyn, by the way,' she said to Seraphine. 'I take it he's one of us? And the rest? You remove them from circulation.'

'Clive is an absolute darling. He was very impressed with you. He said you were elegantly authentic. To be honest, I think he might have fancied you,' said Seraphine.

'No one else goes home,' Jameson said.

'Oh, we give them the chance to go home,' said Seraphine. 'But they always pick the other option. The problem with tasting freedom is that you just want more. So that's what we give them . . . just not here.'

'You send them away? That's . . . an elegant solution,' said Bloom.

'And then what happens to them?' said Jameson.

'I've no idea,' said Seraphine. 'We don't want or need to know what happens to them.'

'But they're people like you,' said Jameson.

Seraphine's expression flashed with disgust. 'Absolutely not.' She reached under her chair and Jameson heard the tear of tape being removed.

He looked at Bloom and Bloom looked back at him. Her eyes were expressionless. He was on his own here. And there were six of them. He didn't want to die. Not here. Not like this. It was insulting and pathetic. He closed his eyes and told himself to man the fuck up. When he opened them, Seraphine had placed a small tin the size of a pencil case on her lap. She took out a syringe and a vial of clear liquid.

'I suppose there's no point promising to keep quiet,' he said.

Seraphine's lips curled as she filled the syringe from the vial. She held it up to the light and flicked it twice with her index finger.

He thought about offering to join forces with them. He had skills. He could offer something of value. But he couldn't do it. 'At least tell me what that is.'

'It is the most logical course of action, Marcus,' said Bloom. She turned to Seraphine. 'I expect this thing only works if no one knows what's going on. The general public need to be oblivious to who we really are and what we're doing. So we can't have a witness walk away with this knowledge.'

'Indeed,' said Seraphine. She pulled her chair close to Jameson's and with one hand began to roll up his right shirt sleeve. 'Certainly not one with all those government contacts.'

It was pointless trying to move his arm away. The ropes were too tight. 'Why the calling cards? Surely that risks exposing all of this?'

Seraphine's brow furrowed. 'It was a risk, yes, but a temporary one.'

'The cards were for me,' said Bloom. 'So I'd try to solve the mystery.'

Seraphine pushed his shirt sleeve higher. His injured elbow protested. She twisted his forearm to get to the veins. A groan passed through his gritted teeth.

Seraphine stopped and met his gaze. 'I can use the

other arm if you prefer.' Her tone was caring, a doctor looking after her patient.

He said nothing. He was not going to discuss with her which arm she should use to kill him.

After a beat she shrugged and gave his forearm a firm twist.

Shards of pain radiated from his elbow straight into his brain. He swore loudly.

'You said no pain.' Bloom's words were detached, a comment on a technicality rather than his distress. But when she glanced at him, he was sure he saw something. It was gone as quickly as it had appeared, but he knew he hadn't imagined it. He had worked with the woman for five years. She might have fooled Seraphine, but not him. He knew her better than anyone else. He had seen her ability to read people, assess a situation and make good decisions. And he knew she'd be relying on him to remember that. That's what he'd seen. A message meant only for him. Brief but clear. A message that said, *Trust me*.

'He wanted me to do it. He enjoys being the macho hero, don't you, Marcus?' Seraphine tapped his arm to lift the veins, then selected a plump one running diagonally across his skin. 'I never took you for the strong, silent type. You were always very vocal with me . . . especially in the bedroom.' She looked at him briefly before refocusing on the vein and moving the needle close to his skin. She sighed. 'I'm really going to miss that.'

Jameson felt the needle make contact with his skin. What if he was wrong? What if he'd imagined that look?

The mind could be a great conjuror when you really wanted to see something.

'What did Libby call your boy, Stuart?' Bloom's question was so out of context that every pair of eyes fell on her, including Seraphine's. Bloom continued to look at Stuart, her eyebrows raised slightly, expecting an answer.

Stuart shook his head gently. He looked from Bloom to Seraphine, then back again.

Seraphine sat upright, the syringe tilted away now from his vein. Jameson studied it in her hand. The taut rope binding his wrists to his ankles restricted his movement, but if he moved his left foot and left hand together, maybe he could reach the syringe?

'Isn't that what your text message was about?' asked Bloom.

'How did you know that?' Stuart's thick black eyebrows bunched together.

Jameson hoped his partner knew what she was doing. This was not a group to fuck with. In the past, he'd sometimes suspected that someone might be a psychopath – the agents on both sides, for instance, who walked away from a killing without looking back. But he'd never been sure. They might simply have been good at compartmentalizing. But these people in this room were self-confessed and validated psychos. The real deal. And he could feel it in the air.

'I expect you instruct your players to dump their phones and acquire pay-as-you-go versions so they remain incognito,' said Bloom. 'Is that something you relax once they're in your pocket?'

'What are you talking about?' said Stuart.

Seraphine sat back further and the syringe moved a little further away. Jameson needed to grab it soon, before she moved again.

'This morning at around ten fifteen, you texted Libby Goodman from your new phone and asked her what she'd called your child,' Bloom said to Stuart.

'So?'

Jameson squeezed his legs together from the thigh to the ankle. His feet and hands had to move together.

Seraphine spoke up. 'So you revealed your new number to your ex and your ex gave it to Augusta, who did what with it, I wonder?'

Bloom looked at Seraphine and smiled.

Jameson took his cue. Time was up. Whatever Augusta had done, Seraphine wasn't going to like it. He swung his whole body towards Seraphine, his feet and hands rotating exactly as planned to bring his right hand up above his left to where Seraphine still held the syringe. He grabbed it, feeling the smooth plastic fit satisfyingly into his palm. And then, as Seraphine protested and tried to seize it back, he stabbed the needle deep into her forearm and plunged its entire contents into her. 'Better in you than me,' he said. Only that morning he'd woken up hoping to spend the rest of his life with this woman.

'That all depends on your point of view.' Seraphine pulled her arm away and removed the syringe that hung limply from it.

A second later, Jameson saw Beardsley's fist coming.

He didn't have time to move his head before his second heavy thud against the concrete.

'Leave him,' Seraphine said. 'There's not enough time. How long do we have, Augusta?' Her voice was as calm as ever and Jameson realized how badly he had read her. He'd thought her so composed and brave. But she was simply detached.

'I couldn't say for sure, but I expect we're talking minutes.'

'Stuart, untie Marcus. The rest of you go,' said Seraphine.

From his position on the floor, Jameson watched Beardsley, Denise and the old chap who hadn't spoken open the large door and leave.

Stuart knelt on one knee and deftly undid the ropes around Jameson's ankles and wrists. 'What's going on?' he said as he stood and pulled the rope away from Jameson.

'You took our phones today so they couldn't be tracked,' said Bloom to Stuart.

Stuart nodded, understanding. 'But you had my phone number.' He stood over Bloom as he spoke. He was a good six foot. Jameson rose to his feet as fast as he could. He didn't fancy Bloom's odds if this psycho took a swipe.

Bloom continued to sit in her velvet chair, facing Seraphine. 'And I'm sure you're aware of how clever today's surveillance systems are. Only last year a number of police forces purchased the technology needed to listen in to conversations via someone's phone microphone.

It's intended for counter-terrorism activities, but people do like to play with a new toy.'

Stuart looked at Seraphine. 'So they've heard every word you've said?'

'Which is why I'm still sitting here,' she replied.

'And you called me by my full name – so I've been identified too?'

'Which is why you are here too, Stuart. It seemed illogical to put the others at risk of exposure.'

'I'm afraid it gets worse than that,' said Bloom. 'You see, as part of our investigation we met a talented young police officer with impressive social media skills. By the time the police arrive, who you really are and the details of your game will be trending across the country, if not the globe.'

Jameson winked at Bloom, then said to Seraphine, 'Not nice, is it? When someone makes a fool of you.'

Seraphine held on to the seat of her chair as if overtaken by a wave of dizziness, then she blinked a couple of times. 'I know you think you know better than me, Marcus, but think about it.' She took an unsteady breath. She was struggling to maintain eye contact. 'Augusta did exactly what I would have done. She played the game. It just so happens she was a move or two ahead of me this time.'

'So because she beat you, she must be like you?'

'To do what she did, she had to know who I was before she came in this room. But she didn't warn you, did she? She never gave you the chance to get away ... and she could have. She could have texted or called

356

you . . . but she chose not to. Because she needed you here to make this little scene work, to make me think I had the upper hand. So . . .' She coughed and took a deep wheezing breath.

'So you would talk,' he finished her sentence. He looked at Bloom. Seraphine had a point. His partner could have warned him, could have included him, and her decision not to had almost cost him his life.

'If that's not a psychopathic thing to do . . .' Seraphine looked at Bloom. Her voice was getting weaker with every word. 'I could have made your life so much better.'

'My life is just fine, thank you.'

Seraphine nodded. 'Go, Stuart.'

The guy turned to leave, but Jameson blocked his exit. 'Oh, I don't think so, psycho.' He wasn't sure he could overpower Rose-Butler with a broken elbow, but he sure would enjoy trying.

68

Seraphine's hands held the chair beneath her as she swayed from side to side. The drug in that vial had been intended for a vein but it had landed in her muscle. Bloom knew this would slow its progress.

Stuart tried to sidestep Jameson. Jameson blocked him and delivered a single punch to Stuart's stomach. He fell to his knees.

Bloom thought about the call she'd made to Assistant Chief Constable Steve Barker from the train. It had been a gamble to suggest using Stuart's phone as a listening device. She couldn't be sure that Stuart would even be there, but it had been the only card she'd had to play. She knew there was a good chance her own phone would be taken away once she revealed who Sarah really was. And so Barker agreed that his team would access Stuart's phone. And if at any point they verified that Bloom, Stuart and Seraphine were together, they'd instruct Libby to send a single text message saying, 'Your son is called Harry.' Bloom would know that anything from that point on would be recorded.

If Stuart hadn't checked his text message, this situation could have ended very differently. Steve Barker had had his doubts about Bloom's plan, but they needed to catch Seraphine revealing everything. She'd have kept her distance from the crimes committed by the players. They had to make her admit to being the orchestrator. Not that any of that mattered now.

'What was in the syringe?' Bloom asked.

Seraphine swayed, but said nothing.

'You need to tell me, Seraphine. The doctors will need to know.'

A male voice outside the room announced the presence of armed police.

'No one's armed!' shouted Jameson.

'And we need an ambulance!' called Bloom.

The door opened and two firearms officers entered with their weapons raised. They scanned the room, saw Stuart on his hands and knees beside Jameson, and Seraphine spaced out in the chair opposite Bloom. They lowered their weapons and radioed for an ambulance.

Bloom moved to crouch in front of Seraphine. She wanted her alive. She wanted more information on the group Seraphine had founded. They needed to know what was coming next. 'What was in the syringe, Seraphine?'

Seraphine's eyes closed and opened slowly. Then, just before she passed out, she said, 'It doesn't matter.'

Bloom and Jameson stood side by side, watching the paramedics attach Seraphine to the monitors in the back of the ambulance.

'Why didn't you warn me?' Jameson said, as the ambulance pulled away.

'You wouldn't have believed me. If I'd texted or called

to say that Sarah was really Seraphine, you'd have said I was talking rubbish – or, worse still, you'd have told Sarah. I couldn't risk that.'

'I could have died.'

'I wouldn't have let that happen.'

'You came bloody close.'

'Marcus?' She placed a hand on his shoulder, taking care not to jar his injured arm. 'I had no choice. I'm sorry. It was your idea though, really. The Romanova play. Make them think they're winning in order to inter-rogate them.'

Jameson looked at her. 'I think she might have been right. I think there's something wrong with you.' He walked away, up the street, then round the corner and out of sight.

69

The sun shone brightly as Bloom walked across Russell Square. She'd visited Libby Goodman and then come straight back to London, eager to get back to the normality of work. But it didn't feel normal any more. Not without Jameson, who'd refused to return. She understood his anger, but it had been three weeks. He'd finally answered her call this morning and had simply said, 'Stop calling me, Augusta.' He'd hung up before she could speak.

Claire had said to give him time. She was sure he'd come around eventually. She said she'd never seen her brother as content as he'd been over the past five years.

'He used to carry around this darkness,' she had said. 'Then, when he started working with you, we got the old Marcus back.'

Bloom asked if the darkness had returned and Claire had replied, 'Not like before. He's hurt and humiliated, but he just needs to lick his wounds and see that he had a lucky escape.'

Bloom had been so focused on confronting Seraphine and making her admit what she was doing that she'd failed to do right by Marcus. She'd said that she had no choice but to keep him in the dark, and she'd meant it at the time, but now, on reflection, she knew she could have done things differently. She could have called him and made him listen.

And she had to face the possibility that he might never come back. Before Marcus, she had been happy working alone. But she didn't want to return to that life. She missed his company and his humour.

She'd called him that morning to tell him that the fitness-to-practise case against her had finally been dropped. Dave Jones had been shown pictures of Dr Sarah Mendax and had withdrawn his complaint. It had been Sarah who'd visited him to suggest an inappropriate relationship between Bloom and Amy, and she was behind the fake images.

Bloom took the pathway through the square, as she did every morning, and walked past the dozen or so metal tables and chairs outside the cafe.

'What a beautiful day.'

It couldn't be. Seraphine Walker was sitting at the table nearest to the hedge with her legs crossed and her hands in her lap.

'What are you doing here?' said Bloom.

The liquid in the syringe had been an anaesthetic dose of ketamine. Just enough to knock someone out and mess with their memory, but nowhere near enough to kill. Within a couple of hours of arriving at Leeds General Infirmary, Seraphine had regained consciousness.

'They released me on bail.'

'I know. That was three weeks ago. What are you doing here now?'

'I thought we should talk.' Seraphine pushed the free chair at her table towards Bloom with one high-heeled shoe.

Bloom didn't move. 'About?'

'About how you ruined my life . . . again.'

'You are joking.'

Seraphine pushed the chair a little further. 'Sit down, Augusta. You can give me five minutes.'

Reluctantly, Bloom walked towards Seraphine's table and sat down. Why was she here?

'I really should hate you, you know.' Seraphine took a sip of espresso from the dainty coffee cup in front of her. 'You ruined my career and threatened my liberty. Not that there's much chance they'll put me away. All they have is that recording and I'm sticking to my story. I was just messing with you.'

Within minutes of the players leaving that room under the arches, all traces of the game had disappeared. The psychopaths had gone to ground and covered their tracks.

'Your little friend and his social media activities, on the other hand, have been impressive.' DC Logan had uploaded a few splices of the recording and shared them widely. 'He managed to select just the right vignettes to undermine our activities.'

'Like the bit where you said that if you were going to convince the world that psychopaths were superior, you had to remove those who muddied the waters.'

Seraphine smiled. 'Yes, that does seem to have alienated both your kind and mine.'

'You said it. You only have yourself to blame. So why not disappear again? You've done it before.'

'I may not be able to continue in my chosen profession, and there is a chance, albeit small, that I may spend some time at Her Majesty's pleasure, but thanks to you I am now the most famous psychopath on the planet . . . and I didn't have to kill a single soul.'

'Didn't you?'

'That's a first, don't you see? I'm already changing perceptions. Psychopaths don't have to be serial killers to be powerful or infamous any more.'

'What about the poor girl you used to fake your own suicide?'

Seraphine shrugged. 'Just one of the drug-addled homeless people I found in Leeds. There were a lot of young girls on the street at that time. It wasn't hard to get one to do what I wanted when I promised her the hit of her life.'

The double meaning wasn't lost on Bloom and she felt a fresh wave of disgust towards this woman. 'What do you want, Seraphine?'

'How's Marcus?'

Bloom said nothing. She refused to discuss Marcus with Seraphine. And, of course, she didn't really know.

'He knows I wouldn't really have hurt him, doesn't he? I like Marcus. He was different to my other men. I think maybe—'

'No. Absolutely not. No. Don't even think about it. He hates you and he always will.'

Seraphine took another sip of her coffee.

'If this had gone to plan and you'd given him that ketamine, what then?' Bloom asked. 'Would you have labelled him a failed game-player and sent him off to God knows where? You certainly wouldn't have let him go, so don't even think about claiming you would have done right by him.' She thought about Lana and Grayson. Geoff Taylor hadn't made it to Peterborough police station in time to collect his son, despite DS Green's best efforts. The officer in charge had released Grayson on bail, and he'd walked out of the station and hadn't been seen since. As for Lana, Jane had confirmed that the necklace Jameson found was the one she'd given to her mother. But as yet, she remained missing.

'Gosh, Augusta. So much anger. Where is this coming from?'

'What. Do. You. Want. Seraphine?'

'You can't stop us, you know.'

Bloom sat back in her chair. She knew Seraphine was right. The psychopaths would learn from their mistakes, regroup and re-launch. 'Seraphine, you messed up. You had all that power, and you lost it all because you wanted to show off to me. Was it worth it? Because I'm not even impressed. I'm actually appalled that you would let your own kind be so callously lured in and manipulated. And you don't even know what happens to them. You wanted me to see what you had learned, how you'd grown and excelled, but you're still that naive little girl unable to grasp the consequences of her actions. You have no empathy, Seraphine, and it makes you stupid.'

Seraphine stood. The anger in her eyes disappeared as

quickly as it had arrived. 'I thought you were the one person who understood me.'

'I am, Seraphine. You're just not listening, and I don't think you ever were.'

Seraphine looked out across the square at the ordinary people going about their day: walking their dogs, commuting to work, checking their phones. 'There are some people in the world that you really shouldn't mess with.' She met Bloom's gaze. 'And I am one of them.'

For a moment or two they watched each other in silence, and then Seraphine smiled the sweetest of smiles. 'It has been so lovely to see you after all these years, Augusta. Let's keep in touch.'

And then she was gone.

Acknowledgements

The journey to publication has been a long process of trial and error during which my lovely family and friends have been called upon to read and comment on numerous stories. I am hugely grateful for their constructive criticism and encouragement. They have taught me plenty, and always cheered me on. Thanks to Liz, Jo and Richard, Barbara and Malcolm Rigby, Catherine Meardon, David Rigby, Elizabeth Kirkpatrick, Dominic Gateley, Kathryn Scott, Nicola Eastwood and, of course, my parents Norman and Jillian. Without you I would never have made it this far.

Thanks also to forensic psychologist Emma Stevenson, who helped me better understand the mind of a psychopath. Your insight was much appreciated and any mistakes I have made are mine and mine alone.

I owe a great debt of gratitude to The Penguin Random House Writers' Academy, not only for introducing me to my wonderful editor Lizzy Goudsmit, but also for the inspiration and insight offered on their Constructing a Novel course. In particular I need to thank my tutor Barbara Henderson, whose enthusiasm and advice were invaluable.

Thanks to the whole team at Transworld for welcoming me into their world and making my story the best it can be. I will be forever grateful to Lizzy for spotting the potential in my idea and championing it with such passion. You are a superstar. Thanks also to Kate Samano for honing my words to perfection and to Joshua Crosley for negotiating those wonderful translation rights.

Finally, a huge thank-you to my beautiful Ella – you never fail to brighten Mummy's day.

Reading Group Questions

The following are just some of the questions you might like to consider:

- 'She knew Jameson was lying. He hadn't called to prevent her feeling ambushed. He'd called to plant a seed because he knew she couldn't resist a mystery.'

  At the beginning of the novel, Augusta and Jameson are presented as a very efficient, capable duo. How do you think their partnership changes as the novel progresses? In what ways do their key similarities and differences affect their working dynamic?

- Why do you think the author chose the title *Gone* for this book?

- There are two epigraphs at the beginning of the book. What do you think these are referring to? Why are they significant?

- 'Bloom didn't have the answer, but she knew not to ignore the question. She often spotted important gaps and links long before she could explain why they were significant. The trick was to note these gut feelings and to interrogate them ruthlessly.'

  How does Augusta compare to other fictional female detectives, either in books or on television and in film? In what ways does she stand out?

- *Gone* is set in a number of different locations, from London and Bristol to Leeds and Manchester. How do the different places affect the story? Where do you think Bloom feels most at home?

- There are many different characters in *Gone* and we see the narrative evolve from a number of perspectives. What were your initial suspicions in the first few chapters? Did they change as new characters were introduced?

- Leona Deakin, the author of *Gone*, is an occupational psychologist. How do you think she has used her experiences to shape the story and the characters?

- The characters in *Gone* frequently have to make difficult moral decisions. Did the book make you question your own decision-making? What would you have done in some of these situations?

- 'Fourteen. You should have one foot still in child-hood at fourteen. Innocence should drift away, little by little: Santa and the Tooth Fairy first; then the realization that your parents are flawed; then that people can be selfish; and finally that the world itself can be unfathomably cruel. Childhood needs to unravel slowly so that the mind can adjust.'

How do childhood experiences go on to shape the key characters in this novel?

HOW DO YOU SOLVE A CRIME
WITHOUT THE CLUES?
THE VICTIM'S MEMORIES ARE
LOST

READ AN EXTRACT FROM THE
SECOND DR AUGUSTA BLOOM NOVEL,
LOST

There is an explosion at a military ball. The casualties are rushed to hospital in eight ambulances, but only seven vehicles arrive. Captain Harry Peterson is missing.

His partner calls upon her old friend Augusta, who rushes to support the investigation. But no one can work out what connects the two incidents. When Harry is eventually discovered three days later, they hope he holds the answers to their questions. But he can't remember a single thing from the last five years.

I

As he walked up the stone stairway, Captain Harry Peterson had no idea that time was running out. In less than an hour, a bomb would rip this building apart.

He looked across the lawn. Everyone was peaceful, content. A hundred officers in full uniform were drinking champagne in front of a marquee. The buttons on their cropped jackets were shining in the sunlight. Their conversation, loud with laughter, mixed with music from the Royal Marines Band.

Harry smiled. He'd seen it all before, many times, but he knew he'd never grow tired of the glamour and decadence of a military ball.

Behind the officer's wardroom at Her Majesty's Naval Base, Devonport, a thin man in dark clothes waited patiently. He paced up and down, up and down. He checked the straps of his backpack and the trigger switch in his pocket.

Harry always thought it was a privilege to be in the Royal Navy, but never more so than when he was at Devonport. He smiled as he walked past the two miniature cannons housed on carved wooden lions on his way into the building. He had never wanted to do anything else but this: as a child he'd dreamt of travelling the world on the ships he'd seen in Portsmouth and as a teenager he'd watched films about fighter pilots and tacked a poster of *The Dam Busters* to his bedroom wall. It wasn't that he wanted to fight but he liked the idea of being a hero. Who didn't? He wanted to be a good person.

The man on reception glanced at the rank insignia embroidered on Harry's jacket cuffs. 'Good evening, Captain,' he said.

Harry nodded. He squeezed past the photographer and collected a glass of champagne from a lady dressed in a red-tailed jacket and a gold waistcoat. The bi-annual balls were themed to separate them from the endless formal dinners and because, as the defender of the seas, the navy felt it was not only the most senior service but also the one with the best sense of humour, and so 'Night at the Circus' had been chosen for this evening's event. Which explained the juggler on the lawn and the man on stilts parading around the concourse.

The room overlooking the lawn had been converted into a complimentary gin bar. Its leather sofas and heavy oak tables had been moved aside and the staff were wearing glittered leotards and feathered headdresses. Harry searched for a familiar face, knowing he was unlikely to find one. He wasn't attached to this base. He'd been invited to attend the ball by Commodore Chris Waite who wanted to sound him out about a job. Harry had no intention of accepting – he didn't want to move back to Plymouth – but it was never a good idea to refuse a courtship flat out. You had to play the game; people in the military had long memories and perhaps he'd be back here one day. But, for now, he needed to be in London and close to his children. He'd missed so much when they were young, and if he didn't take jobs stationed near his ex-wife now, he'd never see them at all.

He nodded to a young lieutenant whose girlfriend was wearing an off-the-shoulder peach dress decorated with diamanté. The dress code had been clear: ankle-length dresses, covered shoulders and minimal bling. No doubt there'd be a coven of military wives discussing the young woman's decision by the end of the evening.

'Lovely dress,' Harry said. He thought he'd put in a good word now, just in case she overheard something different later on. She blushed and thanked him with a delighted giggle.

'Thank you, Sir,' her boyfriend said.

Harry patted the man's shoulder.

The thin man continued to pace up and down outside the officer's wardroom. It wasn't time yet. But he could hear music and the laughter and he hated them for it. He wished he could see their faces when it went off. It was his only regret. But it was a small price to pay.

Harry turned to see Commodore Waite entering the room with his wife, who was wearing a smart black evening gown.

'Evening, Sir,' Harry said, shaking Waite's hand. 'Thank you for the invite.'

Mrs Waite kissed Harry on the cheek. 'When we were out for dinner last month, you called him Chris all night,' she said. 'But now it's "Sir".'

'That was pleasure, Mrs Waite,' said Harry. 'This is work.' She was the Commodore's second wife and still new enough to the military world to be fascinated by its quirks.

She looked at the gin bar surrounded by well-dressed guests. 'You think *this* is work?'

Harry and Chris exchanged a smile.

'How's it feel to be back? I bet you've missed the old place,' Waite said. It was true that Harry had always had a fondness for Devonport.

'The place, yes. The people . . .' He scrunched up his face.

The Commodore laughed, a loud boom fitting for a man of his status. 'No doubt you'd whip 'em into shape.'

Waite held up his hand to greet a group of officers on the other side of the room. 'I better get over there,' he said. 'Let's catch up later, I want to talk about your next move.'

'Drinks first,' said Mrs Waite, looping her arm through her husband's and navigating them towards the gin bar.

'We better see what they have,' said Waite.

'Everything from black pepper to raspberries, I believe,' Harry replied. He was sticking to his one glass of champagne. He liked to stay in control at work events. He walked to the window and his eyes immediately fell on an elegant redhead in a floor-length dark-green gown cinched tightly at the waist with a bronze bow. She was standing in the middle of the lawn. Her hair was tied up so that her face was framed by just a few loose curls. She'd said that there was absolutely no way she'd make it, that work was crazy.

Harry rushed back towards the reception. He loved that she'd decided to surprise him. It's exactly what he'd have done.

At the door, a grey-haired, muscular officer blocked his way.

'Sir,' he said. 'Sub-Lieutenant Philips from Joint Forces Command. May I have a word in private, please?'

Dinner was announced and the other guests started moving out of the building and towards the marquee in typical military compliance.

'Now?' Harry said. He leant to the side, trying to see Karene through the moving crowd. He wanted to find her, to kiss her.

The man stepped a little closer and spoke in a low voice. 'Yes, Sir,' he said. 'I've come here especially. I need to brief you in person.' The man turned and began walking back to the bar.

Harry knew he couldn't refuse Joint Forces. He was one of them and it would be impolite at best and dangerous at worst. Plus the sub-lieutenant wasn't in dress uniform – just his white shirt and his cap under one arm – so he'd been sent unexpectedly. The brief was clearly urgent.

Moving against the flow, Harry followed the man through the crowd. Commodore and Mrs Waite were lingering at the door of the bar as the final group of officers made their way outside.

The sub-lieutenant strode towards the window on the other side of the room so that they were out of earshot.

'What's so important?' asked Harry. He checked the man's rank and frowned. The epaulettes decorating his shoulders were upside down. That was a rookie mistake. Or perhaps he'd dressed in a hurry.

'This will only take a minute, Sir.'

Harry peered through the window and back out to the lawn. He could see Karene on the concourse looking for him in the crowd. A man on stilts stomped past the window. Karene glanced up and her eyes met Harry's. He raised his hand to wave and she smiled.

And then the room exploded.